Charles F. D. P. Dumouriez

Memoirs of General Dumourier

Part 1

Charles F. D. P. Dumouriez

Memoirs of General Dumourier
Part 1

ISBN/EAN: 9783337093693

Printed in Europe, USA, Canada, Australia, Japan

Cover: Foto ©Andreas Hilbeck / pixelio.de

More available books at **www.hansebooks.com**

OF

GENERAL DUMOURIER,

WRITTEN BY HIMSELF.

.... VITAM QUI IMPENDERE VERO.

TRANSLATED BY JOHN FENWICK.

PART I.

PHILADELPHIA:

PRINTED BY SAMUEL HARRISON SMITH,

CHERRY-STREET, ABOVE FOURTH-STREET.

1794.

CONTENTS OF THE FIRST PART.

PREFACE.

IT is among the misfortunes that attend General Dumourier, to be abandoned by the world; to be the outcaft of fociety; to be compelled to fly from city to city to feek an afylum from the rage and madnefs of countrymen who imagine they will ferve the public caufe and rid the world of a traitor if they can but plunge a dagger into his breaft; and to avoid the wretch whofe avarice would tempt him to gain the price offered for his blood by the Convention. Compelled to live among ftrangers under the difguife of an affumed name, and to fubmit to the pain of liftening to opinions on his conduct, equally fevere and unjuft, that are induftrioufly circulated by the hired journalifts of the different courts of Europe, who beftow their praifes only on the fuccefsful, and every where encountering emigrants, who deteft him with as little reafon, and as much ferocity as the Jacobins, this man, whom Minifters and Courts received with flattering careffes when he quitted the army, but afterwards calumniated and perfecuted, for having publifhed memorials which contained his real and ferious opinions, at length obeys the call of his duty, by giving to the world the Memoirs of his life.

B   The

The moſt extravagant and contradictory tales reſpecting him have filled the journals of Europe, and portraits have been drawn of him ſo unlike each other, that not only his character, but his exiſtence is become an enigma.

The Courier of Europe repreſents him with the force of Hercules, the licentiouſneſs of Mark Anthony, the treachery of Hannibal, the cruelty of Sylla, and the military and political talents of Caeſar; they have alſo attributed to him, the poſſeſſion of immenſe riches in the Engliſh funds. On the contrary the Journal of the Lower Rhine deſcribes him as poſſeſſing talents, but being deficient in judgment. This opinion, Dumourier regards as true praiſe, for he was never deſirous of being thought ſubtile or practiſed in the art of changing his opinions according to his intereſts. He has always had fixed principles and a determined character. His mind was formed by the ſtudy of Plutarch; and he has mixed too little with men, to be known by any but a ſelect few. Excepting during his travels and his wars, he has lived ſurrounded only by his books, and his choſen friends, of whom the greater part no longer exiſt. Far from eſteeming the maxim of the Epicureans, which recommends the concealment of our actions, his whole life ſhall be expoſed to the obſervation and judgment of his contemporaries. He has nothing to loſe by his conduct; already he is poor, calumniated, proſcribed, all that mankind regard as miſerable; but he has every thing to gain, ſince men of elevated

and

and upright minds, who read thefe Memoirs, will become his friends. With fuch men only he defires to live, and to whatever nation they belong, he fhall always regard them as his fellow citizens.

The celebrated Dictator Fabius Maximus, he who alone could check the victories of Hannibal, and whom Dumourier earneftly endeavoured to imitate in his campaign againft the king of Pruffia, made this obfervation to Paulus Emilius, when he went with Varro, to command the army, " *Let him not fear who thirfts for glory; for, although we often find that true merit is eclipfed for a time, we have never known it to be entirely loft; it burfts at laft through the clouds which encircle it, and appears arrayed in its bright and genuine colours.*"

Dumourier thought like Fabius, but their fituations were widely different. Fabius refided on his eftate with his family, expofed indeed to the calumnies of a faction, but honoured in the Senate, and by all the fages of Rome. They ftill regarded his counfels and preferved him in the command of the army, nor had ingratitude effaced the many fervices he had hitherto rendered his country, or deftroyed the expectation of his ftill rendering them many more. Fabius was thus enabled to follow the bent of his mild and moderate difpofition ; and wait, in tranquillity, the progrefs of truth and juftice. Such are not the happy circumftances of Dumourier ; and however fhort a time he may have to live, it will be too long if

it

it be stained with the injustice of the public opinion. Not only therefore for himself, his contemporaries, and his country to whom he may one day be useful, but in justice to his friends, his relations, his advocates, he is obliged to repel the calumnies which follow him, and to dissipate the cloud which obscures the truth. This he will do by an honest and accurate detail of such facts as are important, and of which he was a competent witness.

For these reasons he is obliged to change the order of his Memoirs, and to submit to the public opinion the third volume, which contains the circumstances of the year 1793. These are the more important as they will enable the reader to foresee the issue of the strange events that have lately happened in Europe, in studying the nature of their motives and causes. If General Dumourier have stated any of them erroneously, his contemporaries are competent to detect his injustice, but he has surely this great reason for speaking the truth, that he may not increase the number of his enemies. He describes the French as they really are, and not such as Europe has hitherto regarded them, who seem to believe that the whole French nation are without religion, without honour, or humanity. The French are engaged in a bad cause. We are compelled to regard them with horror; but prudence will not permit us to despise them. They have displayed a magnificent courage ; and, had they followed the opinion of virtuous and experienced

rienced men, this period of their hiſtory would have been as honourable as it is now diſgraceful and wretched.

Unhappily, their licentious exceſſes have deſtroyed the liberties of Europe. The example of their misfortunes, has induced every people to believe that they had better wear their chains in peace, than fall into an anarchy that can never end but in abſolute deſpotiſm.

There are two queſtions that naturally preſent themſelves to which Dumourier's juſtification ought to reply, by ſtating the motives of his conduct, which appears to be in contradiction with his own opinions.

It is aſked, *why did Dumourier, after the arreſt of Louis on the 10th of Auguſt, refuſe to obey the orders that he had received from another general, to make the ſoldiers renew their oath of fidelity to the king?*

Dumourier had then under his command 10,000 men in the camp of Maulde near Tournay, and the Auſtrians who had a much larger army, were indefatigable in harraſſing his troops. Dillon had been ſent to remove the general in his command. The miniſters were then evidently inimical to the revolution; and, as we ſhall ſee in the ſecond volume of theſe Memoirs, purſued a conduct that was the cauſe of the king's misfortunes. The circumſtances of the frightful ſcene of the 10th of Auguſt, were not accurately known in the camp. To engage the troops to renew their oath, according to the orders of General Dillon, was to prejudge the

the cause of the people, to unfold the standard of rebellion against the nation, and to engage the army in a dispute respecting parties, at the very moment when we had a foreign enemy to combat; and the inevitable consequence would have been to have exposed the unfortunate Louis to the daggers and vengeance of the populace.

Again it is demanded, *how can Dumourier justify his conduct at the time when a Convention was appointed for the purpose of abolishing the monarchy and establishing a republic, in acknowledging the authority of this Convention, giving his sanction to the destruction of the monarchy, and to the assumed power of the republic.*

It was shortly after the general's refusal to give the oath to the troops in the camp of Maulde, that Fayette deserted from his army, and Dumourier was ordered to take the command in his stead. The king of Prussia entered Champagne with a formidable body of troops; and terror and treason ensured his success. Longwi and Verdun were taken. Dumourier, being in force in his camp at Grandpre, assembled his army at St. Manehould. The history of France does not present so dangerous a crisis. The 20th of September, the day on which the Convention declared France to be a republic, Dumourier and Kellerman repulsed the Prussians, who had attacked them at Valary. The two armies were in sight of each other and every day threatened to come to an engagement; and this surely was not the moment to enter into quarrels respecting the

form

form of government! The enemy were to
be driven from the territories of France.
The country was to be faved. Befides, the
people were incenfed againft the king, whom
they regarded as a traitor. At fuch a period
to have maintained his prerogative, would
have been the fignal for his maffacre. The
people would have looked upon fuch an attempt as an act of treachery, which would
have deprived Dumourier of the confidence
of his countrymen, and thereby have left
France an eafy prey to the enemy.

As foon as the Pruffians had retreated,
Dumourier began the campaign in the Low
Countries, and it was not till he had gained
the Belgians for allies, and had acquired influence by his fuccefs, that he had any reafon to hope that he could give peace to his
country, deliver the imprifoned king, and
eftablifh on fecure foundations the conftitution of 1789. After that period, circumftances arofe fo extremely contrary to all
poffible expectation, Dumourier's journey
to Paris, and the horrible murder of Louis
XVI. fo clearly convinced Dumourier of the
guilty aims of the Convention, and the im-
placability and power of the Jacobins, that
the general refolved at all hazards to fepa-
rate the caufe of the country from that of
the monfters by whom it was governed. His
plan was bold. No other perfon in France
had means in his power, for that purpofe, fo
apparently well founded. But every circumftance turned againft him, and, above
all, the inconftancy of his army.

The

The apparent contradiction between Dumourier's political principles and his military conduct have drawn upon him the unjust reproaches of many of the Emigrants, and of several persons of good sense, who could only judge from their mistaken view of the facts. As minister of foreign affairs, Dumourier certainly has shewn a sincere attachment to the Constitution; of this his dispatches, his discourses to the Assembly, are an abundant proof. He has equally opposed Republicans and Royalists. He procured the dismission of three ministers of the former party, without leaguing himself with the court faction, and in consequence he was exposed to the fury of the Jacobins, who loudly demanded his being sent to the prison of Orleans. The public opinion of Dumourier's principles at that period, was so decided, that the following couplet was placed at the bottom of his portrait.

> Inflexible foutien du trone, et de la loi,
> Il fut ami du peuple, il fut ami du Roi*.

Afterwards appointed to the command of the army, he had neither time nor inclination to concern himself in the intrigues and crimes of Paris. He was solely employed in repelling the enemy.

He is reproached, however, with never having changed his party, till he was no longer victorious, but the reproach is unjust;

---

* Inflexible supporter of the throne and of the law, he was at once the friend of the people and of the king.

juft; for, in the firft place, he never changed his party, fince, although he quitted the
Republicans, with whom he had been long difgufted, yet he did not join the Royalifts; and
that no doubt might remain refpecting his opinion, he inftantly proclaimed his defire of
re-eftablifhing the conftitution of 1789. Secondly, his fentiments were conftantly in
oppofition to thofe of the Convention, the
Jacobins, and the Minifter of War, during
the time of his expedition into Belgia, from
the month of November, as may be feen
in his correfpondence with Pache, publifhed
in January 1793. In this fame month of
January, he fent to the Convention four
memorials, againft the tyrannical decree of
the 15th of December, and he neither prefented himfelf to the Convention, nor the
fociety of Jacobins; on the contrary, he
gave in his refignation at that period. Thirdly, compelled for his perfonal fafety to return to the army, he perfevered in oppof-
ing the tyranny and injuftice of the Convention. It was on the 12th of March that
he wrote the well-known letter to the Convention, which was confidered by the Jacobins as fo great a crime. Hence, before he
went to engage the Prince of Cobourg, and
to decide the fate of France and her enemies on the plains of Nerwinde, his quarrel with the Convention was open and proclaimed. He was profcribed. He was,
therefore, compelled to overthrow the Convention, or perifh.

The

The reproach that General Dumourier never quitted the Republican party till he was vanquished, was expressed with the greatest bitterness, in a letter written by the Elector of Cologne, to the General, which was published with a cruel oftentation which that prince might have foreborne against a man then unfortunate and a fugitive. But furely it is to be fuppofed, that this Prince will regret the injuftice done to General Dumourier, when, by the reading of thefe Memoirs, he fhall be convinced that it is an injuftice. None of the wrongs the General has endured, has afflicted him fo much as this, fince the author of it is held in fuch juft eftimation throughout Europe.

Every nation in Europe muft be convinced, that its moft important interefts are involved in the cataftrophe of the French Revolution. If the belligerent powers fhould re-eftablifh the monarchy, the vengeance of the nobles, and confequent profcriptions will fall on the greater part of the people. But, as the people are fortunately the moft numerous body, as they have enjoyed the bleffings of Liberty, and felt the advantage of holding the fovereign power in their hands, the triumph of the nobility and clergy, would be but momentary; it will endure no longer than while the foreign troops are enabled to fupport them. Every day will be productive of frefh rebellions, and another Revolution ftill more deftructive

tive and terrible than the prefent, will reftore the people to the exercife of the fovereignty. But if, by the imbecility of the allied powers, the National Convention and the Jacobins are enabled to maintain the republic, then will their fyftem of fraternization be exercifed with irrefiftible force; and finally, not only the neighbouring nations, but the moft diftant countries will imitate the rebellion of France, and all Europe be reduced to a ftate of anarchy, while by a grand and rapid Revolution, the exifting governments of the world will be haftened to deftruction. There is a juft medium, however, which the fenfible part of the French nation eagerly defire to be adopted, and which would infure general tranquillity to Europe; it is that France fhould become a limited monarchy.

It is to this end the fovereigns of Europe ought to direct their efforts; and it is by fo doing only they can fecure the fafety of the monarch who fhall mount the throne of France. It is the only bond of univerfal peace.

If it be true that the ancient monarchy cannot be reftored in France, it is no lefs certain that the fpecies of Democracy, which exifts there at prefent, cannot be of long duration.

Abftract notions have been too much confulted in this important matter, which may eafily be reduced to a few fimple truths. There is no political conftitution which will

not

not render a people happy, if it be the choice of the people, and if the government be enabled to act without any other reftraint than that of the law. The monarchical form of government is exclufively fuited to large and populous nations, becaufe fuch only are enabled to provide for the expence of monarchy. The republican form is better fuited to fmall and poor countries, becaufe it is adminiftered with lefs expence. In the former, there is a unity of power, which coftitutes the perfection of government; and it alfo includes fecrecy and promptitude, without which great and complicated affairs cannot be fuccefsfully conducted. Ariftocracy is neceffary in a Republic; drawing together the authoritics that otherwife would be without union, and excluding the tyranny that refults from the arbitrary will of a people governing themfelves. Pure democracy will always produce an inconfiftent and ineffectual government, becaufe it neither admits of union of opinions, nor of prudence, promptitude, nor fecrecy; and it includes in itfelf principles that beget diforders among the people, and are entirely fubverfive of their happinefs.

All the Republics that we are acquainted with, ancient or modern, have been meliorated by Ariftocracy. We muft not even except Athens, which was devoid of fuccefs and fplendor, excepting when its councils were directed by Ariftides, Themiftocles, Cymon,

Cymon, and Pericles; and was reduced to flavery, at firft by Sparta, and afterwards by Philip of Macedon, when the democracy triumphed, and when celebrated men were no longer at the head of its affairs.

The civilization of our manners, the extent of our commerce, our wealth, our luxuries, in a word all the enjoyments on which are founded the fplendor and happinefs of our age, are oppofed to the eftablifhment of a Republic. If we will have a perfect equality among men for the bafis of our political union, we muft go back to the fimplicity of the firft ages, caft away our advantages, and return to a ftate of nature. A government founded on equality can be nothing more than the contract of a favage people, who, for the firft time, have affembled in fociety.

The French have erred ftrangely in this refpect. They compare themfelves to the firft Romans; but Brutus, in freeing Rome from the Tarquins who were deteftable tyrants, in abolifhing royalty, was better informed of the interefts of men, than to eftablifh equality and democracy. He preferved the royal authority while he divided it between the Confuls, to whom he left the Lictors, the Fafces, and the Ax, as well as all the real attributes of royalty. He new modelled the fovereign power, by ordaining that the hands which held it fhould be changed every year. Yet the Confuls were taken from the Senate, that is to fay, from the

the Aristocracy. Afterward, indeed, new changes took place in the government, when bold plebeians attacked the privileges of the senate by their decemvirs and tribunes. But the government remained five hundred years an aristocracy; and when the people had made innovations, if the senate had not conceived the sublime policy of rendering the Roman people a nation of conquerors, its government would have resembled that which we have since seen in the Republic of Florence: Always feeble, always agitated by civil wars, and open to the invasion of every ambitious neighbour, Rome would have been conquered, or would have become, a dower, or a heritage like Florence; and scarcely would history have spoken of that city, which her aristocracy rendered the most celebrated of the whole world.

But even this species of republic which Brutus founded, and which may be considered as a mixed government, extending only over a small territory, it would have been impossible to have re-established, after the death of Cæsar, or Tiberius, or Nero. The circumstances of the Roman Empire, at that period, would have destroyed the Republican spirit in its birth. The bounds of the empire were too much enlarged; the Romans were too rich; luxury, arts, and all the enjoyments that spring from them, had spread their influence too much to accord with the austerity of a Republic. And liberty does not necessarily demand a Republican

publican government. England is a proof, that a people may be free under a monarch. Liberty confifts in being free from obedience to all laws but thofe that the people themfelves have made. The law is the fanctuary in which the fovereignty refides; and kings or other magiftrates to whom the executive power is delegated, being fubject to the law, the people are as free as they can be confiftently with their happinefs. Such are the bounds of a true liberty, and all beyond is anarchy.

Nothing can be better proved than that a republic cannot now be eftablifhed, without the deftruction of thofe very advantages which diftinguifh the age. We cannot obtain the object, without confounding property, and forcing the minds of men to fubmiffion by terror and crimes. To be a Republic, we muft firft be in a ftate of anarchy; but does anarchy conduct to equality and liberty? No. It overthrows all eftablifhed order; and, in the place of hereditary authority, fubftitutes that of the populace, which being directed by lefs reafonable principles, neceffarily exercifes an infupportable ryranny : Of which France is an example. The palaces and rich property of the nobility and clergy cannot be equally divided, and they become the prey of thofe mifcreants that are the moft depraved and daring, and perhaps, one day we may fee the Ex-capuchin Chabot, Lord of Chantilly; Bazire, Lord of Chambord, and Merlin,

Lord

Lord of Chanteloup; and filling the places of the great Conde, the Marefchal de Saxe, and the Duke de Choifeuil. Perhaps we fhall fee changes a thoufand times more extravagant and ridiculous. And what good will refult to the people by thefe hideous changes? They will ftill have mafters. But of what a new and contemptible race!

This difaftrous ftate of things is at prefent confined to France, but its democratic or rather monftrous Republic cannot exift but by the fpreading of anarchy among all its neighbours. Thus her intereft, and every part of her policy, (which fhe is not even defirous of concealing) confifts in preaching and propagating anarchy. As experience proves that it is eafy to deceive and betray a people in preaching liberty to them, (fince it is lefs difficult to create confufion than to reftore order), and as the poor are more numerous in every country than the rich and the noble, it is to be feared that, tempted by the example and fupport of the licentious people of France, all nations will imitate her exceffes, and turbulence and anarchy become univerfal.

This confufion, accompanied with all its miferies, is inevitable, if the foreign powers are unable to ftop the progrefs of the French Revolution. The forces employed by the allies are fo great that fuccefs is infallible if they be directed by wifdom and prudence. But if the allies abufe their power and rob the unfortunate family, whofe defenders they

avow

avow themselves to be, the excess of the French people will be justified, and the same dangers and misfortunes will again desolate Europe.

General Dumourier has discussed this subject more fully in another work, which he has delivered to persons who have promised to convey it to the Emperor, and he hopes for the sake of mankind, that it will not be neglected or forgotten.

Although General Dumourier has asserted the necessity of founding every stable government on an aristocracy, it is not to be understood that he would grant all right and privilege to the nobles and nothing to the people. Nobility was in its original the reward of virtue; and the titles, honours, and feudal rights attached to it, are the legitimate property of their descendants, and nothing could be more unjust than to deprive such of the nobility as have not borne arms against France of any part of their hereditary rights. But nobles should have no privileges in the eye of the law, either in engrossing of places, or in exemption from duties. In a free government, all are equal in this respect, and a nobleman is a simple citizen. He has no just claim to the acquisition of places but by his services, his talents, and his virtues. He has the advantages of education, leisure, and the example of his ancestry. Of these it is his duty to avail himself; but these are his only just advantages; and in this system is to be found the only true equality that has existed in any age, or among any people.

D

It

It is not becaufe all the members of the Convention, and the generals of the armies of France have been raifed from among the vulgar that the decrees of the former, or the military conduct of the latter, excite the difdain and the indignation of Europe, but becaufe they are abfurd, criminal, ignorant, and cruel.

Certainly a ftate may exift without a king, a court, or a nobility ; but it is not true that a great and powerful nation can exift without nobility ; for nobility being the reward of virtue, becomes a motive not eafily to be deftroyed in the defcendants of the virtuous man.

This applies only to nobility, as it exifted in its origin, for that which is fold by kings is a wretched abufe, the offspring of the avarice of kings, and will ceafe of itfelf as a ridiculous vanity, when titles fhall no longer be attended with pecuniary privileges, which the public opinion has forever abolifhed in France, and which if an attempt be made to reftore it by foreign powers will but ferve to produce another Revolution.

The ariftocracy that General Dumourier regards as neceffary to all government is that of virtue and talent. To govern men, to fit in judgment upon crimes, or to decide on queftions of property, to inftruct men in the duties of religion, to conduct the citizens of a great empire in war, are employments that muft be ftudied as other employments are. The declaration of the Rights of Man, and the Conftitution to which it
ferved

ferved as a bafis, will inſtruct the future
king of the French, in what manner it is
his duty to felect thofe who are to aid him
in the government of the kingdom. The
right of choofing fuch men is the nobleſt attribute of royalty. Let us examine that fublime Conſtitution, and we will find that no
condition can be found more happy for a
wife and virtuous man than that of a king of
France.

Frenchmen, liſten to the temperate and
informed part of Europe, again adopt with
fincerity, that true code of philofophy, and
your monarch will be refpected and powerful, your nobility will again become worthy of their anceſtors, your clergy pious,
worthy, and ufeful, and you will become the
happieſt nation of the earth !

Such is the zealous wifh of a man whom
you would deſtroy, becaufe he faved your
country, and has always fpoken with fincerity ; whom the emigrants load with calumnies, becaufe in quitting his country he
would not turn his arms againſt her like
themfelves ; whom the miniſters of foreign
courts declared to be a dangerous man becaufe he aſſerts that the fovereign power refides in the people. No fufferings will induce him to change either his opinions or
his conduct, or his wifhes for your happinefs,
fince reafon and not the chances of fortune
ought to conduct the wife man.

And you alfo, fovereigns of Europe, be
perfuaded that the perfecuted man whom
you feem to condemn, to whom you refufe
the

the afylum which he ought to find among
you, although he brings no other title than a
pure and honeft mind, be perfuaded that he
is influenced by the love of mankind, which
infpires him with refpect for all juft authority, that he is actuated with the defire of
feeing peace reftored to all nations, that he
abhors war, and renounces it for himfelf,
even in the fervice of his country, excepting
when he believes it to be neceffary to arreft
the courfe of ambition and injuftice.

A BRIEF

BRIEF ACCOUNT OF THE

LIFE OF

GENERAL DUMOURIER.

EXTRACTED FROM A LETTER WRITTEN TO A FRIEND.

————AT prefent, my dear friend, let us quit thefe abftract notions, too fublime to be the general fubject of a letter, and let us enquire what is the refult of fuch principles. It is that we ought to do all the good we can in our ftations; to be humane; but, above all, to be juft. It is never our duty to enquire what the opinions of men refpecting us will be, and our actions ought never to be influenced by an attention to the queftion of what may be thought of them. It is in times of great public commotion, during the revolutions of empires, that this principle ought to be maintained with the greateft firmnefs. It is then that the juft man will call forth his talents to fave his country, exert his genius to reprefent the dangers of excefs, and his courage to ftand between the nation and a great crime.

He will be hated and perfecuted by all parties, fince he will not flatter the paffions of faction; but he confoles himfelf in recollecting that he performs his duty. Perfecutions appear but an incident that he was to expect; and he fupports them with fortitude, becaufe he knows they are the effect of miftake that cannot be lafting.

Hiftory reftores the virtuous man to his juft rank among his fellow-citizens. My enemies cannot deny that I have acquired great military fame; but, to obfcure it, they paint me as a faith

E   lefs,

less, immoral, unprincipled man. They would drive me from the theatre of Europe to make room for meaner actors. I am willing to remain a spectator of the scene, but I cannot consent to descend from the stage with opprobrium. These considerations have driven me to two decisive measures. The first, to publish the facts that justify the latter period of my public life, which has been the most calumniated. The second, to deliver myself up into the hands of the emperor, who, instigated and deceived by the gross calumnies of my persecutors, has given orders to have me arrested. Prudence perhaps would dictate a different conduct on my part, but duty rests on other calculations. These are mine: that this voluntary surrender of myself into his power ought to convince the emperor of my innocence, and incline him to lay aside his prejudices. He is represented as a just man; I believe him to be such. He will value the confidence I place in his character, he will produce the accusations they have urged against me, and I shall prove their falsehood. These memoirs will have appeared, in the interval, to justify me to the world; and, having gained the confidence of a monarch even more than any other interested in the re-establishment of peace and order, I may again render services to humanity and my unhappy country. Should the emperor refuse to hear my justification, and consign me to the oblivion of a prison, I shall only have to suffer and to die. But this history of my life will vindicate my name. The consequences of the treachery and injustice of my persecutors will fall on themselves; and the emperor himself will regret me.

In the approaching month, I shall be fifty-five years of age. Shall I really suffer less, if, by shamefully concealing myself, I can escape a few days of reproach or imprisonment?

I will

I will now give you a short history of my life, which may serve as a supplement to my memoirs, if I am not allowed time to finish them. I was born at Cambray in 1739, of parents not affluent, although noble. My father was a man of great virtue and understanding; he bestowed on me a very careful and extensive education; at eighteen years of age I became a soldier; and at two-and-twenty I was honoured with the crofs of St. Louis, and had received twenty-two wounds.

On peace being made in 1763, I began my travels, to study the languages and manners of different nations. The Emigrants have said, that at this time, I was employed as a fpy by the French miniftry. It is not improbable that the *petit-maitres* of Tarentum and Athens (if there were any fuch men there) have faid as much of Pythagoras and Plato.

In 1768, I was put upon the ftaff belonging to the army in Corfica; and, having ferved with reputation in the two campaigns of 1768 and 1769, I was raifed to the rank of Colonel.

In 1770, the Duke de Choifeuil appointed me minifter to the confederates of Poland; and I commanded a body of men in that country during two campaigns, and conducted feveral very important negotiations with various fuccefs. As the meafures of the confederates were ill concerted, their revolution was unfortunate, and ended in the partition of Poland.

In 1772, the Marquis of Monteynard, minifter of war, employed me in correcting and revifing the military code of laws; at the end of the fame year, this minifter by the exprefs order of Louis the XV. entrufted me with the management of a fecret negotiation relative to the revolution in Sweden; but, having received my inftructions on this affair immediately from the king himfelf, and unknown to the Duke D'Aiguillon, minifter

E 2   of

lefs, immoral, unprincipled man. They would
drive me from the theatre of Europe to make room
for meaner actors. I am willing to remain a
fpectator of the fcene, but I cannot confent to
defcend from the ftage with opprobrium. Thefe
confiderations have driven me to two decifive
meafures. The firft, to publifh the facts that
juftify the latter period of my public life, which
has been the moft calumniated. The fecond, to
deliver myfelf up into the hands of the emperor,
who, inftigated and deceived by the grofs calumnies of my perfecutors, has given orders to have
me arrefted. Prudence perhaps would dictate a
different conduct on my part, but duty refts on
other calculations. Thefe are mine: that this
valuntary furrender of myfelf into his power
ought to convince the emperor of my innocence,
and incline him to lay afide his prejudices. He
is reprefented as a juft man; I believe him to be
fuch. He will value the confidence I place in
his character, he will produce the accufations they
have urged againft me, and I fhall prove their
falfehood. Thefe memoirs will have appeared,
in the interval, to juftify me to the world; and,
having gained the confidence of a monarch even
more than any other interefted in the re-eftablifhment of peace and order, I may again render
fervices to humanity and my unhappy country.
Should the emperor refufe to hear my juftifica-
tion, and confign me to the oblivion of a prifon,
I fhall only have to fuffer and to die. But this
hiftory of my life will vindicate my name. The
confequences of the treachery and injuftice of my
perfecutors will fall on themfelves; and the emperor himfelf will regret me.

In the approaching month, I fhall be fifty-five
years of age. Shall I really fuffer lefs, if, by
fhamefully concealing myfelf, I can efcape a few
days of reproach or imprifonment?

I will now give you a short history of my life, which may serve as a supplement to my memoirs, if I am not allowed time to finish them. I was born at Cambray in 1739, of parents not affluent, although noble. My father was a man of great virtue and understanding; he bestowed on me a very careful and extensive education; at eighteen years of age I became a soldier; and at two-and-twenty I was honoured with the cross of St. Louis, and had received twenty-two wounds.

On peace being made in 1763, I began my travels, to study the languages and manners of different nations. The Emigrants have said, that at this time, I was employed as a spy by the French ministry. It is not improbable that the *petit-maitres* of Tarentum and Athens (if there were any such men there) have said as much of Pythagoras and Plato.

In 1768, I was put upon the staff belonging to the army in Corsica; and, having served with reputation in the two campaigns of 1768 and 1769, I was raised to the rank of Colonel.

In 1770, the Duke de Choiseuil appointed me minister to the confederates of Poland; and I commanded a body of men in that country during two campaigns, and conducted several very important negotiations with various success. As the measures of the confederates were ill concerted, their revolution was unfortunate, and ended in the partition of Poland.

In 1772, the Marquis of Monteynard, minister of war, employed me in correcting and revising the military code of laws; at the end of the same year, this minister by the express order of Louis the XV. entrusted me with the management of a secret negotiation relative to the revolution in Sweden; but, having received my instructions on this affair immediately from the king himself, and unknown to the Duke D'Aiguillon, minister

of

of foreign affairs; I was arrested at Hamburg in 1773, and conducted to the Baſtile by the orders of that miniſter. The irreſolute Louis XV. yielding to the importunities of Madame du Barry his miſtreſs, and the Duke Aiguillon, diſgraced the virtuous Monteynard, forebore to inform the Duke of the authority he had given me to nego-tiate, and ſuffered me to bear the weight of a criminal proſecution, which the Duke D'Aiguillon ſuſpecting the truth, feared to carry to all its ex-tremity. I rejected offers of friendſhip and pro-tection made me by this deſpotic miniſter whom I did not eſteem; and after lying ſix months in the Baſtile, I was baniſhed to the Caſtle of Caen for three months.

Louis XV. died ſoon after; and D'Aiguillon was diſgraced. I had no inclination to take advan-tage of the expiration of the *Lettre de Cachet*, for the purpoſe of regaining my liberty; I was anxi-ous to be completely juſtified, and therefore peti-tioned Louis XVI. to remove me to the Baſtile and to order a reviſion of my trial. The king would not permit me to remain in priſon, and com-manded M. du Muy, M. de Vergennes, and M. de Sartine to reviſe the trial, and thoſe three miniſters ſigned a declaration that I had been un-juſtly proſecuted. Immediately after I was ſent to Liſle, in my rank of colonel, to make a report reſpecting the new military manœuvres which the Baron de Pirſch had brought from Pruſſia. I had alſo a commiſſion to examine a plan for improving the navigation of the river Lys, and another plan of forming a harbour in the channel at Ambleteuſe. And theſe employments occu-pied the latter end of the year 1774, and the whole of 1775.

In 1776, I was joined in a commiſſion with the Chevalier D'Oiſy, captain of a man of war, and Colonel la Roziere, one of the ableſt engineers in

Europe

Europe, to determine on a proper place in the channel for the conftruction of a naval port. I paffed the year 1777, in the country twenty leagues from Paris. It is the only period of re-pofe in my life. At the end of that year, I was invited to Paris, by M. de Montbarey, minifter of war, on account of the rupture between England and her colonies, which I had long predicted.

In 1778, I procured the office of commandant of Cherbourg to be revived and given to me. Being perfuaded that Cherbourg was better calcu-lated that any other place in the channel for a na-tional harbour, and being aided by the zeal, acti-vity, and influence of the Duke d'Harcourt, governor of the province, I obtained a decifion, in favour of Cherbourg, of a queftion that had been agitated during an hundred years, concerning the preference to be given to Cherbourg or La Hogue, for the fite of a naval port. From that time till 1789, I was occupied in fuperintending the works of Cherbourg; and, during that period, I was but three times at Paris. When I firft arrived at Cherbourg, it contained no more than feven thoufand three hundred inhabitants, and when I quitted that place it contained nearly twenty thou-fand inhabitants.

The emigrants, not contented with faying I was a fpy from the miniftry while I was on my travels, have alfo reported that I was employed by the war office as one of the tools of its fecret intrigues, although the time that I have paffed at Paris, in the different journeys I made to that place during twelve years, did not altogether amount to fix months, and although in thefe journeys I very rarely vifited Verfailles.

Let us review this hiftory : twenty two wounds received in battle, fix campaigns made in Germany, two in Corfica, and two in Poland, important trufts difcharged, a city raifed from obfcurity to a

flou-

flourishing condition, a naval port established, fortified, and rendered fit for the purposes of the navy, twenty years spent in travels, that had a knowledge of mankind for their object, and in fine the study of languages, of the military art, and of the policy of nations; such are the events of which it is composed. It will be happy for France if she produce many such designing and selfish men. If those who were called by their birth, their wealth, and their dignities to maintain the honour, and produce the happiness of their country, had qualified themselves with equal care, France would either have needed no revolution, or the revolution would have been more happy and honourable. For my part, the revolution was not necessary to raise me to dignities. I should soon have been lieutenant-general in the ordinary course of promotion, and was on the point of receiving honours that men at that period sought after. I possessed an income of 20,000 livres, which was equal to my wants and desires. Yet I could not but see that France was disgraced abroad, and ruined within. I foresaw that she hastened to this latter period of her misery; and have often warned those of the ministers, whom I esteemed to be honest men, of the event.

When the revolution commenced, I deprived its character of much of its evil in the place where I commanded. At Cherbourg, the excesses of the populace were punished by me with death; but the people could not accuse me of being inimical to their liberty. Those who were placed in like situations would have rendered an inestimable service to their country, in exerting the same firmness with the same discernment.

The military governments of towns in France being suppressed, I went to Paris, where, during two years, I studied the influence and character of the revolution. The flight of the princes of France

was

was an irreparable injury done to the cause of the king. I foresaw that the exercise of the *Veto* would not produce the end that was proposed by it, and would occasion the ruin of the monarch's cause, and I opposed it by all the means that were in my power.

In 1791, I was appointed to the command of the country from Nantes to Bourdeaux. At that period a religious war raged in La Vendee, and the people laid waste the castles and lands of the nobility. I had the good fortune to calm the minds of the people, and to preserve tranquillity in that country till the month of February, 1792, when I was recalled to Paris, was raised to the rank of lieutenant-general, and appointed minister of foreign affairs.

I am reproached with having caused the war by my counsels; but I shall prove that the war was already inevitable, when I began my administration, and that indeed it might be said to have commenced. I acknowledge, however, that my opinion was decidedly for the declaration of war, as was also that of the king, who, not only approved of my memorial to the National Assembly on that subject, (which was three days in his hands) but made corrections in it, and himself composed the discourse he delivered to the assembly on that occasion.

At the end of three months, finding myself embarrassed by the various factions, and being sincerely desirous to see the king's council possessing proper dignity, and his measures governed by constitutional principles, I changed the ministry, and obtained a promise that the king would sanction two decrees which appeared expedient to his service. Having done so, I would have retired from the administration. The king would not grant me his permission; the ministry was again changed by his order, and I took the war department. But,

soon

foon perceiving that the court had deceived me, I resolved not to be the instrument of their intrigues. I predicted to the unhappy king and queen all the misfortunes in which they were involving themselves, and I gave in my resignation three days after being appointed minister of war.

I was not driven from the councils of the king as the emigrants have asserted, but resigned in opposition to the entreaties of Louis. He was two days before he would accept of my resignation, and he did not suffer me to depart without expressing the deepest regret.

After that period, I commanded the armies with the greatest success. If the French had displayed as much moderation and virtue as they have enjoyed of success, peace had been long since restored to Europe; Louis would have been on his throne; and the nation would not have been, as now, stained with crimes, and the slave of anarchy. France would have been happy and illustrious under her constitution and her king.

I have now, my worthy friend, given you a short history of my life, and it will stand in the place of one more circumstantial, if opportunity be not given me to prepare a fuller account for the public. My heart is unburthened in sending you this letter. Here, I wait the orders of the emperor, and the decision of my fate, without inquietude. My mind, far from being weakened is fortified by disasters; and I shall be always myself.

MEMOIRS

OF

GENERAL DUMOURIER.

FOR THE YEAR 1793.

BOOK I.

CHAP. I.

Of the General State of Affairs in France.

IN the early periods of the Revolution we have seen the French combating for their independence with courage. But there was too much violence in their mode of acquiring liberty to afford any hope that they would enjoy either that or their subsequent successes with moderation. Having been hitherto victorious, they had no doubt that they were now invincible. They no longer thought of maintaining the good-will of a people who had received them with open arms. They beheld nothing but conquests before them; and, while they tyrannized over the minds of their newly adopted brethren by turbulent clubs they robbed them of

F   their

their property; and left them without any species
of liberty either moral or physical.

Every person of character and political experience had retired from the management of affairs,
to escape the persecutions of an *Ochlocracy* that governed under the sanction of the dreadful society
of Jacobins. The King was in prison. The
worthy of every description were persecuted under the names of Feuillans, Moderes, and Intriguers. The constitution was destroyed. Paris
was in the hands of the federates, invited there
by the Girondine party, but who, on their arrival at Paris, had been gained by the Jacobins.
These federates now threatened to bring to the
scaffold Pethion, Briffot, and all the leaders of the
Girondine party. But their threats were loudest
against General Dumourier, whom Marat, Roberspierre, and the other heads of the Jacobins pointed
out as the instrument and protector of that party,
then distinguished by the name of *the politicians**.
This was a prejudice against the general altogether
unfounded; for he was unconnected with either
party, having no more esteem for one than the
other, but regarding them as equally adverse to the
tranquillity of France, which he saw no means of
establishing but by a revolution capable of de-
stroying the influence of both. To this end his
army was his only engine; and it will soon be
seen how little there was to be relied on.

France at the period of which we are now speaking, assumed an appearance of prosperity that deceived and elated the people; and more especially,
the predominant party. But she had rendered
herself odious to foreign nations; and was, in
truth,

---

*. The word in the original is *Politiques*. At Paris, the Girondists were called *Les Politiques*, or *Les Hommes d'Etat*. But these
epithets were used in disdain, because the politics of Statesmen
were deemed to be unworthy of the simplicity of freemen.

truth, divided and weakened within herself. On the side of Italy, the French army was extended among the Alps by the acquisition of Savoy; and was further aggrandized by the addition of the county of Nice. These territories had incorporated themselves with the Republic, but violence alone was the author of the union.

Clubs composed by a few corrupt men, who could exist only by a change in the government, were established in every city by the Jacobin soldiers that were scattered throughout the different armies. Their violent resolutions at once acquired the validity of law. Questions were not even put to the vote. Every thing was carried by menaces and force. And patriotic addresses arrived at Paris from the foot of the Alps, from the mountains of the principality of Basle, from Mayence, Liege, and the cities of Belgium. The National Convention believed, or affected to believe, that the blessings of our condition were ascertained by foreigners ranging themselves under our colours.

Geneva became a club instead of a republic. Claviere gave a loose to old resentments that he harboured against his country; and being appointed minister of finance by the Girondine party, he sacrificed General Montesquieu, who, in discharge of his duty as general of the army in the neighbourhood of Geneva, had attempted to save that city and Switzerland from the baneful influence of the Jacobins.

The principality of Porentruy, deceived by Gobet bishop of Paris, and by his nephew Ringler, two despicable adventurers, had also incorporated itself with France, and had adopted its dangerous reveries.

Custine was master of Worms, Spire, and Mayence; but he had neglected to enter Coblentz, and had evacuated Franckfort, after having excited the detestation of the inhabitants against the avarice

F 2   rice

rice and turbulence of a people in whose hands the torch of philosophy had lighted up the flames of discord.

Between Custine's army and that commanded by Dumourier in the Netherlands, another had been placed under the orders of General Bournonville. But this army had been nearly annihilated in a disgraceful expedition undertaken by its general against Treves, after he had lost the opportunity of attacking that city with advantage. One third of his army being thus destroyed, the remainder retired for the purposes of recruiting into cantonments in Lorraine. The Prussians and Austrians took possession of the intervals left open by this retreat; and their position, connected with Coblentz, Treves, and Luxembourg, entirely cut off the communication between Custine and Dumourier; so that there was no longer any concert in the efforts of the two armies. And indeed Dumourier's plans had already been deranged by the stupid pride of Custine, by the ignorance of the convention, and by the treachery of Pache, Meunier, and Hassenfratz, who having the direction of the war department and resolving to ruin Dumourier, had disorganized the armies and with-held their means of subsistence. The Netherlands were in the hands of the French army called the army of Belgium, composed of that of Dumourier and the army of the Ardennes commanded by General Valence. The latter was not more than 15,000 strong. The two armies occupied Aix-la-Chapelle and the banks of the Meuse. Clubs agitated all the cities of Belgium. The convention had sent commissioners to execute the odious decree of the 15th of December, that sequestered the public property of Belgium; and so had frustrated the hopes of uniting those rich provinces to the French republic although that union was the very object of this oppressive decree. But the convention

vention were eager to seize on the wealth of Belgium previous to any union. Such was the plan of the financier Cambon; and he boasted of the project.

The immoral and ferocious dispositions of the six commissioners employed in this affair were well calculated to ruin the scheme. Danton was a man of great energy of character; but was without education and equally detestable in mind as, he was coarse and disgustful in appearance. La Croix was an adventurer, a debauchee, and a braggart; and was destitute of all sense and honour. Camus, the most rugged, haughty, aukward, and pedantic of the Jansenists. Trielhard, little differing from Camus. Merlin of Douay, a well-meaning man; but splenetic, and infected with extravagant and theoretic notions. And Gossuin, a monster of a brutal and sordid spirit*.

To these commissioners were joined thirty-two others named by the executive council, but recommended by the club of Jacobins at Paris. The greater part of these assistants were miscreants who came only to massacre and pillage throughout the rich provinces of Belgium. They over-ran the unfortunate country; and while, by the terror of
sabres

---

* These portraits seem to be drawn with too much severity. If much may be said against these deputies, it is also well known that they have rendered many services to their country. We should have been unwilling to have published these and other personalities that are to be found in General Dumourier's Memoirs, if we had had any right to suppress them, and if we are not moreover persuaded that the important facts, extensive views, and useful objects of the work would amply compensate for some intemperate passages. Besides when we recollect the ingratitude and gross calumnies that have pursued General Dumourier (who probably has discovered more talent and conduct than any other person in the revolution, and who certainly as a general has gained the most important victories and acquired the greatest glory) we cannot wonder that in writing of his bitterest enemies, he has indulged himself in writing satire instead of history. *Note by the* British *Editor.*

fabres and fufees, they drove the inhabitants to demand their being incorporated with the French
republic, thefe men plundered the churches and
palaces, emptied the coffers and fold the furniture
of all who fell uuder their difpleafure, and whom
they marked with the odious name of Ariftocrats;
and whom often confifting of fathers of families
and old men, and women and children, they fent
as hoftages into the fortified towns of France.

The north and weft of France began to unfold
the feeds of difcontent againft this bloody and
horrible anarchy. The revolters of La Vendee
were not however dangerous as yet; and there
had been no difficulty in crufhing them utterly, if
any forefight had exifted in the National Convention, or in the Councils of the executive power.
But what is to be expected from a government in
which while the wife hefitated, mad men ftep in
and decide.

Two factions equally attrocious, the Mountain,
and the Girondine party, divided the Convention.

The former, made up of the moft furious Jacobins, neither palliated their wicked principles nor
their crimes. They fpoke of nothing but blood
and death. And, being without capacity to govern,
having neither knowledge nor digefted plan, they
would fuffer no dominion whatever. Not even the
principal men of the faction could boaft of ruling
it; and the liberty of the faction confifted in anarchy.

The other faction, compofed of metaphyficians
and intriguing ftatefmen, had long abufed the
fuperiority acquired by their talents, and their
more cultivated education. They had treated the
Jacobins with difdain. The executive council was
their inftrument. And they imagined they fe-
curely held the reins of government. But the
Convention had been difgufted by their infolence
and pride; and it was known, that this faction
were

were the enemies of royalty only becaufe they afpired to fill its place. Hence the independent part
of the affembly, thofe men who execrated the atro-
cities of the Jacobins, ftood yet more in fear of the
ambition of Condorcet, Briffot, Pethion, Genfonne,
Guadet, Vergniaux, &c. And thus all other
parties became united to humble the prefumptu-
ous Girondifts.

The meafure of bringing the unhappy king to
trial, refulted from the hatred of the two factions.
It ferved them mutually for food; but the Girondifts have too late difcovered how fatal it has been
to them. Louis, the victim of their ambition and
of their cowardice dragged them down in his fall,
and left the field open to the triumph of the Jacobins.

The factions that fplit the affembly, divided the
departments alfo; each efpoufing the paffions of
their deputies. Bourdeaux, Marfeilles, and Lyons,
hated the Mountain; and were the firft to begin an
oppofition, that has fince degenerated into a civil
war.

The Pyrennees and the inclemency of the fea-
fon, ftill fecured the frontier provinces of Spain;
and that kingdom, at its leifure, collected the
forces that were afterwards directed again Rouffil-
lon; while the Convention, occupied entirely by
their own quarrels, and by the ftate of Paris, provided none of the means of repelling the attack.

Paris, the moft miferable and moft guilty city
that has exifted, thought herfelf the rival of Rome,
becaufe in the fpace of a few months, fhe had become the fcene of crimes, maffacres, and cata-
ftrophes, that were the accumulation of ages in
the capital of the Roman empire. Forty theatres,
always crowded, amufed her trifling, cowardly,
and cruel inhabitants; while a fmall band of villains, no lefs ridiculous in their pretenfions, than
barbarous in their deeds, fupported by two or
three

three thousand dependants, the outcasts of the provinces; and many of whom, indeed, were not Frenchmen, destroyed the memory of the massacres and horrors of each evening by those of the succeeding morning. The frightful cavern of the Jacobins vomited forth every ill, and spread terror through every house. All men of property trembled, and citizens, who, in peaceful times would have been mild and virtuous, hardened their hearts against pity, and were ready to applaud guilt, lest they should become its victims. All who had the remains of virtue or shame were fled or were driven from the administration of the department, of the municipality, and of the sections. An infallible sign always precedes the fall of nations. Then good men hide themselves; and the wicked and violent alone remain in the conduct of affairs. And in this crisis, it is not even in the power of supernatural aid to save the people from the effects of public phrenzy.

Such was the terrible situation of France in the beginning of the year 1793. Such is the gulph to which democracy leads, when the populace takes the place of the nation, and tyrannizes over it by the Oligarchy of a few depraved wretches selected from the refuse of the people. At Rome a senate, during many ages, controuled popular vehemence; and directed it, not towards happiness, but to the aggrandisement of the nation; for Rome turned her arms abroad, that she might not destroy her own offspring. France has no such counterpoise as that of the Senate of Rome; and the want of virtue in the governing party can bring nothing but disgrace and misfortune on her head.

CHAP. II.

Of the State of the Armies.

ALTHOUGH the political condition of France had even poſſeſſed more ſolidity, and had been regulated by a prudent aſſembly, although France had gained the hearts of the nations to which her arms had opened her the way inſtead of having diſguſted them by a tyranny more offenſive than that of a formal deſpotiſm, it had been impoſſible that this new Republic ſhould ſupport herſelf againſt the intereſts of the whole of Europe, unleſs ſhe had eſtabliſhed a military ſyſtem capable of making head againſt a univerſal attack upon her territory by ſea and land. The National Convention, never miſtruſting themſelves on any ſubject, becauſe they were ignorant of the political combinations of things, iſſued a decree on the 19th of November, 1792, againſt every deſpot in the univerſe, and invited the people every where, to throw off their yoke; promiſing them protection and fraternity on condition of their adopting the French Syſtem. But they ought to have humbled the Empire, Pruſſia, Spain, and Ruſſia, before they made ſo proud a declaration. A juſt aſſembly, an aſſembly regarding the rights of man united in ſociety, (for man in a ſavage ſtate has no rights, and a ſtate of nature confounds all rights) would have perceived ſuch a decree to have been unjuſt. The maxim of *compelling men to come in* is not more philoſophical in a ſocial view, than it is in theology. The Jacobin preacher is not leſs unjuſt, than the preacher of the church of Rome; and it is unbecoming of liberty to be propagated, like the alcoran, by the ſword.

But

But in taking the violent step of the 19th of November, it will at least be supposed, that the Convention, desiring to range all men on the side of liberty, had taken due precautions that the decree should be something more than a vain and dangerous boast, and consequently that they had placed their military establishment on the strongest footing. General Dumourier, on becoming minister of the war department (which situation he held but three days, being appointed on the 13th and quitting it on the 16th of June, 1792) read a bold memorial to the National Assembly, proving clearly, that they thought not of the army, and that far from placing it in a state to support the war, they were trifling with the public liberty and safety. This memorial was forgotten. The campaign was begun. The General's success which ought to have gained him the confidence of his fellow-citizens, if no further yet as far as respected the military department, served merely to throw suspicion on every advice he gave them. They not only altered his plan of the campaign, but they were desirous of retarding his too rapid progress. The Girondine party frankly told him, they should be extremely sorry to see him force the enemy too promptly to demand peace, since they feared the consequence of the return of the army before they should have finished the constitution.

The Jacobins, who supposed the General to be connected with the Girondine party, accused him of ambition. Their contemptible journals, especially that of Marat, affected to make him at one time dictator, at another Duke of Brabant, and at another head of the Orleans faction, and under this last fiction, described him as intending to place the eldest son of the infamous and odious Philip, on the throne. Nothing could be more contradictory than these calumnies; for if Dumourier desired to be dictator, he surely was not the agent of the house

of

of Orleans; if his aim was to be Duke of Brabant, he had then an interest foreign to the party intrigues of his country. But the absurdest accusations were sufficient in France to tarnish innocence. It has however seen that calumny was too feeble to stop the progress of a victorious general; and machinations of a more effective nature were employed, and which ended in the destruction of the miliary resources.

Servan, having discovered the difficulties of the war department, feigned sickness; and while he declared the insufficiency of his strength for the fatigues of his situation, he appointed himself general of the army of the Pyrenees. Servan was lieutenant colonel in the preceding month of May. His health unequal to the duties of the cabinet, was robust enough to support the fatigues of the field. Yet the Revolution, it seems, was undertaken to reform the improper distribution and abuse of employments!

Roland, minister of the interior department, was the most intriguing and least capable of the Girondine party. He had a friend, named Pache; a man of talents and great zeal, who had formerly been secretary to the Marefchal de Castries and had educated his son. Roland imagined he could make himself master of the war department, in procuring it for Pache. We shall afterwards see how far the result was favourable to the designs of Roland.

Pache now became minister of war, chose the following men, or was obliged to appoint them, to fill the principal departments of his office; Meusnier, an academician and a man of sense, but of as depraved a mind as could be found in France; another academician, named Vandermonde; a Jacobin who had rendered himself ridiculous by the affected vulgarity of his manners, and dangerous by his intrigues, and who had assumed the name of

Haffenfratz

Haßenfratz to conceal the name of le Lievre, under which he would have been recognized to his difgrace ; and Audouin who was Vicar of St. Euftache and fon-in-law of Pache.

Thefe new minifters threw every thing into confufion in the different departments of the war office, during the moft important and hazardous campaign. The few perfons of experience that remained were difcharged and their fituations filled, not merely by Jacobins, but by fuch of them as had diftinguifhed themfelves in the maffacres of the firft fix days of September. The adminiftrations eftablifhed for the fupply of arms, cloathing, provifions, and for regulating the hofpitals, were abolifhed. The old and experienced commiffaries and contractors were either difmiffed, or calumniated, or dragged to the bar of juftice ; or thrown into prifon, and rendered infamous without being heard. As thefe imprudent and unjuft meafures equally affected all the armies, although particularly aimed at that of Dumourier, the complaints of the generals were univerfal. Commiffioners from the Convention were fent to examine into the truth of the complaints. Their reports were alarming. But the committee of military affairs, who in no cafe could have any other effect than to embarrafs the meafures of the war department however wifely concerted, was now made the inftrument of juftifying the falfe ftatements of Pache in direct oppofition to thofe of the generals and commiffioners. The Convention paffed to the order of the day ; and Pache efcaped with having been fimply ordered to the bar, and with the reproaches which the generals continued to lay upon him.

The commiffioners Camus, Goffoin, Danton, and la Croix, were themfelves witneffes in the month of December, of the diftreffed condition of the army in the camp of Liege ; and rendered an

account

account of it in their reports to the Convention, but without applying any effective remedy to the evil. The army was composed of forty-eight battalions ; the completeſt of which were from three hundred and fifty, to four hundred men, and many of them were not more than two hundred : the whole amounting to between fourteen and fifteen thouſand foot. The cavalry were about three thouſand two hundred. Moſt of the ſoldiers were without ſhoes, and encamped in the mud, their feet being protected by nothing but hay twiſted together. The reſt of their cloathing correſponded with this deplorable appearance. Clothes had been diſtributed to ſome, but thoſe, to the number of fifteen hundred, deſerted and returned to their reſpective homes. The ſick filled the hoſpitals, where they were in want of every thing. To ſuch a ſtate was the victorious army of Jemappe reduced after the conqueſt of Belgia.

This army had been obliged to ſtop ſhort on the banks of the Meuſe for want of proviſions ; and, if its diſtreſs had been known to general Clairfait, he might have engaged it with great advantage, for the carriages of the artillery were almoſt entirely deſtroyed, and in the preceding month of December ſix thouſand artillery horſes had died at Tongres and at Liege for want of forage. The foot had but ten thouſand fuſees in a condition for ſervice. The cavalry were in want of boots, ſaddles, cloaks, carbines, piſtols and ſabres. The army was without money ; and often the ſtaff officers raiſed contributions among themſelves to make out the ſoldiers ſubſiſtence-money for the day.

General Dumourier could have ſupplied all theſe wants in Brabant, Liege, and Holland ; and had even entered into the neceſſary contracts and made reports reſpecting them ; but every plan was rejected and all his arrangements deſtroyed. The
commiſ-

commissary Ronsin, had orders to condemn, embarrass and retard every measure. His hostility was open; he paid no regard to the opinion of the general: for he was certain of the support of the military committee, of the financier Cambon, of Pache and his dependants, together with the secret protection of the commissioners of the Convention, who appeared to blame these disorders, but suffered them to remain without a check, and in the account they rendered in the month of January excused Ronsin although they acknowledged him to be unfit for his situation.

Manufactures were established at Paris for every thing wanted in the armies. Cloth was conveyed from Liege to Paris to make clothing for the troops. Leather was bought at Liege, at Dinans, and all along the banks of the Meuse, to make shoes at Paris, which were sent to the army at nine livres each pair, altho' at Liege shoes cost no more than four livres, or four livres ten sous per pair. Cloaks that could be manufactured at Antwerp for nineteen or twenty-one livres each, cost fifty livres each at Paris; and cloaks were sent from Paris to the army. The corn of the Netherlands was sent to Nantz, from Nantz to Paris, was ground in the mills of Mont Martre, near Paris, and sent back to the Netherlands.

The greatest evil that resulted from these disorders, was their influence on the conduct of the soldiery. We have already taken a review of the character of these troops, and have seen how difficult it was for General Dumourier to avail himself of their courage. It may even be said, that he had accomplished what seemed to be impossible; and that in beating the Prussians and Austrians, he had obtained a victory more tedious and difficult over his licentious soldiers, having introduced discipline and love of order into an army, one fourth

part

part of which was composed of troops of the line, infected by the spirit of the times, and the other three parts of volunteers, each having an opinion of his own, and each proud of his victories, and rendered susceptible of more mischief than good, by his notions of equality.

In the beginning of the campaign of 1792, the battalions were in want of officers. The superior officers were ill chosen, and were without influence. The soldiers themselves chose their captains, lieutenants, and subaltern officers, and hence these officers were subject to the caprice of men, who acknowledged no superior. A single Jacobin was sufficient to ruin a battalion by his licentious discourses; and it was only by culpable condescentions that an officer could preserve his rank, or obtain promotion.

The city of Liege was the tomb of Frenchmen. They died there of hunger and every species of distress. And this city, where the army knew nothing but wants, was more fatal to it than Capua, with its enjoyments, had been to the Carthaginians.

The people of Liege had carried the Revolutionary spirit to an excess, proportioned to the excess of their sufferings when they were betrayed and subdued by the Prussians. They had therefore withdrawn their confidence from the leaders of the Revolution, who laboured to secure liberty on the foundations of wise principles. Fabry and Cheftrel, who were very honest men, and wished only for the welfare of their country, had entirely lost their influence. The populace of Outremeuse, perhaps the most dangerous in Europe after those of London and Paris, had made themselves masters, not of the government, for there was none, but of the public force. Those unhappy men thought only of vengeance and punishment. They conducted the French soldiers into the
houf

houses of their particular enemies, whom they treated as Aristocrats; that is to say, they pillaged and murdered them. This cruel intestine war, in which each French soldier took an active part either for or against his host, destroyed the little discipline and good conduct which had hitherto existed in the French army in the midst of misery, want, and complicated distresses. But it was impossible to punish, for it was impossible to discover the guilty. The people of Liege cast the fault upon the French; and the French recriminated upon the people of Liege. The General would have established the punishment of death for such crimes. It had even been demanded of him by his army in a moment of enthusiasm. But the Commissioners, while they seemed to approve of this severity, secretly and effectually opposed it. Since that time, we have seen that one of the causes of the execution of the unfortunate Custine, was the having established the punishment of death in his army.

Dumourier's army occupied cantonments from Aix-la-Chapelle to Liege, in which cities were all the officers who could not procure quarters with their battalions. So that the soldiers were almost left without commanders. Want had carried marauding to its utmost pitch. The soldiers robbed in bands from village to village; and the peasants took their revenge in killing such as, at any time, they found single.

General Dumourier, prevented by these circumstances from pushing on to Cologne, and forcing Clairfait to repass the Rhine, resolved at least to secure the Meuse. He therefore ordered the army of the Ardennes, consisting of 15000 men, and commanded by General Valence, to join him; and placed them on his right, in the countries of Stavelo, Malmedy, Spa, Verviers, and Huy. A body of 18000 men under the command of Gene-

ral

ral d'Harville, occupied the Meuse from Givet to
Namur; having his out-posts at Ciney, Marche,
and Rochefort. The army under General Miranda
occupied the left from Tongres to Ruremonde. It
consisted of 18000 men. New battalions, lately
arrived from France, formed the garrison of the
Netherlands. And this line along the Meuse a-
mounted to from 65,000 to 70,000 men; and would
have been sufficient to have seized upon the country between the Meuse and the Rhine, and to have
occupied the banks of that last river from Burick
to Cologne, if it had been possible, first, to take
Maestricht, which General Dumourier was not
permitted to do, although he had proposed it in
the beginning of December, and had it then in
his power; secondly, to place a garrison in Juliers,
which was also forbidden him because it was
deemed necessary to keep terms with the Elector
Palatine, lest he should deliver the passage of Man-
heim to the Imperial army, by which means they
would have cut off the army of Custine from
Alsace; and, lastly, if the army of Belgia had been
provided with provisions, arms, cloathing and
money, so that it might have marched in the month
of December, and have forced the Imperialists to
repass the Rhine.

General Dumourier was persuaded of the impossibility of his preserving his position on the
Meuse, while he should neither be in possession of
Guelders, Venloo, Maestricht, nor Juliers. He
wrote to the Convention and the Minister of the
War Department to that effect. The reasons of
his opinion will be found in his correspondence
with Pache, printed in January, 1793. It was toward the close of the preceding November that
his quarrel commenced with that Minister, with
the Jacobins who supported him, and with the
Convention who had not discernment to foresee
the effects of his criminal conduct. In December

H   began

began the trial of the unfortunate Monarch, whose mild character conducted him to the scaffold. From that instant, the general foresaw the crimes and misfortunes that have since sprung from the chaos in France. He attempted to sound the dispositions of his army respecting the King, but his Staff-officers whom he employed in the task effected nothing, and thenceforward the general was proscribed. Not one soldier, not one officer would consider the case of the king. Every one discovered the same apathy; and this cold disposition in the army on that point, hastened the General's design of visiting Paris.

C H A P. III.

General Dumourier departs from Leige for Paris.

GENERAL Dumourier was thus a prey to various chagrins in the palace of the Prince Bishop of Leige; and, if it can be a consolation to that Prelate, he may read with pleasure that after the most splendid victories, this general was more unfortunate than himself. He had been harrassed by the calumnies of the Jacobins from the moment that he had saved France by driving a formidable foe out of her territory. The conquest of Belgium had increased the *column of his enemies*, to express himself in the words he used to the National Convention after the battle of Jemappe. He almost reproached himself with having lost the opportunity of quitting the command that was offered him on his return from Champagne, by the ingratitude of his fellow-citizens. He had caused the war to be declared,

in

in his former situation as minister of foreign affairs; he had afterward conducted it with glory as a general; he had nothing wherewith to reproach himself on these accounts; but he saw the successes of the war mouldering away, and he could not but be penetrated with grief, since the important share he had taken in the public concerns during nine months, had identified his fate with that of his country.

All his letters and memorials were either rejected or misinterpreted;. and his counsels slighted. Cambon declared, nothing could be more dangerous to a republic than a victorious general. It was laid down as an axiom in the tribune of the National Convention, that ingratitude was a necessary virtue in Republicans. The Convention with-held the recompences due to the heroes of Champagne and Belgium, because the General had demanded them. By a decree, they authorized the minister of war to annul the nomination of officers made by the Generals. The corps were left destitute of officers. New and ignorant men came from France, to gather the fruits of the army's toils. The General complained of these things to the National Convention; and declared, if they would not do him right respecting them, both as to the wants of his army and the other evils which were the cause of its destruction and disorganization, he should be compelled to give in his resignation.

He demanded as an indispensible step, the revocation of the impolitic and unjust decree of the 15th of December, that had driven the Belgians to despair. Notwithstanding the remonstrances of the General, it had been resolved in the Convention that the decree should take place on the first of January. Cambon had obtained this decision; the four Commissioners Camus, Gossuin, Danton, and La Croix, supported him; and the

two

two latter boasted that they had done so, to a-
venge themselves for an insult they had received
at Ath, where they had been refused a lodging.
The General's honour was concerned in preventing the execution of the tyrannical decree,
because when he entered the Netherlands on the
third of November he had published, with the
sanction of the National Convention, a proclamation declaring to the Belgians, that the French
entered their country as friends and brethren;
that they came to give them entire liberty; and
that the people should be left to chuse their own
constitution and mode of government, without
interference from the French. The decree not
only destroyed the force of this proclamation, but
also robbed the unhappy Belgians of all remains
of liberty. The Commissioners sequestered the
public property and that of the clergy; and this
nation no longer possessed any public revenue,
nor the authorities necessary to preserve even the
form of government.

Cambon expected to find money for the expences of the war, in this plunder of a country
that was the friend of France, and that had not
been conquered, but had voluntarily associated
itself with the Republic. This criminal and
sordid conduct produced no benefit to France;
on the contrary, it deprived her of 40,000 men,
that the Belgians were willing to furnish, and fifty
millions of livres that they would have poured
into the French treasury, to contribute to the defence of their liberty; and was followed by the
loss of those fine Provinces, and excited a detestation of the National Convention and their
Commissioners, that will be eternal.

By an article of the decree the generals were
charged with its execution, and were required to
place the seals on the public property. General
Dumourier rejected this dishonourable employment;

ment; and the commissioners gave the charge to Ronsin, who employed as his instruments, soldiers and clerks of office, all Jacobins, who stole half the wealth they were ordered to secure in the name of the nation.

The general, being unable to prevent these base actions, resolved, at least, to mark his disapprobation of them as much as he could, to the Belgians, by being absent, if that were possible, while they should be transacting. On these, and all the other subjects of his vexation, he explained his views so clearly to the commissioners, and General Valence supported his reasonings with such force, that in a conference held at Leige between the commissioners, the generals, and the administrators that were entrusted with providing subsistence for the army, it being clearly shewn to these administrators that they could not furnish him provisions even to remain at Leige, much less to march forward, it was decided that Camus, the President of the commission, should return to Paris, attended by General Thouvenot, the first to make a suitable report to the National Convention, and the second to lay before the military committee an account of the wants of the army, and to obtain the necessary arrangements, and also solid and ample contracts for establishing magazines on the Meuse, and more than all the rest, to obtain a revocation of the decree of the 15th of December, which added the whole Belgic nation to the number of our enemies. General Thouvenot took with him also written observations of generals on the plan of the campaign, as laid down by the minister of war, and was to bring back with him a decision on that point.—— The journey, however, was altogether unsuccessful, notwithstanding the talents of General Thouvenot, because Camus, opiniated, deceitful and vulgar, and not contented without engross-

ing

ing all the honour of the embaſſy, aſſumed the ſole right of ſpeaking, ſupported the decree, and yielded to the will of others reſpecting the article of the committee of contracts. Thus, inſtead of removing the evils complained of, he only increaſed the difficulty of the general's ſituation.

Meanwhile General Dumourier ſhut himſelf up in the palace of Liege, and was employed in ſolliciting leave to return to Paris, and in reflecting on his miſery. He continued to declare in his letters and memorials that it was impoſſible for him any longer to hold the command if the Convention did not aboliſh the committee of contracts, which was no better than a den of knaves, and had cancelled his bargains of every kind with the Belgians; and if they did not change the miniſter for the war department, who had nearly ruined the armies, and if they ſhould continue to treat as conquered countries the provinces that ſhould be allied to France.

Such were the oſtenſible motives on which the general demanded leave to go to Paris. He had another, however, much more eſſential; but which he concealed with the utmoſt care. It was to endeavour to ſave the unfortunate Louis the XVIth, by repreſenting to the governing party the danger to which the nation was expoſed without; and the neceſſity of forming a ſolid plan for the campaign, which it would be neceſſary to commence at a very early period. He hoped the weight of this conſideration, aided by other motives, he meant to urge on the different factions in the convention, would ſecure a ſuſpenſion of the abominable trial.

General Dumourier was in this embarraſſed ſituation at Leige, and his mind agitated in the manner we have ſeen, at the very moment when the Jacobins were contriving to bring him to

trial;

trial; and when they pretended that he paffed
his time furrounded by courtezans and actreffes.
The miniftry indeed had fent him a detachment
from the opera; but thefe returned to Paris after
a ftay of no more than twenty-four hours. This
expedition, and that of a troop of comedians
from the theatre of Montanfier, coft the nation
more than 100,000 livres, the government pretending to inculcate French revolutionary principles to the Belgians, by exhibiting democratic
pieces in their theatres. The general difdained
to be the protector of fuch follies. All that he
faw of thefe deputies from the opera was at his
table, having invited them to dinner. And
certainty they conducted themfelves with much
decency and good fenfe; and difcovered much
more fagacity than the minifters that had fent
them.

The general found it extremely difficult to obtain his leave of abfence. Pache and the Jacobins feared his prefence at Paris. And having in vain urged the ftate of his health and his
need of repofe, he was at length compelled to
engage the commiffioners to demand the leave of
abfence directly in their own name, and to declare folemnly his determination to refign in cafe
of refufal.

In the midft of the vices that infected the
army, there remained a fentiment of juftice a-
mong the foldiers which fecured their attachment to a general with whom they had always
been victorious, and to whom they could no
way attribute their prefent diftrefs. The commiffioners therefore declared in their letters that
the army would certainly difband themfelves
fhould the general refign. The leave of abfence
arrived; and the General prepared inftantly to
depart, although La Croix propofed to make a
tour with him to Aix-la-Chapelle, in the hope

of

of detaining him still longer in that country. But Dumourier had secretly determined never more to resume the command; and was not willing by visiting the quarters, to make a tacit engagement with the soldiers for his return.

He arrived at Brussels; the command of which he had given to General Moreton. This man, who died in good time at Douay, had played a very curious part at Paris in the Revolution. He was an Aristocrat, taking that word in its most odious acceptation. He had been colonel of the regiment of La Fere, and he had been broken under the old government for the vilest acts of military despotism. Resentment threw him into the hands of the Republican party; and his influence in the councils of the Palais Royal had made him one of the chief actors in the Revolution. Become secretary of the Jacobins he plotted to procure a revision of his former sentence; but the sentence remained in its original state. He was afterwards appointed colonel in the army of the north, and as he was well acquainted with all the parts of the discipline of the infantry, and had considerable ability, General Dumourier appointed him chief of the staff to the army of the North. When Dumourier took upon him the command in Champagne, Moreton, who could not penetrate the veil that covered that affair, although perfectly brave, misconducted himself at the breaking up of the camp of Maulde; and was in danger of being massacred by the people of Valenciennes. General Dumourier's return to the army of the north, then become the army of Belgium, replaced Moreton at the head of his staff. But as Thouvenot possessed qualities for the situation which Moreton wanted, Dumourier made the latter lieutenant-general by seniority (for six months was sufficient to advance men to the highest rank by seniority in this revolutionary army)

army) and gave him the command at Bruſſels and in Brabant, in order to make General Thouvenot head of the ſtaff. Moreton then threw off all reſtraint toward General Dumourier, and entirely gained by the Jacobins, to whom he already owed many obligations, he oppoſed the ſentiments and judgment of his General in every poſſible way. He adopted the decree of the 15th of December; and became hateful to the people of Brabant. General Dumourier found him ſurrounded by the Jacobin populace. He had raiſed a corps that aſſumed the name of the Sans Culottes. Theſe came to make an harangue to the General; and uſed the phraſes *thou* and *citizen*. Dumourier was offended with this groſſneſs; and plainly told them that being chiefly French ſoldiers, they ought not to addreſs him in ſuch familiar phraſes, becauſe ſuch expreſſed an equality inconſiſtent with the diſcipline of an army; that they ought to call him *General* or *Citizen-general*, but never *citizen*, without ſuch like addition. He ordered their ſtatutes to be brought to him, and told them, that on his return from Paris, he would decide reſpecting them: for this mob demanded pay; and were really paid, though unknown to the General, with the conſent of the commiſſioners, as a recompenſe for their ſervices, or rather for the atrocious vexations they had committed.

General Dumourier had before this, ſent a proclamation from Liege, to engage the Belgians ſpeedily to hold their primary aſſemblies, and forthwith to chuſe a conſtituent aſſembly; becauſe in the decree of the 15th of December it was ſaid, that the ſequeſtration of the public property ſhould ceaſe when the people of Belgia ſhould have choſen their repreſentatives. The commiſſioners ſaw clearly enough that the appointment of an aſſembly would reſtore the Belgians to their liberty, and would deprive the commiſſioners of the admini-

ftration of the public revenue, and especially of
the plundering of the churches. They therefore
delayed the publifhing of the General's proclamation ; and afterwards its execution, and prevented
the holding of the primary affemblies at Aloft, the
place Dumourier had appointed, with a view to
counteract the influence of the populace of Bruffels. The General had been warned by the example of Louis the XVI. who might have avoided
the influence of Paris, by affembling the ftates-
general at Tours, Orleans, Blois, or Bourges.
But feeing, now, that the only means of fnatching
Belgium from the tyranny of the French Convention had failed, he continued his journey without
delay to Paris.

CHAP. IV.

General Dumourier's abode at Paris.

GENERAL Dumourier arrived in Paris on the
firft of January. Having reflected that, on his
vifit to that place after the expulfion of the Pruffians from Champagne, Marat and the other Jacobin journalifts had reproached him with fhewing himfelf at the theatre, and with feeking popularity, he refolved to avoid all places of public
refort, to live as privately as poffible, and to fee
only his particular friends, or fuch perfons as
might be ufeful to him in the objects of his journey.

He was five days without leaving his apartments, during which he compofed four memorials : the firft on the neceffity of recalling the de-

cree of the 15th of December, which had been confirmed and even aggravated by two decrees paſſed on the 28th and 31ſt of the ſame month; the ſecond, reſpecting the ill effects of the committee of contracts, and the neceſſity of replacing on the old footing the ſupplying of the army with proviſions, forage, horſes, clothing, &c. by the appointment of intelligent contractors; and the third and fourth on military affairs and the plans of the enſuing campaign. He concluded each of theſe memorials by a new declaration of his reſolution to reſign if the National Convention ſhould neglect any of theſe objects. He accompanied them by a letter to the Preſident, requeſting him to engage the Convention to form a new committee for the purpoſe of treating with the Generals, both as to the wants of the armies and future military operations. On the 7th of January, he ſent the memorials and his letter to the preſident, whoſe name was Treilhard, who had formerly been an advocate, and who ſhortly after this was joined with Merlin of Douay, another advocate, to the four former commiſſioners of Belgia. The preſident neglecting to communicate the papers to the Convention, General Dumourier wrote him another letter, very ſhort and peremptory.

On the 11th of January, a ſummary account of the affair was given to the convention. The letter was read. The memorials were ſuppreſſed there, and ſent to a committee of twenty-one members recently eſtabliſhed under the name of the committee of general ſafety. The moſt popular members of the other committees had been ſelected for this committee. They opened their ſittings on the 13th, and the General was invited to aſſiſt. The memorials were read. Ignorant and frivolous diſputes ſucceeded. All ſpoke together. And, after ſitting three hours, they broke up without making the leaſt progreſs. A further memorial,

memorial, more detailed on certain points, was
demanded of the General. As to the plan of the
campaign, the members unanimously agreed utterly to decline the confideration of it, alleging
that it belonged properly to the executive council. The General attended a fecond fitting of
the committee, held on the evening of the 15th
with a memorial containing a minute ftatement
of the required information. There were not
more than half of the members prefent. They
dropped in one after another; and, running
flightly through the memorial, which was very long
and intricate, no more was faid of the matter.

General Valence arrived previous to this fitting;
he was admitted, and read a memorial refpecting
the recruiting and new modelling of the army.
He propofed that the infantry fhould be divided
into brigades, by incorporating two battalions of
the National guards with each battalion of the line.
This project, adopted by the Convention in the
midft of the enfuing campaign, completed the
ruin of the French army, by rendering it a body
of mere volunteers without reftraint or difcipline.
The attention of the committee, whofe trifling and
inquifitive difpofition was equalled only by their
ignorance and indifference to the public welfare,
was caught by this novelty, although it ought never
to have been difcuffed but in a time of peace, or
at leaft not till the conclufion of the campaign;
and the committee entirely threw afide the important objects contained in the General's memoirs.

General Biron, having quitted the army of Alface to take upon him the command of that in the
country of Nice, affifted alfo at the third fitting;
and read a very preffing memorial refpecting the
new contractors and the committee of contracts.
The minifter of war being ordered to attend, and
not being able to anfwer the accufations of the
three Generals, was very groffly treated by the
committee

committee, charmed with finding an opportunity
of humbling a minister. They had, however, a
just occasion in the present instance, for the minister had no other defence to offer than the presenting of statements taxed with being false. And
the whole affair was referred to the military committee, the least respectable of all the committees
of the Convention.

General Dumourier afterwards attended a fourth
sitting. There were but five members present.
They discussed nothing. And, when they separated, they told him they would send for him
when they should have occasion to consult him
again. Immediately the General retired to a small
country house at Clichy, from whence he came
every day to Paris in the prosecution of his greatest object, that of saving the king. He was never
again called to attend the committee of general
safety. All the important affairs of France were
suspended during that moment for the pursuit of
a measure that involved the ruin of the nation.
The Convention were occupied by nothing but
the trial of the king; which was prosecuted with
the greatest bitterness and most indecent barbarity.

It was from the fate of his memorials that General Dumourier expected the salvation or the
ruin of his country. Had they been adopted, he
designed to have presented himself to the Convention, to have appeared in public, and openly
to have canvassed for the unfortunate monarch.
He might then have promised himself an important influence. He would have been surrounded
by a number of officers and soldiers of his army
who were on leave of absence at Paris. And,
by adding other means to these, he would have
commanded a party sufficiently strong to counteract the Jacobins, and their support, the federates.
This resource was lost; and, far from being able
to

to save the king, General Dumourier, destitute of power and influence, and considered as a man dangerous to the republic, because he disapproved of the crimes that were committing, feared only to injure Louis XVI. to precipitate the horrible catastrophe, which thenceforward appeared inevitable, and which has cost the General nothing but anguish.

A contemptible man, a man without knowledge and capacity, General La Bourdonnaye, the personal enemy of General Dumourier, in revenge for having lost the command of the army of the north in the preceding year, in consequence of complaints made against him by General Dumourier, published throughout Paris that the General had no other object in coming there than to save *the most honest man in the kingdom.* It was an appellation that indeed General Dumourier had very justly given to the king in a letter written in 1791 ; and which had been printed, with the other papers found in the iron chest, that Roland had lately delivered up to the Convention.

The same report was spread by the Jacobins, especially by Marat and his too active faction. It was said that the General held consultations with Roland and the Girondists every evening. And these last, offended that he was as unwilling to visit them in private, as the Jacobins, spread the rumour that he secretly saw *Philip Egalite*; that man unworthy of bearing the name of Duke of Orleans.

Dumourier went each day to the council ; and returned in the evening to Clichy. But he never dined with any of the Ministers, except Le Brun and Garat. He avowedly shunned the houses of Monge, minister of the marine ; Roland, minister of the home department ; Claviere, minister of the finances ; and above all, that of Pache, minister of the war department.

The

The war-office was become the filthiest place imaginable, where 400 clerks, and numbers of women, affected to carry slovenliness of dress and coarseness of manners into a system: Nothing was forwarded in the office, and nothing but rapacity was to be seen on all hands. Several of the villains employed in this department, having Hassenfratz and Meusnier at their head, worked day and night to collect false depositions, and to forge papers, to substantiate the accusation that Hassenfratz had made at the Jacobin society against the General, charging him with having embezzled twelve hundred thousand livres in his contracts in Belgium. They excited the hatred of the federates against the General; and often passing by groupes of these, he has heard them propose in a loud voice to place his head on the top of a pike. One day in particular, he thought himself happy in escaping through a narrow passage from a gang of those federates in the street of Montmartre, being warned against them by a tradesman who knew him, he having formerly lived two years in the same street. In the general meetings of the sections and in the coffee-houses, men were paid to declaim against him; and it was more than once in contemplation to seize upon his person.

The frightful Santerre, commander of the National guards of Paris, professed a great attachment to General Dumourier; and frequently pressed him to dine with his brother-in-law. His design was to entice him to dine with Marat. The General always declined the invitation, but on the politest pretences; obliged, in order to escape assassination, to behave with seeming respect to this execrable man.

A circumstance that happened at this time, rendered the situation of the General more critical, although he had no concern in it. Colonel Westerman had caned Marat on the Pont-neuf, for
having

having in his journal accused the Colonel of being the creature of General Dumourier, and the principal instrument of his robberies. Marat thirsted to revenge himself on the General, whom he supposed to be the author of the insult. Dumourier every day received intimations of Marat's designs against him, both from particular friends and by anonymous letters. And the General, for the first time in his life, adopted the precaution of carrying pistols in his pocket.

Du Bois de Crancé, the most cowardly and barbarous of the Jacobins, being one day at table with the General, shewed a disposition to offend him, imagining that the General, would be terrified by his great bulk and the ferocity of his air. General Dumourier laid hold of him, and imposed silence upon him very effectually. Du Bois de Crancé, in revenge, repeated every day in the Convention that Dumourier despised its members, painting it as an assembly consisting of four hundred fools headed by three hundred robbers. Thus a violent storm gathered round the General; and his enemies waited only for his resignation to arrest and try him. He had long before been proscribed.

CHAP.

CHAP. V.

Trial of the King.

IT was in the fame temper that this horde of cannibals pufhed on the trial of the King with the bitterest fury and the most horrible joy. The trial is in the hands of all the nations of Europe. The proofs, documents, and pleadings are published, and will remain the dishonour of the French nation to all posterity. Never was crime committed with fuch cowardice, fuch cold bloodedness, and fuch deliberation of mind. More than an hundred and fifty members of the pretended tribunal, had printed and published their opinion even before they had been made acquainted with the facts and papers, on which it ought to have been founded. They ought therefore to have abstained from giving their vote, or their vote ought to have been rejected; but the unfortunate Louis XVI. had none of the privileges of an accufed man on his trial. It is astonishing that the three hundred and ten members, who had the courage to vote for preferving the king's life in fpite of the daggers at their throats, had not refolutely insisted that each of the judges who had given his opinion publicly in writing, should be incapacitated from voting. But those friends of humanity will pardon this reflection in an historian, who, far from defigning to caft a reproach upon them, wishes to have the power of raifing a column to their names, as deferving of remembrance, as were the names of the heroes at Marathon. In the unwor-

K   thieft

thieft affembly in the world, were found three hundred and ten men, who acted with confcience and courage in the midft of general depravity and cowardice, and to whom the royal family of France has an eternal obligation. Juft and humane citizens, receive the homage of a foldier, who acknowledges more courage in your conduct than he has fhewn, or than he has feen, in all his battles where he commanded with fuch fuccefs and glory!

This homage is pure and difinterefted. He who pays it expects nothing from kings, and is the friend of liberty; and, having ferved his country honeftly has renounced her, whether fhe again be brought under the terrible yoke of defpotifm, or, by the ignorance and falfe policy of the combined powers, fhe fhall remain a republic under the iron fyftem of the Jacobins: For he no longer has any hope of feeing France governed by a conftitutional king, fubject to the law, and the fupport of the law. Your virtue fhall be more refpected in after times, inafmuch as it fhall appear in the fame page with the conduct of the Girondifts, whofe intrigues, as far at leaft as they are known to General Dumourier, fhall be delivered over, one by one, to hiftory whofe province it is to punifh crimes.

It has often been demanded if it were the intention of the Girondine party to fave the king. The queftion is difficult to anfwer; and it does not feem that we can difcover the truth, but in diftinguifhing two periods of very different characters in the exiftence of this faction, and confequently in its ambitious members, that varied with the change of circumftances.

It is certain that this faction, after having long fwayed the Convention and the miniftry, elated by the excefs of their influence, openly afpired to the eftablifhing of a Republic, as the means of perpetuating their power. They had fubdued the

feuillans,

feuillans, the moderate party, and the royalifts. They had enlifted moft of the daily journals on their fide. The Paris Journal, the Chronicle, the Monitor, the Patriot, the Thermometer, the Journals of Gorfas and of Carra, in a word, all that were efteemed, and in great circulation, were compofed, corrected, and edited by the members of this faction. The beft orators of the Convention, Gaudet, Vergneaux, La Source, Briffot, Genfonne, and Condorcet, gave reputation and currency to the opinions of the faction. They had feized upon the direction of the principal committees. Sieyes and Condorcet were at the head of the committee of the conftitution. Briffot and Genfonne governed the diplomatic committee affociated with that of general fafety. The committee of finances was entirely at the devotion of Cambon, whom the Girondine party at that time believed to be their partizan. And they ruled Paris during all the mayoralty of Pethion.

This faction may be called the Jefuits of the Revolution. They acted on the fame political fyftem; they poffeffed at firft the fame unlimited power; blinded, afterwards, in a like manner, by pride, they committed the fame faults, and underwent the fame fate. During their reign they contemned and infulted the royal family. Pethion, in the fame carriage with the King and Queen, on their return from Varennes, took every occafion to declare that he no longer defigned to fupport the monarchy. The unfortunate Queen related the fact to General Dumourier; and Pethion afterwards acknowledged it, on his naming it to him.

But in the month of November 1792, circumftances were entirely changed. The popularity of *King Pethion*, for fo he was called in Paris, had funk under the afcendancy of the Jacobins, and the Marfeillois, whom the Jacobins had gained by patriotic orgies. A weak but honeft

man,

man, named Chambon, had succeeded Pethion in the mayoralty. He was despised, and without power. The Jacobins tyrannized over the sections; and the commune of Paris assumed an authority independent of the Convention and frequently superior to it.

Barbaroux, deputy from Marseilles, one of the Girondine party, relying on his influence in that city, undertook to bring a new body of men from Marseilles; and, mean while, the party employed Roland, the minister of the interior, to invite the deparments to find Federates to relieve Paris and the Convention from the tyranny of the former body of Marseillois. Nothing could be more imprudent than this measure. It could not fail to produce a civil war, unless the new Federates, should strengthen them against their antagonists: gained like the former by the Jacobins, which happened in the sequel.

The intrigues of the Girondists were unmasked with great capacity, by Danton, La Croix, Roberspierre, and Marat. Impartial men in the Convention, saw the dangerous ambition of the Girondine faction. It was then that the party ought to have adopted a decisive conduct in defending the innocence of the king, and opposing the sentence of death; and then, had they fallen, they would, at least, have fallen with honour. But it it is most probable that, on the contrary, their efforts would have been successful, that the departments would have joined them to save the king and the country, and that the Jacobins would have been crushed. But the Girondine party possessed not the courage their situation demanded. They contented themselves with proposing an inadequate appeal to the people on the fate of Louis XVI. And this was considered as holding out another signal of civil war.

The

The Girondifts were terrified, and yielded to the torrent; but they did not fave themfelves by their cowardice in voting with the Jacobins againft the unfortunate monarch, who thus fell the victim of the united villainy of implacable monfters, and ignorant intriguers. Pethion had the bafe cruelty, in a moment, while pity yet hefitated to condemn the king, to recall the remembrance of the violence that was afcribed to him on the unhappy days of the 9th and 10th of Auguft. Having thus incenfed his hearers by an unworthy charge, he concluded by voting for death. The veiled opinion of Condorcet, amounted to the fame fentence. The conduct of this artful fchoolman, abounding in fubtlety, and deftitute of feeling, has been equally atrocious in every ftage of the Revolution.

Briffot, Gaudet, Genfonne, and Vergniaux, were even eager to vote contrary to their known fentiments.

The accufation againft Louis XVI. contained no article fufficienty weighty to fanction the judgment. The cataftrophe of the 10th of Auguft, was no crime to be imputed to the king. Carra had the impudence to publifh in his journal, and declare in the Convention, that the event of that day had been prepared by a committee of five perfons, among whom were Pethion, Roberfpierre, and he, Carra; that the committee met in a fmall public houfe in the Fauxbough St. Antoine; that the fcheme of obliging the king to arm and oppofe the people, had failed twice, and had even been on the point of failing on the 10th of Auguft. Hence it is clear, had this paper of Carra, been produced on the trial, it had juftified the king, by proving the neceffity of his taking up arms in his own defence. But neither juftice nor policy, nor good fenfe, were concerned in his trial.

Providence

Providence feems to have deftined the arrival
of this period, fo difgraceful to France, and fo
decifive of her fate. All things confpired againſt
the unfortunate and innocent victim. Even the
Emigrants, in the zeal of a miſtaken attachment,
adopted meaſures that were fatal to him. Bertrand, ex-miniſter of the marine, a refugee in
England, imagined he could fave the king by fending to the Convention authentic papers, proving
that the leaders of both parties had negociated with
the king in fecret. Danton and La Croix, efpecially, were fo directly implicated in the papers,
that their credit had been utterly ruined, if Danton, maſter of the *mountain*, that is to fay the Jacobin party, and La Croix, who influenced the
Plain, that is to fay, the independent part of the
affembly, had not united their efforts to bury the
memory of thofe papers with the ill-fated king.
The zeal of Bertrand, inſtead of faving Louis,
haſtened his death. The murder was committed.
On the guilty evening all the theatres were full.
Unhappy Frenchmen! When you ſhall read this
chapter, bathed with the tears of him who offers
the picture of the greateſt of your crimes to your
view, you ſhall tremble for yourfelves, and you
ſhall acknowledge the terrible vengeance that
awaits you to be juſt.

Fruitless attempts of General Dumourier in beha'f of the King.

AMONG the abfurd and unjuft accufations of the Emigrants againft General Dumourier, that which has obtained moft credit with ignorant and fuperficial men is, that he did not avail himfelf of the afcendancy which his victories gave him over his army, to lead it to Paris, and liberate the king. But it is to be confidered, firft, that his influence with his army was always very precarious, and events afterwards proved that it was not to be relied on; fecondly, that this army was more than a hundred leagues from Paris, was in want of every neceffary for a march, not being able even to quit the country of Leige, without great hazard of lofing its artillery for the want of horfes; that this ftep would have abandoned that country to the Auftrians, who alfo would have followed him; and that it would have been a degree of treachery to the honour and interefts of the French nation, which would have coft the General and all his principal officers their heads before they could even have entered France; thirdly, that this army had for fome time been in an abfolute incapacity of proceeding even to the Rhine, which was only twenty leagues diftant, and confequently could not accomplifh the longer march to Paris.

General Dumourier, however, did entertain the project of conducting, not the whole of his army to Paris, but a chofen detachment of troops of the line. But the example of Fayette, taught him

him to regard this meafure as a perilous extremity; and fome legal form and pretence was wanting to give it colour, and to preferve to him the confidence of his foldiers in the execution of it. He had declared, and written and repeated often to the leaders of the Girondine party, and efpecially to Barrere, who has fince occafioned fuch mifchief by his verfatility, that, if the convention were overawed, they had to write but four lines in the form of a decree, and he would forthwith march 20,000 men to their affiftance. Whether it were the effect of timidity, or a confidence in their own means and intrigues, the members that were ftill confidered as the moft refpectable in the affembly were unwilling to employ this refource. Indeed their views, fuch as they have fince been difcovered to be, would naturally prevent them from placing much confidence in the General, whom they knew to be perfectly attached to the conftitution and to the re-eftablifhment of order. Seeing no hope of fuch a decree as the General had pointed out, and governed by the motives that have been amply detailed in the foregoing chapters, he departed fingly for Paris; but he had fent before him, on leave of abfence, many of the officers commanding corps, and other officers, and foldiers, both of the line and national guards, and among them fome Parifians, all of whom had promifed him their fervices in behalf of the king. It is to be obferved alfo that at the time of his departure, although the trial of Louis XVI. was begun, it could not be forefeen, efpecially by one at the diftance of an hundred leagues, that the iffue would have been fo fpeedy and fatal. The General well knew that the criminal ferocity of the Jacobins would incite them to prefs forward this hateful and bloody cataftrophe by every means within their reach: but he thought that
the

the Girondifts, not for honeft reafons, but for
political reafons and for their own fafety, would
fpin out this affair, and fo give him time to take
meafures for the refcue of the king. It was not
till his arrival at Paris that he knew the true ftate
of things, and faw how inadequate his refources
were to the magnitude of the tafk.

General Dumourier had been on terms of
friendfhip with Genfonne, a deputy of the department of Gironde, and had found an opportunity of pardoning fome hoftile meafures of that
deputy toward him the preceding year, when
Dumourier quitted the miniftry. He had difcovered in Genfonne great capacity and judgment and a humane difpofition; and he willingly
renewed his connexions with him. General Dumourier opened his mind to him relative to the
king. He expreffed his horror at the crime that
was about to ftain the nation; he made him fenfible that fuch a detestable triumph given to the
Jacobins would end in the ruin of all the honeft
part of the nation, and would render the anarchy that afflicted France incurable; that fuch
of the nations of Europe as had regarded with
indifference and perhaps with pleafure our interior ftruggles, our war with Auftria and Pruffia,
and perhaps were not unwilling to fee our fuc-
ceffes againft thofe two powers, could not but be
fhocked at the barbarity of murdering Louis
XVI. and would be thenceforward engaged in
honour to join the enemies of France, till we
fhould have every power in Europe againft us
without one ally. Thefe reflections feemed to
make great impreffion on Genfonne; but to
whatever caufe it was owing, he undertook nothing, and even avoided the General, who had
afterward little opportunity of feeing him.

Dumourier converfed with feveral other deputies of the fame party, as well as with many

L   of

of the independent party in the Convention, to
whom he reprefented that, the nation being now
a republic, Louis was to be treated fimply as an
individual; that it was indecent, impolitic, and
unreafonable to wafte time, that ought to be employed in preparations againft the dangers of the
enfuing campaign and in reinforcing the armies,
in the profecution of the trial of a fingle man,
whofe fate was of no importance to the nation;
and that it would be wife at leaft to fufpend this
ufelefs meafure till after the war. The more
reafonable of them acknowledged the trial to be
an unjuft and unwife proceeding, but faid, that
the members of the *Mountain* had taken their
meafures, and, fhould the trial now be abandoned
by the Convention, the Jacobins would excite an
infurrection, fall upon the temple, and maffacre
the whole of the prifoners. The General then
told them that he could not think they were fufficiently authorized by their conftituents to try
the king; that, fince they made an affair of
confequence of the trial, it appeared to him it
would be neceffary to their own fecurity to demand inftructions in precife terms on the point
from the departments, leaft one day they fhould
be reproached for the deed by the nation, and
leaft they fhould one day become perfonally ref-
ponfible for the irregularity and violence of the
act. They anfwered to this, that the imprudent
propofal of appealing to the people made by the
Girondine party had deprived them of the refource the General now propofed; fince it was
feared the convoking of the primary affemblies
for fuch inftructions would be the fignal of a civil war.

It then occurred to the General to fuggeft an
idea that feemed to have great weight with thefe
deputies, although in the end it failed of effect
like all the reft, becaufe every man feeing a
poiguard

poignard at his breast, chose rather to be a mur-
derer than a victim. The idea was, that a long
war had existed between the nation and the king,
that the day of the 10th of August had decided
the fate of both, that the king had fallen into
their hands, and could no longer be considered
as any thing but a prisoner of war, yet without
criminality, because both parties had in like
manner had recourse to arms; that a foreign war
raged against the nation, and that they ought to
deem themselves fortunate in having a precious
hostage in this prisoner, who might serve them in
a case of extremity. The General added, that
should they persist in thinking the king guilty,
they ought to form a tribunal authorized to collect facts, to examine and confront the witnesses,
and to prepare the way for a final decision, with a
deliberation due to the subject; that this act of
justice would satisfy the bitterest enemies of royalty, would give the people time to reflect, and to
the Convention an opportunity to finish the constitution, which was the grand object of their
mission; and when the primary assemblies should
be convoked for the acceptance of the constitution, all the proceedings of the tribunal might
be laid before them, and they be called upon to
decide the fate of the king.

Having spread this opinion in conversation
and even in writing, the General saw Pethion,
with whom till this period he had been on terms
of friendship, and represented to him that it became him personally to interest himself in behalf
of Louis XVI. since otherwise, a malignity of
mind would be imputed to him that certainly was
not in his character. Pethion appeared to be
moved by the General's reasoning; and declared
that personally he *loved* the king, and that he
would exert his utmost influence to save him.

General

General Dumourier then addreſſed himſelf to Roberſpierre, by the medium of one of his friends. He repreſented that it was entirely in Roberſpierre's power to ſave Louis XVI. that the magnanimity of the action would immortalize his name, and that in conſequence of it the generals of the army would look up to him as the firſt man in the ſtate, and that the dictatorſhip would be the reward of his virtue; but that otherwiſe he would fall into the ſame contempt and execration as Marat, with whoſe name that of Roberſpierre would thenceforth be conſtantly aſſociated. This idea the General knew to be peculiarly odious to Roberſpierre.

General Dumourier knew that the Jacobins deſpiſed the Convention and hated the Girondine party. He inſinuated to them by ſecret agents, that if they wiſhed to become maſters of France and Europe, and to riſe on the ruins of the National Convention, they had only to declare their will that the trial of Louis ſhould be ſuſpended, and that a more important object, the ſtate of the war, ſhould be taken into conſideration.

Drouet, poſt-maſter of St. Menehould, who had arreſted the king at Varennes, was a deputy of the Convention and a Jacobin. The brother of Drouet, a very honeſt and faithful man, was in the General's ſervice, and was greatly attached to him. Dumourier gave this man inſtructions to prepare his brother's mind for the impreſſions he wiſhed it to receive, and afterwards to bring him to Clichy. The General painted to Drouet the crime he and his aſſociates were committing againſt the king, with ſuch energy, that Drouet, ſtruck with horror, promiſed to move for the ſuſpenſion of the trial both in the Convention and in the club of the Jacobins. Had there been

one

one member sufficiently resolute to make the proposition, the king had been saved. No one had
the courage. Drouet fell sick and was not present when the sentence was passed.

Each day the General visited various parts of
Paris, went into the shops and houses of individuals, and took occasion always to turn the
conversation to the king's trial. He observed
how strange a circumstance it seemed that the
Convention should suddenly become a tribunal ;
that if Louis were still king, the nation ought to
decide by whom and with what forms he should
be judged ; that if he were no longer king, it
was unfit that time so precious to the nation,
should be lost in enquiring into the guilt of an
individual. And to these considerations he added
reflections on the mild virtues and misfortunes of
Louis XVI. Sometimes he was listened to with
eagerness and pity; but frequently, he was requested to forbear speaking of so *dangerous* a to-
pic ; and sometimes condemned for introducing
it. At times, he exposed himself to serious danger, by expressing his surprize, that in a great
city like Paris, there should not be five or six
thousand men with courage sufficient to rise a-
gainst two or three thousand villains, who calling
themselves Federates, held the city in absolute
subjection. A well informed tradesman, casting
down his eyes and blushing with shame, made
this answer one day to the general : *Citizen, I see
what you would have us to do. But we are cowards and the king will be sacrificed. What do you
hope from a city that, having 80,000 armed men,
suffered itself to be intimidated on the first days of
September, by less than 6000 Marsellois and Bretons ?* The general left the man's house, and retired to an unfrequented part of a public walk,
to indulge in his melancholy reflections.

Those

Thofe foldiers of his army that he met with from time to time, feemed to be devoted to revelling, and to be wholly infected with the phrenzy of the Federates; and fome even joined the party of his enemies, filling the different clubs and meetings of the fections with abfurd accufations againft him.

From all thefe attempts to ferve the king, which the general renewed every day in various forms and difguifes, and with much rifk to his own perfon, he reaped nothing but the dreadful certainty of the king's ruin. Paris feemed indifferent on the fubject. During the twenty days previous to the death of the king, that he ftudied the temper of that city, he perceived not the fmalleft commiferation, neither among individuals nor in the public, in behalf of the unfortunate Louis. Nor indeed any abftinence from their amufements in the frivolous and favage Parifians.

CHAP. VII.

Death of the King.

ALTHOUGH General Dumourier's conftitution was robuft, his health yielded for a while to the acute vexations of his mind. On the 18th of January, he fell fick and was confined at his houfe at Clichy, till the 22d. He now refolved to quit Paris in a few days; and never to enter it more till he fhould come to difperfe that un-

worthy

worthy affembly, who were bafe and wicked enough, wantonly, precipitately, and without proof, to condemn to death an innocent king, who had ever loved his people, whofe faults were not his own, who had banifhed the torture from criminal trials, who readily adopted every propofal for the public benefit, and had himfelf invited the nation to remedy all abufes and to provide for its happinefs. Kings are fubject in common to many of the caufes by which Louis XVI. was reduced to this unhappy condition; they are befieged and betrayed; they are kept in ignorance and fee nothing as it really exifts; nor have they power to quit the circle in which they are placed, in fearch of the virtuous man whofe pure dignity fhuns the corruption and infolence of courts.— But it muft have been the completeft diforder that could hurry a whole nation to the murder of their king, after having often bleffed and adored him; and having compared him to Louis XII. Henry IV. and all the beft and moft beloved of their monarchs. The club of Jacobins conducted the French to this pitch of folly and wickednefs.

The 21ft of January, the day of the death of Louis XVI. is the true epoch of the ruin of the Republic, of the reftoration of the monarchy, and it may be feared of the triumph of defpotifm. The French nation began the career of liberty glorioufly. Their firft exceffes were pardonable, as they refulted from the obftinacy of the abufes it was neceffary to deftroy. A noble conftitution, although in fome degree it was imperfect, feemed to fecure the happinefs of France. General Dumourier's journeys into England, Germany, Switzerland, and Italy, at that period, convinced him of the general approbation it obtained. But the king, feduced by his perfidious counfellors, attempted to efcape from his people, after having

fworn

sworn to maintain the constitution. He was discovered and taken. The National Assembly of France acted as became a great nation. They restored the king to his rights; and from that instant the king ceased to be dangerous to the liberties of the people. He was governed faithfully by the principles of the constitution. They were engraven on his heart. And if his ministers or his courtiers still sought to violate the law, the constitution had provided a remedy for the evil. The agents of the executive power were responsible with their lives for misconduct in the government, but an absolute inviolability was attached to the person of the king. The third legislature of France however, tended visibly to Republicanism; they were bent on the overthrow of the constitution. It was necessary to raise new accusations against the king for his destruction; and to this object the Girondine faction proceeded with the most refined perfidy, while the Jacobins openly acted in the same cause with a wild and brutal insolence. Carra and the journalists of the Jacobins have placed this subject in the clearest light, in tracing the intrigues which engendered the catastrophe of the 10th of August.

The affair of the 21st of June, was a prelude to that catastrophe, although directly it produced nothing more than a disgusting insult to the nation and the constitution, in the unfortunate person of the king. The ferocious Santerre was heard to say on that day, *We have failed now, but we will return again.* The National Convention neither punished nor resented the insult. On the contrary, the two factions, which notwithstanding their mutual hatred had many wicked objects in common, were preparing for the execution of a greater plot; and had assembled the Marsellois and Bretons from the extremities of the kingdom, to insure success.

These

These were the true causes of the bloody and
decisive 10th of August. The ministers and generals, it is true, took measures, on their part,
against the assembly, and the Jacobins; supposing
however, that they were culpable, the law was
armed against them, but ought to have had no operation on the king, who was both innocent and
inviolable, and who was to be considered merely
as the occasion and not as the author of the steps
taken in his name. The nation was convinced of
this truth; and if Louis had been firm he had not
fallen. His assassins basely punished the mildness
of his character with death; and the mildness of
his character should have pleaded for mercy.

But this good and weak monarch found in his
religious principles, a strength that bore him he-
roically through his martyrdom. The particulars
of his death are preserved, and are inestimable
aids in the study of the human heart. They add
new aggravations to the crimes of the Parisians.
An innumerable crowd attended the execution.
Barbarous joy, or an unfeeling curiosity, were the
only impressions that appeared in the guilty spectators. No one had the courage to shed a tear;
and it will scarcely be believed, that the domestics of the good king pressed nearest to the scaffold, and were the most implacable of the multitude.

On arriving at Paris, on the 22d, General Dumourier went to the house of Garat, minister of
justice, who seemed to be extremely affected by
the death of the king, but more especially by the
duty that had been imposed on him, and the other
ministers, of reading the sentence to the king.
The unfortunate Louis during the solemn office,
remained standing, and assumed a tranquil and ma-
jestic countenance, without offering remonstrance
or complaint. He said only, that it was not just
to charge him with treason, since his intentions

M   had

had always been pure, and since he had constantly desired the welfare of his fellow-citizens. After requesting a little time to prepare for his death, he dismissed the ministers with an air of dignity and gentleness, the remembrance of which affected Garat very much in speaking of it. General Dumourier, Cabanis the friend and physician of Mirabeau, and the minister, were mutually affected. They read over the will of this unfortunate prince. It had been written with his own hand, in some places there were erasures, but the writing was clear, and without any marks of being written with agitation. It contained four pages written on letter paper. The first was consecrated to religion, and the homage was just; since, in that principle, he found courage, support and consolation. The three other pages exhibited an example of magnanimity, reason, and philosophy. This will, since published to the world, is one of the noblest writings that the mind ever produced under suffering circumstances. The monsters of the National Convention have said, that this writing justified the king's sentence; because, having no object in common with the world, on the point of becoming the victim of the ingratitude of his subjects, he had employed in two or three places the language of royalty, and disdained to flatter their prejudices.

During the existence of a monarchy of fourteen hundred years the French have assassinated many of their kings. But the deed was always the crime of an individual; the rage of the nation against the perpetrator was extreme; and the villain was punished with the most horrible tortures. It was reserved to an enlightened and philosophical age to produce a like crime, committed in the name of the whole French nation, approved by the majority, and regarded as an act of Heroism.

Is

Is the continuance and prosperity of a republic, founded on such guilt, soberly to be expected?—certainly not. The monsters have killed Louis XVI. but they have restored royalty. This inconsiderate and changeable nation, always running to the extremes of passion, will herself massacre her iniquitous judges and her furious Jacobins, and run to adore new kings. The efforts for a reasonable liberty that have been made during three years by true Patriots will be lost; and France will present the picture of a monarchy crowded with disgraces and crimes, dismembered and ruined, in which a rigid despotism must long combat a destructive anarchy before the reign of the laws can be restored: and then it shall not be the laws of the people. The whole of this generation, even those that are but newly born, shall endure the punishment of the atrocious crimes of four years: crimes that posterity will scarcely be persuaded to credit.

CHAP. VIII.

General Dumourier's Conference with Cambon.

HAVING particularly traced the transactions that most affected General Dumourier in a catastrophe that he could neither prevent nor foresee, it will be necessary to pursue the account of his other occupations in Paris during this unhappy month of January. An essential object of his journey was to obtain the suppression of the decree of the 15th of December, or at least a tacit agreement from the Convention, that it should not be put in execution in Brabant. He demonstrated to

the

the Convention that the people of Brabant were
wholly alienated from the French; than an open
rebellion was to be feared if the decree should be
executed; that on the appearance of the Austrians
in force the French would have an additional enemy in the Belgians, who might easily attack their
weakened garrisons, cut off their provisions and
render their retreat impossible. The Convention
were too presumptuous, and too much taken up
with the king's trial to attend to these remonstrances.

One individual of the Convention controlled
the department of the finances with the most absolute sway. This was Cambon a man of a most irregular mind; ignorant and destitute of found
principles, yet scheming and unrelenting in his
projects. D'Espagnac had been arrested on the
22d of November, along with Malus, for fulfilling
an engagement that they had made with Servan
respecting carriages for the army, and which was
very important to the nation. He was still a prisoner at Paris; but at liberty to go about with a
guard. He possessed a mind abounding in resources. He had gained the confidence of Cambon on
all the subjects of finance, and offered to procure
the General a conference with this dictator of the
national treasury; the General consented and they
went to breakfast with Cambon. This man boasted of having obtained and supported the decree of
the 15th of December. His reasons for the project
he said were that the treasury was empty; that
France had six hundred thousand troops on foot,
and paid two hundred million of livres per month
for the expences of the war. The General observed that six hundred thousand men ought not to
cost two hundred millions per month, and that the
armies of France did not amount to more than
three hundred thousand effective men. Cambon
answered, that the national guards of all the frontier

tier cities received the same pay as the army, as
well as part of the national guards of Paris; he
declared he saw no other resource, than the execution of the decree, for carrying on the war; that
specie already cost the nation fifty per cent. and
that soon it would not be procured even at cent.
per cent.; that he had but one remedy against this
evil, which was to seize on all the specie in Belgia, and the silver in the churches and banks. He
acknowledged this to be unjust, but he thought it
unavoidable; he said, that when the Belgians
should be ruined and reduced to the same distress
as the French, they would necessarily unite their
fate with that of France, as the people of Liege
had done, who threw themselves into our arms,
being poor and involved in debt. He added,
that then France would admit the Belgians as
members of the Republic, and with the same policy they might hope to proceed conquering people after people; that the decree of the 15th of
December was well calculated for this purpose,
because it tended to disorganize the neighbouring
states, that being the most fortunate thing that
could be done for France.

The General objected that, beside the barbarity
of the project, it was impracticable; that we
were now in the middle of the month of January;
that our armies were weakened; that no one
thought of the means of recruiting them; nor of
the plan of the ensuing campaign, although on the
eve of being opened; that the people of Belgium
were entirely averse to the disorganizing principles of our Revolution; that we had neither
time before us to remove what he (Cambon) called their prejudices, nor to crush them; that in
the beginning of the approaching March, the
enemy would attack the French posts upon the
Meuse, which were too distant from each other,
and not sufficiently strong; that, masters of the
passage

paſſage of Maeſtricht, they would penetrate the centre of the French line; that the Belgians, finding a power to protect them, would take up arms every where at once, and would put to the ſword the garriſons in the interior part of Belgium, compoſed of feeble battalions of new levies; that, occupying the poſts behind the French, they would not only cut of the proviſions of the army, but its retreat; that in this ſituation the army could not gain France, but would be entirely ruined, and thus all would be loſt to the Republic. General Dumourier repreſented, moreover, that theſe odious robberies would not produce as much to France as would a juſt conduct toward the Belgians; that it would be more prudent to borrow part of the treaſures of the clergy, and ſo to intereſt them in our ſucceſs, than to ſeize upon the whole by violence; that, as to ſpecie, there would be no neceſſity for ſending any from France into Belgium, where it was in abundance; that the true means of putting it in circulation, and at length to replace it by aſſignats, was to engage the rich merchants of Antwerp, Bruſſels, and Ghent, in the furniſhing of proviſions, clothing, and all the neceſſaries for the war; that, in this way, the ſupply of every thing would be ſecured, and the expences reduced to one half; that the contractors would receive aſſignats in payment, and would be compelled by their own intereſt to give them currency. The General obſerved that the Convention, by annulling the decree of the 15th of December, would effectually free the Belgians, whom they had reduced to a ſlavery more revolting than their former ſervitude; that in this caſe the Belgians would form a free conſtitution, raiſe troops, and join our arms; that this fraternity of arms and mutual ſervices would induce them, more effectually than any other means, to demand at leaſt a

permanent

permanent alliance with the Republic, if not an entire union.

Cambon feemed inclined to yield, efpecially when the general promifed him that, fhould thefe juft, moderate and wife means be adopted, he would not only forbear longer to demand any thing for his army, which the refources of Belgium could provide for in abundance, but that he would procure the French treafury feveral millions by way of loan. He well knew that the Belgians, to withdraw themfelves from their prefent ruinous flavery, would fulfil the promifes which he now made in their name.

After this firft conference, Cambon went to the Convention, and, in the heat of the debate, faid in the tribune, that if the decree of the 15th of December was not executed, it would be becaufe Dumourier had oppofed it by the prerogative of his *Veto.* Notwithftanding this dark treachery, in which, to render General Dumourier odious, Cambon affimilated him with the king, whofe trial was then profecuting with bitternefs, the General confented to have another interview with him, and even invited him to dinner, together with a deputy named Ducos.

The fecond conference, which lafted more than fix hours, was not carried on with much temper. General Dumourier having faid that if Cambon was refolved upon oppreffing the Belgians, he might feek another General, fince Dumourier never would confent to become an *Attila* to a people who had received the French as friends and brethren ; Cambon took an opportunity to tell the Convention that nothing could be more indecent than to hear a General threatening to refign in confequence of every decree that was paft contrary to his opinion ; that the Republic muft not reft upon one man, and that they ought either to impofe filence on the General, or to punifh him.

In

In this fruitlefs manner terminated the General's conferences with Cambon, whom he exprefsly warned againft the events that have fince happened.

It was not without reafon, Cambon had faid, that he was devoid of refources for the war. In January, there was no more in the national treafury than an hundred and ninety-two millions of livres in affignats, and from fifteen to twenty millions of livres in fpecie. Thefe fums were not fufficient for the army till the month of April, and the whole prefumed value of the lands of the clergy was already confumed by the emiffion of affignats on that fund.

Dumourier acquired this knowledge in the fecond fitting of the committee of general fafety. As it was then refolved to augment the army to three hundred and feventy thoufand men, he reprefented to the committee, that the decree for that purpofe would be ufelefs, as was the cafe with others of the fame kind the preceding year, if the minifter of war did not at the fame time prefent a ftatement of the fums neceffary for each particular article belonging to the augmentation, fuch as clothing, arms, horfes, &c. and if the Convention did not place thefe fums at the immediate difpofition of the minifter of war. Cambon, who affifted at the fitting, acknowledged the truth of the General's obfervation, but ftated the poverty of the treafury, and faid he knew not on what fund to iffue new affignats, fince the only refource that remained was the national forefts, and the eftates of the emigrants. Inftantly, the violent part of the committee cried out, they had nothing to do but to fell thofe eftates forthwith. Difputes fucceeding, the General requefted leave to give his opinion.

He defired the committee to confider that the lands of the clergy had fold exceedingly ill; that

a part

a part still remained unsold, the general apprehension being such that there were no buyers;
that, if under these circumstances, they should
order the sale of the estates of the emigrants, valued at more than twelve hundred millions of
livres, this great addition to the lands on sale
would still further diminish the value of the whole,
and complete the ruin of the nation; that the discredit of assignats recently issued would be still increased by this fatal operation; since the public,
judging by the price of the lands, would doubt the
sufficiency of the funds on which the assignats were
grounded; for, supposing they should hazard the
emission of twelve hundred millions on the estates
of the emigrants, as some members had proposed,
either they would not find purchasers, or the produce of the sale would not amount to the third of the
enormous sum; that then the state would lose the
other two thirds of that sum, and would be menaced with inevitable bankruptcy.

As to the national forests, he represented that
wood was already very scarce in France, and, if
they alienated these forests, the purchasers would
cut down the whole; that, besides the enormous
consumption of wood for articles of every kind,
France had not a sufficient quantity of coal for firing; and that, independent of this inconvenience,
which France would feel for more than a century,
this resource would not produce, at the utmost,
more than two or three hundred millions of livres,
although it stood valued at eight hundred millions.

The weight of these considerations was acknowledged, and it was agreed to leave these two objects untouched; and thus, General Dumourier
saved the estates of the emigrants for that time:
but, neither this service, nor many others General
Dumourier has rendered the emigrants, could
ever obtain him justice or candour on their part.

N   The

The committee refolved upon propofing to the Convention the iffuing of fix hundred millions of livres in affignats, on the grofs fund of all the national lands, without appropriating any fpecific part for the fecurity.

This mode of iffuing paper on vague funds is a dangerous practice in finance, and it was this kind of abufe of confidence which ruined *Law*'s fyftem in 1720. However, the committee had as yet kept it within bounds. It has fince been carried to twelve hundred millions of livres. This is a fmooth defcent that leads to bankruptcy; but bankruptcy is the laft refource of Cambon. He has himfelf faid that it is inevitable. As to the Convention they are not employed in confiderations fo profound. They have no object but to exift from day to day, without the trouble of inquiring what will be the refult. In fuch hands is the richeft kingdom in the univerfe.

CHAP. IX.

Interview of General Dumourier with fome Jacobins.

DUMOURIER had been a member of the fociety of Jacobins in the early part of its career; but, at that period, neither Marat, Camille Defmoulins, Bazire, Merlin, Chabot, nor Bourdon, were known in the fociety, nor the reft of that lift of contemptible characters, afterward chofen, to the furprife of all juft men, to form the moft atrocious affembly in the univerfe. The General never attended their meetings very affiduoufly; although

although the adventure of the *red cap*, which he was obliged to put on when he went to the Jacobin society on his being made minister, might beget an opinion that he was a zealous partizan of the sect.

The following is the history of the fact. Dumourier told the King, that he imagined it would be useful to the King's personal interest, but especially to the public concerns, for the new ministers, named by him on the recommendation of the people, and who were members of the Jacobin society, to present themselves to the society, lest they should now be suspected of joining the aristocracy; and he proposed to attend the sitting of that evening himself. The King perceived the importance of the measure, and approved of Dumourier's design. Some days previous to that, the factions had adopted the *red cap* for the emblem of liberty. Dumourier, and the Girondine party, who had hitherto professed to be the friends of order, and who, indeed, cannot be reproached with having flattered the Jacobins at any period, convinced Pethion, then mayor of Paris, then beloved by the Jacobins, then all-powerful, that this badge assumed by the people, might be productive of the greatest disorders, if not of the horrors attending the contest of the white and red roses in England, and that of the times of the hoods in King John's reign at Paris. Pethion, at that period, possessed an absolute ascendency over Roberspierre and the Jacobins; and promised that he would write a note to them on the subject, and that the red cap should be suppressed. The day on which Pethion was to write was the same that Dumourier had chosen for paying his respects to the Jacobins. The letter was indeed written, but had not arrived when Dumourier entered the hall of the assembly. All the mem-

bers

bers had red caps on their heads, and a cap was offered to Dumourier as he was mounting the tribune. He was compelled to put it on, or imprudently to subject himself to very great risks.—— Dumourier said little in the tribune. Having assured them that, when war should be declared, he would quit his pen to serve them with his sword, he left the hall. He was scarcely gone, when Pethion's letter was announced and read, and produced the desired effect, in banishing the caps from the assembly; so that half an hour would have saved the minister this disgrace. The public, misled by false royalists, that is to say, by the anti-constitutional party, have misjudged this fact, which was but a mere accident.

At the time of Dumourier's quitting the administration, the Jacobins were become his bitterest enemies. The General's success in Champagne, had restored him a little to their favour, in spite of Marat's accusations; and he appeared at the club, for a quarter of an hour, on his being at Paris, in October 1792. But he never held any correspondence with the society, nor with any one of its members.

Hassenfratz, Andouin, and the other clerks of the war-office, were never absent from the meetings of the Jacobins. They multiplied accusations against the General; and often demanded that he should be compelled to appear at the bar to answer their charges. But in the midst of these intrigues, the Jacobins were desirous of attaching the General to their party. The majority usually opposed his enemies; and, when Hassenfratz produced his grand accusation respecting the embezzlement of two hundred thousand livres, together with the papers to substantiate the charge, the society silenced him, and passed to the order of the day.

The

The Jacobins even employed several of their emissaries, to induce the General to attend their sittings. Anacharsis Clootz, used various arts to that end; but the General always excused himself, on the ground that he could not appear at the society till he had offered his homage to the Convention. Doctor Seyffer made attempts of the same nature; as well as Proli, an adventurer of Brussels, who was desirous of procuring at least an interview between the General and one Desfieux, a celebrated Jacobin, and one of the most active itinerants of the sect, who, arriving at Bourdeaux, found means of disgracing the members of the Girondine party, and of exciting the populace against the honest part of that great city. Jean-Bon St. Andre, who was a member of the Convention, and an enthusiastic Jacobin, notwithstanding he had the reputation of being an honest man, having conceived a great esteem for Dumourier, although he had no personal acquaintance with the General, was extremely anxious to bring about this interview, and requested that he might be present. The General was not satisfied that the adventurer Proli, whom he despised, should be the medium of this negociation; however, for many important reasons, he, at length, consented to the interview.

On the day appointed, the General was indisposed; but as he would not, by a violation of his word, seem to be wanting in respect to Desfieux and St. Andre, to both of whom he was a stranger, he made another appointment to meet them at the house of Bonne-Carrere, who was the intimate friend of these two persons.

The interview took place at the house of Bonne-Carrere. Desfieux appeared to the General to be a man of mean capacity, and of a violent disposition. Jean-Bon St. Andre seemed better

better informed, and more moderate. No arrangement could be made respecting the mode of the General's presenting himself to the Jacobin society; nor on the conduct the society would observe towards him, governed as it was by Marat. Dumourier, therefore, declined entering into any engagement to present himself to the society; nor did he make any declaration of a contrary intention.

As to the trial of the King, which the General feared to touch upon, excepting very slightly, lest he should injure the cause by seeming to be interested in it, he saw that Desfieux and Jean-Bonne St. Andre, were governed by savage rage against the King, which vented itself in the vilest and most unjust terms; and he perceived clearly, that he had nothing to hope on that point from these men.

They vehemently supported Pache and his associates, and Desfieux, who called himself the organ of the Jacobins, requested Dumourier to withdraw his accusations against the minister of war, whom the Jacobins, he said, were determined to preserve in his place; and invited the General to join their faction in disgracing Le Brun, Garat, Claviere, and above all, Roland; which ministers they considered as the agents of the Girondine party.

The General now resolved to break off these negociations entirely; and informed Bonne-Carrere of his determination. But he felt the danger to which he should expose himself in taking this step; and especially in pursuing the plan he had laid down, and which he had announced to the convention, of resigning the command. He well knew, that thenceforth he must either join the Jacobins, and become the accomplice of their crimes, or deprived of the command, his only shield against his enemies,

he

he should be pursued on the unjust accusations of Hassenfratz, and delivered over to the execrable Revolutionary Tribunal, that has since murdered Custine on the slightest pretences.

Dumourier therefore made up his mind upon the course he should pursue; and which he afterward adapted to the political circumstances that will be related in the following chapters. Losing all hope of saving the king, he now thought only of the means of avenging his death, of saving his unfortunate queen and her son, and, by the establishment of a limited monarchy, of putting an end to the frightful disorders that were compleating the disgrace and ruin of France.

C H A P. X.

Of the Executive Council of France.

IT was with the six ministers exercising the executive power in France, that General Dumourier transacted the chief part of his business during the twenty-six days that he passed at Paris. And here it will be necessary to observe that, in a writing he published after that period, by an error in the press, twenty-six hours were put for twenty-six days. In consequence of which error, a criticism appeared in one of the English papers, in which the general was seriously reproached with asserting he had performed, in twenty-six hours, the business of twenty-six days.

The ministers were Roland, to whom we will give a chapter apart. He was hated by the other

five,

five, who concealed all they could from him. They were themselves divided into two very opposite parties. One was composed of Le Brun, minister of foreign affairs, whom Dumourier had made first clerk, and who was very fit for that situation, being industrious and well informed ; but he had neither sufficient dignity nor energy of mind to act for himself, and was rendered deceitful by his timidity of character, even toward his benefactor, although he still regarded him as necessary to his support. He had dismissed from his office Marat and Noel, two men neither deficient in talents nor honesty ; had appointed no person to superintend the business of the office, and to distribute the work to the different superior clerks ; and he had taken for his principal secretary a man of the name of Isabeau, whose reputation was none of the fairest. Occupied, like ministers of former times, by intrigues for the preservation of his place, he was more influenced by the Jacobins than became a man, to whom Briflot, Condorcet, and the other heads of the Girondine party dictated the policy of his foreign negociations.

Of the faction of Le Brun was Garat, minister of justice, a man of an able and upright mind, and to whom no reproach could be made excepting that, by an adulation unworthy of himself, he had endeavoured to apologize for the well known murders of the first days of September. Grouvelle, although only secretary of the council, may be considered as having all the influence of a minister, since he assumed much authority and gave his opinion, and decided on every thing.— He was a man of letters, overbearing, and open in his avowal of bold and extravagant notions of liberty.

On the other side was Pache, minister of war, a man of sense, and possibly an honest man, but

ignorant

ignorant and blindly devoted to the Jacobin party.
He had a wife and daughter, equally ugly and ill
tempered, who frequented the clubs and even the
haunts of the Marseillois, to demand the king's
death. The war-office was become a club, breath-
ing nothing but blood and carnage. The clerks
always wore the red cap at their desks, and used
the phrases *thou* and *thee* to every one, even to
the minister, who himself affected a slovenly dress,
and courted the Parisian populace, by assuming
their manners.

The same disgusting scene presented itself in the
office of the marine department, from which all
the clerks of character and experience were driven,
to make way for ignorant and furious Jacobins,
who, notwithstanding the filthiness of their appearance, have acquired immense fortunes.

The war-office and that of the marine department, united in presenting an address to the National Convention, signed also, as it was said, by
the two ministers, demanding that the king should
be put to death. Monge, the minister of the marine, was an academician, had been an excellent
lecturer in hydrography, and seemed a man of
simple manners, but was a little ungracious in his
behaviour. He was entirely devoted to Pache;
and, in concert with him, supported the Jacobin
faction in the council.

Claviere, minister of the finances, although he
was connected with and supported by the Girondists, and was the relation of Brissot, frequently
joined the other faction, from a love of contradiction, and because it was the most active and powerful. Like the rest, he thought of nothing but
of preserving his place, which Cambon, and the
committee of finance were endeavouring to suppress.

Such was the executive council of France, in
the most critical period of her existence. An ob-

O

vious and sad reflection naturally presents itself; the French Revolution, under the pretence of equalizing all men, has debased all men. Most of the Jacobins, belonged to the lowest class of the people; and, unable to find among themselves persons equal to the first stations, they lowered the nature of those stations to their own level. Hence, there is neither dignity, nor character, in the government: nor respectability, nor a sense of duty in the people; and the populace, unlike the Athenian democracy, are drunken and savage slaves, usurping the place of the Spartans. The ancient government was destroyed to remedy the abuse of distributing places among the nobles, without any regard to their moral capacities. Yet, instead of the Revolution replacing them by men of talents, it has filled their seats with artful and impudent plebeians.

France cannot escape her entire ruin, but in freeing herself from the subaltern tyrants that invade every department. Unhappily, she no longer has the means in her own hands, since these tyrants are masters of the money, arms, power, and authority of the nation. But the ignorance and barbarous rage of this horde is destructive of itself; and foreign arms will restore the ancient despotism, instead of forming that just equilibrium between the talents of men and the employments of the state that constitutes the perfection of government. This state of things however, cannot remain long; because the love of liberty is too deeply rooted in France to be ever again wholly destroyed; and the restoration of despotism will beget another revolution, the moment that foreign troops shall be withdrawn from the country, and shall leave the nobles of France, scattered over that vast kingdom, to the vengeance of the people, called down on their heads by the abuse of their short lived triumph.

The

The council did not interfere in the fate of the king. Le Brun and Garat, seemed to apprehend the consequences of the trial; but they feared to employ the means, or to indulge in the idea, of putting a stop to it, or of suspending it; and confined themselves to a declaration, that it was unfortunate for France that such a trial had commenced. Roland was the most terrified of all the ministers at this trial; because, in reflecting on the imprudence, and on the injustice of his former complaints against the King, no doubt he felt that he was the principal cause of the king's danger. He relented and was silent. It belonged to the malignant mind of Claviere, to rejoice at the trial; and besides, he had always discovered a personal hatred against Louis XVI. As to Pache and Monge, they canvassed openly for the king's death. And Grouvelle declared, that it was necessary to the honour of the Republic, that he should die.

The open and bitter quarrels that existed between the minister of war and the generals, on the complaints made by the latter respecting the armies, and the providing of necessaries for the troops, could never bring the council to take any step in its collective capacity relative to those subjects. Every one of the members reserved an exclusive authority in his own department; and Pache laid before the council, as well as before the committee of war, statements which were altogether false, and which were uniformly opposed by new complaints from the Generals, and by the reports of the Commissioners of the Convention with the armies. The council heard all the reports and complaints, but they still upheld the committee of contracts, which was secretly influenced by Claviere, the friend of Bidermann, who was at the head of the committee; and the affairs of the armies were conducted as before. No provision was made either for the clothing, subsist-

ence,

ence, or accoutrements of the troops, nor for the hospitals, nor for the ammunition that was wanted in the frontier places, nor for the works necessary to put them in a state of defence. At that time the Jacobins had resolved to place one of their faction at the head of the municipality, and had promised to make Pache mayor of Paris; he, therefore, gave himself little uneasiness respecting the future embarrassments of the war department; which Haffenfratz and Meusnier were to quit along with him.

The more we reflect on the conduct of the Jacobins, the more are we lost in conjecture respecting the spirit by which they were guided. It is certain, that they have been continually industrious to disorganize France, and to render useless the immense resources she possessed for the defence of her liberty; they have ruined the fleets and armies; they have imprisoned or driven out of the kingdom, the ablest officers; they have lavished the treasures of the nation in wild and ineffectual expences; they have destroyed the commercial and political connections of France with other nations; and have set every nation at defiance; and it cannot be doubted, that the society has been influenced by English, Italians, Flemings and Germans, pretending to be furious Jacobins, and who were known to be the spies of foreign governments. In this class may be ranked Clootz, Marat, Chabot, Pio, the Jew Ephraim, De Bufcher, and many others.

The decree of the 15th of December, far from being disapproved of by the Council, was supported by every one of the members. Le Brun had been secretary to the people of Liege, during this revolution, to which he had given his support by a periodical work, entitled, "The Journal of Europe." This paper was not ill written; and it was in consequence of seeing it, that Dumourier

mourier had placed him at the department of foreign affairs. Le Brun was of opinion, as well as most of the other revolutionists of France, that a revolution could not be successful without being attended by a complete disorganization; so that he could not fail to approve of a decree, calculated to disorganize a people, who had the misfortune to call upon us for aid. The principles of Dumourier, which inclined him to respect the liberty, property, and opinions of others, could not be very acceptable to Le Brun. But Le Brun was silent on the subject to Dumourier, although he, in concert with Marat, Chepy, and his other emissaries, had established a destructive engine in Belgium, under the name of the Revolutionary Committee. The General complained to the minister of the language and conduct of Chepy, desiring he might be recalled, as being dangerous to the affairs of France in Belgium. Le Brun, however, not only countenanced Chepy, but gave him new instructions that greatly extended his power.

In the same manner while the General was soliciting the revocation of the decree of the 15th of December, the council appointed, on the recommendation of the Jacobins, thirty-two commissioners of the Executive Power, to whose situation was annexed the salary of 10,000 livres, besides the expences of their journey, and the profits of their robberies. These commissioners were furnished with ridiculous instructions, in which the council feigned to confine their authority within narrow bounds; but the commissioners paid no regard to their instructions, having themselves given an arbitrary latitude to their power. These miscreants inflicted the greatest wrongs on the Belgians, and caused among that people an utter abhorrence of the French name.

The

The plan of the campaign remained yet to be
settled. Cambon had afferted that France maintained 600,000 troops. It was now the 15th of
January, and the council knew not how many
troops France really had on foot, nor how many
enemies fhe would have to contend with, in the
campaign. The General ftated to the Council that,
although all Europe fhould declare againft France,
fhe having no civil war, (for the revolt in La
Vendee had not yet broken out) might defend her
frontiers with three hundred and feventy thoufand
men (the fixth part of them being cavalry) exclufive
of the garrifons and troops of the fleet, by ftanding
on the defenfive on the fouth and on the banks of
the Rhine, and confining their offenfive operations to the frontiers extending from the Mozelle
to Dunkirk. The General propofed to diftribute
the troops in the following manner : 80,000 men
to compofe the army of Belgium ; 40,000 men
that of the Ardennes ; a corps of 20,000 to be
pofted on the Mozelle, to keep open the communication between the armies of the Ardennes and
that of the Rhine ; 50,000 to compofe the army
of the Rhine ; a referve of 20,000 men to be
placed at Chalons or Soiffons ; a corps of 15,000
at Lyons, to watch Switzerland and Piedmont ;
40,000 for the army of Savoy and countries of
Nice and Provence ; 25,000 for the army of the
Pyrennees ; 40,000 for the coaft of the Weft, from
Bayonne to Breft ; and 40,000 for the coafts along
the channel, from Breft to Dunkirk. All thefe
armies might mutually affift each other; and, as
the whole of France was armed, even fhould the
enemy penetrate any part, it was not to be doubted
they would be repulfed or overwhelmed.

General Dumourier alfo propofed that Cuftine's
army, which had already evacuated Franckfort,
fhould fall back upon Landau, leaving a garrifon

in

in Mayence fufficient to compel the king of Pruffia to lofe three or four months before that place,
which would afford time to put the fortified towns
of Alface, Lorraine, and the Ardennes, into a
proper ftate of defence, and to make the enemy
on that fide lofe the reft of the campaign.

The General further propofed that the greateft
efforts fhould be made to pufh the campaign on
with vigour on the fide of Belgium, becaufe that
being a flat country without fortified places, or
even without any of thofe naturally ftrong fituations of country which ftand in the place of fortreffes, the fate of the war in thefe provinces muft
be decided by battles. On this fcheme, if the
French fhould be victorious, the greater part of
the French army might pafs the Rhine : and if
unfuccefsful, might retire behind the fortreffes of
Flanders and Artois; however the whole campaign might pafs without the French lines being
broke in upon in this quarter.

Inftead of this plan, which Dumourier laid
before the Committee of General Safety, as well
as the Executive Council, La Clos, who had juft
been appointed to the command in India, propofed
that they fhould inftantly fend him out with fifteen
veffels and 15,000 men, which meafure neceffarily involved a war with England and Holland,
although it had then been very eafy and was very
neceffary to the fafety of France to have avoided
that war.

The object of this expedition of La Clos was to
make himfelf mafter of the Cape of Good Hope
and the ifland of Ceylon ; and afterwards, to join
Tippoo Saib and to attack Bengal.

Kellermann, on paying his refpects to the National Convention, on his departure to take the
command of the army of Dauphine, which amounted to nearly twenty thoufand men (exclufive of
the army of the country of Nice, under General
Biron,

Biron, from ten to twelve thoufand men) received orders from the Prefident to go and conquer Rome; and the General gravely anfwered, that he took his leave to go to Rome. This army had alfo been weakened by drawing between feven and eight thoufand men from it, for the fleet that lay at Toulon, deftined to conquer Sardinia. This expedition was undertaken in the moft ftormy part of the year, in a narrow fea, abounding with rocks and iflands; and part of the fleet was loft, and the expedition failed.

The army of the Pyrennees confifted only of an extenfive eftablifhment of ftaff officers, without troops. Yet the Convention had refolved upon conquering Spain, and had deftined 40,000 men, that were not raifed, and General Servan, for the purpofe. There were no troops on the coaft of the weft and north; excepting fome weak garrifons at Belleifle, and at two or three other places on that coaft. There was no army of referve. Fifty thoufand men were wanting to complete the army of Belgium and that of the Ardennes; the army of Alface did not amount to 20,00 men, exclufive of 22,000 fhut up in Mayence; and the army of the Mozelle did not amount to 12,000 men.

In order therefore to put the plan of General Dumourier in execution, there were wanting more than 150,000 men; together with the provifions, arms, and clothing, for this large body of troops. Above all, France was in want of cavalry. The armies of Belgium and of the Ardennes required a body of 20,000 cavalry; and the two armies had not 6,000; and they were in want of 15,000 artillery horfes.

The General's plan was adopted; the 370,000 men were decreed to be raifed; and a few alterations made in the diftribution of the troops; but
this

this was all that ever was done towards the execution of the plan. However, the General obtained an order a few days before his departure for 15,000 men of the new-raised battalions to march from the third line in Picardy, Flanders, and Artois, where they were altogether useless, into maritime Flanders.

- Independent of the Executive Council, from which (as Le Brun and Garat suspected) a great many projects were concealed, especially those respecting foreign politics, there were two private committees held at the house of General Dumourier, which seemed to dispose of the fate of the empire; and which in fact produced nothing. They were composed of the two ministers Le Brun and Garat, and those members of the Girondine party, Condorcet, Pethion, Genfonne and Briffot. It is probable that the only object of the party, in establishing these committees, was that their existence should be known to Paris, in order to beget an opinion that the General was entirely devoted to them; and thereby to strengthen the party, by the acquisition of his friends. Le Brun even seemed unwilling that the negociations then carrying on with England and Holland should be at all enquired into by the committees; and requested the General to forbear touching on the subject; and it was never introduced.

Briffot boasted of his plans for the conquest of Spain and Italy; but the General easily detected the folly of his calculations.

The situation of the Republic with Switzerland, was an interesting subject. The malignity of Claviere, had been lately gratified, in compelling General Montesquieu to become an exile to escape the fangs of his persecutor the vile Du Bois de Crance; and, in disorganizing Geneva, his native country. Briffot and his adherents maintained, that it was necessary to compel the Swifs Cantons

P

tons

tons to abandon their neutrality; or, in cafe of
refufal to attack them; and it is probable that in
this they were acted upon by the agents of the
combined powers, to whom it was very important
that Switzerland fhould join the confederacy.
The General proved by arguments, drawn from
the relative fituations of France, Switzerland,
and the Combined Powers, to which thefe metaphyficians were ftrangers, that it was prudent to
conciliate the good difpofitions of the Helvetic
body towards France; yet, at the fame time to
maintain an army of 15,000 men to cover Lyons,
and to be ready on any emergency on that fide.

Dumobrier was the more defirous of preferving
this neutrality, becaufe it was during his admini-
ftration, that the event of the difarming the regiment of Erneft happened at Aix. At that period,
he made every compenfation he could to that brave
regiment, for the injuftice of his countrymen; he
prefented the red ribband to the two principal officers, and provided for the fafety of their retreat
with their men to the frontiers.

General Dumourier always exerted every means
in his power to preferve peace with Switzerland;
a meafure that was fo juft, and fo neceffary to
the welfare of the two nations. But he muft
own, that his efforts have lefs contributed to that
difficult tafk, than the prudent and firm conduct
of Colonel de Weifs, a member of the fovereign
council of Berne, and a writer diftinguifhed by
works which difplay extenfive knowledge, energy
of mind, and goodnefs of heart. This officer,
without poffeffing any oftenfible diplomatic character, was refpected by the miniftry, was liften-
ed to in the committees, and had even acquired
an influence in the convention. Tranquil when
furrounded by danger, and uncorrupted in the
midft of crimes, he had the courage to fay to one of
the leaders of faction, *I know that you can caufe me*

to be arrested or massacred; but proofs of your villainy that would bring you to the scaffold in eight days, are within my reach: I demand that a peaceable conduct on the part of France, toward my country, be the price of my silence.

On another trying occasion, when a superior officer had bluntly interrupted him, in the midst of a sentence, to demand if, daring to speak the language he held, he had a 100,000 men at his beck in the Fauxbourgs of Paris, *No,* he answered haughtily, *I am single; but I have a hundred thousand republican sentiments in my heart of which you are destitute.* He was applauded by his audience; and continued his discourse.

His work entitled, *A rapid survey of the relative interests of the Helvetic body, and the French Republic,* which was published in a crisis of great danger to both countries, exposed and defeated the hostile projects of a faction, towards Switzerland, on the eve of execution; and it is very probable that, without the foresight and courage of Colonel de Weiss, war had been declared against the Helvetic body before the end of February. Various secret preparations were already making for an attack upon Switzerland, in pursuit of an ill digested plan of Robert, Claviere, and other Swiss emigrants. The attack was to be made on three points at once. A column, composed of part of the army of the Upper Rhine, and augmented by new levies, was to take Basle by surprize, or assault, and keep the Austrians in check. Another column, drawn from the army of the Alps, was to blockade Geneva, where the French had numerous partizans, and to penetrate by Versoix into the Pays de Vaud. The third division, composed of chosen troops, was to march suddenly by the Pass of Potentru, already occupied by the French, against Berne, whose treasury, granaries, and arsenal, excited

the

the cupidity of the projectors of this plan. Berne
had been already fecretly reconnoitred ; and, although it be nearly furrounded by a rapid and
deep river, it was expected that the place would
be carried, by pouring in bombs and red-hot
balls from the neighbouring heights, before the
Swifs militia could affemble with force to oppofe
the attack. The projectors of the plan alfo expected a powerful diverfion to be made in their
behalf, by the difcontented party, (whofe numbers were greatly exaggerated) of the Lower Va-
lais, Neuf-Chatel, Pays de Vaud, Soleure, Lu-
cerne, and Fribourg. This laft city was deftined
to be an object of fignal vengeance, on account of
fome offence fhe had committed refpecting the
affignats. The popular governments were to be
informed that thefe hoftilities would not affect
them, and that France would continue to preferve
peace with them. As to the other cantons, the
commiffioners and other feditious preachers were
to overthrow their conftitutions, ftir up the poor
againft the rich, maffacre, imprifon, or banifh
the magiftrates and principal citizens, feize upon
fpecie, provifions, horfes, and arms, compel
men of property to emigrate that their eftates
might be confifcated, outrage religion, and in the
name of liberty and the public good to ruin this
free and happy people, and reduce them to flavery. The expedition was to have been prompt;
but the explofion was prevented, and Claviere
and Briffot, overawed by Weifs, laid afide a project in which Switzerland, from the character of
the times, had every thing to hazard.

The conqueft of Rome and Spain, were defer-
red till armies could be raifed to march againft
thofe countries. As to all other affairs, the fit-
tings of thefe two committees were as fruitlefs as
were the deliberations of the committee of general fafety, and thofe of the executive council.—
Dumourier

Dumourier could not, by any motive, obtain of them the accomplishment of any object, calculated to serve the nation.

CHAP. XI.

The Retreat of Roland from the Administration.

AT the time of the king's death, Roland, who had long strove to maintain his situation in the ministry, against the will of the Jacobins, as well as against the real inclinations of his own party, sent a letter to his colleagues announcing his resignation. The ministers never appeared more chearful than on the day they received this letter, and the council appeared more like a school relieved from the restraints of a troublesome pedant, than a grave meeting of Statesmen. Roland's resignation, made part of a compromise between the Jacobin and Gironde parties, in which it was agreed, that both Roland and Pache should quit the ministry. But the consequences were very different to those two ministers, the latter of them acquiring a situation of more real importance than any in the ministry; while the former remained more than ever exposed to the insults and persecutions of the Jacobins.

This sacrifice made of Roland by his party, is another instance of the cowardice of that faction, which ought never to have abandoned a man, of whose

whose services they had availed themselves, without any respect to his peace or safety. In truth, the whole conduct of Roland, in his public character, was a mistaken policy, which exposed himself and his party to continual danger. Roland did not possess much strength of mind, but had acquired extensive information on the different branches of trade and manufactures; and, if it had been expedient to divide the duties of the administration of the home department, which was too extensive and too complicated for a mind of such little energy, it is probable, he would have made an excellent minister of commercial concerns. He was upright in his designs, and was possessed of a mild and philanthropic disposition; but the desire of appearing a rigid moralist induced him to assume a severity of character unnatural to him. He hoped to resemble Cato the Censor, and had adopted his turn of conversation, at once cold and repulsive, but without the genius and boldness of that celebrated man. In his dress he was nice and singular, following the fashions of former times; but this was at least less displeasing than the slovenly affectation of the Jacobins. His deportment was grave, and not unbecoming the dignity of his station. He was indefatigable in the application of his talents. But he loved too much to gratify the will of the people, and was too ready to believe that the higher orders were oppressive and unjust; and this disposition, that becomes dangerous when it is too generally indulged, conducted him habitually into precipitate and imprudent measures.— He was candid in his examination of the subjects belonging to the other departments of the government, such as those relating to the armies, the marine, and foreign negociations; and supported, with great sincerity, all propositions that came before the council of a just and reasonable nature.

ture. Perceiving the equivocal conduct of the other ministers, mistrusting their talents and perhaps their good faith, he would no longer admit of any responsibility of the council in a collective capacity: and his pertinacity in refusing to answer for any measures but those that were the consequence of his direct orders begat a greater hatred of him than ever among his colleagues.

The temper and qualities of Roland would have fitted him well enough for the ministry had the republic been settled on its foundations, and if the times had been more free from the violence of party rage, for he was a rigid republican. This disposition was the cause of his ill conduct to Louis the XVI. and of the imprudent step of delivering into the hands of the Convention the fatal chest containing the monarch's *passive** correspondence, in which those base men found pretexts for the martyrdom of that unfortunate prince.

Perhaps it was prejudicial to the interests of Roland that he was governed by his wife, who was a woman of fine talents, and whom he acknowledged to be the critic, that gave a polish to his numerous works; but certainly it was among his misfortunes to be surrounded by ignorant and designing journalists, who composed, under his directions, those verbose harangues that covered the walls and public buildings of Paris; for the Jacobins

---

* *Passive!* Such is the word in the original, and it is printed in Italics. Dumourier seems to have thought that Louis XVI. was innocent, because he had not courage or capacity to *contrive* the means of injuring the nation. Supposing he is not mistaken in that conclusion, he seems to have forgotten, that he was conceding one of the great points, insisted upon by the friends of Democracy, that it is in vain to have an innocent king, if his ministers, mistresses, wives, or favourites, be not innocent also; as it would be in vain that these latter should be innocent, if the king be avaricious, deceitful, or tyrannical.　　　　　　　　　　　T.

Jacobins had the address to turn this engine of faction against him and his party.

Among the women who have risen to celebrity during the French revolution, no one has acted a more conspicuous or noble part than that of Madame Roland. She was between thirty and forty years of age, had a lively and healthy countenance, and a most interesting figure ; she dressed with great taste ; conversed with ability, although perhaps with too much wit and refinement ; she was innocently gay, and had placed herself at the head of a party consisting of metaphysicians, scholars, members of the Convention, and ministers. Every day these partizans of Madame Roland paid their respects to her, and on the Friday of every week they dined at her house, where the conduct and politics of statesmen took their character from Madame Roland's opinions.—— None of the wives of the other ministers were admitted to these meetings.

It would be unjust not to notice the spirit with which Madame Roland conducted herself under an insult of the Jacobins, at a time when her husband's name had already fallen into great discredit. Interrogated at the bar of the Convention, respecting the injurious accusations of an unprincipled man named Viard, she said, *I am the wife of citizen Roland ; I bear the name of a virtuous man, to whom I am proud to be allied.*—— Certainly it required all the malignity of the Jacobins to persecute such a woman.

Although Madame Roland possessed much good sense, she permitted it to be seen that she governed her husband, and thereby did a disservice to his reputation, for which she could not compensate by the value of her councils. It was Madame Roland that selected Pache and Lanthenas to aid her husband in his administration ; and the former of them so entirely gained the confidence

dence of Roland, that he was appointed minister of war through Roland's interest. Pache was no sooner the colleague of Roland, than he became his enemy, and fought by every means to ruin him, and for that purpose he did not hesitate to become the partisan of the most intemperate men among the Jacobins. The contest between those two ministers was open, and their hostile attacks were without measure or decency. They both descended from their situations, but with Pache it was only to rise to higher power. Roland was to be subjected to new and more bitter misfortunes.

Other women have also distinguished themselves during the revolution, but without the dignity that has been preserved by Madame Roland; excepting, indeed, it be Madame Necker, who, in many respects, may be considered as the rival of Madame Roland's fame, and whose age and experience, if it rendered her less agreable to the thoughtless, gave her the advantage as the counsellor of her husband. Mademoiselle La Brousset, Madame de Stael, Condorcet, Pastoret, Coigny and Theroigne, were either artful females, like those who haunted the courts of former times, or differed in nothing from the vulgar and furious women of the Fauxbourgs of Paris.

One unfortunate woman, Elizabeth Corday, has consigned her name to history, by an act, which happily for humanity will find few imitators, although it delivered the earth from a monster.

The executive council seemed to have undergone no change by the retreat of Roland from the ministry. During a considerable period before his resignation, he had been entirely occupied in brooding over his vexations, the attacks of his enemies, and the means of his defence. Every satire of the Jacobins that was directed

Q

against him, begat in his apprehension the obligation of justifying himself to the Convention; and
the members of the Convention, who, perhaps,
were more irritated by the austerity of Roland's
virtue, than by the petulance of his spirit, saw
nothing in those homilies but an insupportable
pride. His own party, no longer deriving reputation from his name, had, in truth, renounced
him; and had very ignorantly resolved to sacrifice him. Roland flattered himself that his resignation would not be accepted, and he remained
in the house appropriated to the minister of the
Home Department, till he was no longer permitted to doubt of his fate. During the latter
part of his administration, he seldom slept in this
house; as the Jacobins, to terrify him, frequently
sent bands of the fœderates to make excursions
during the night round the house. In this manner were the representatives of the executive
power treated in France. Le Brun and Claviere
have been since accused and imprisoned; and
Garat was accused and arrested after having resigned. So ferocious has been the character of
this revolution that, of the men who have had an
eminent part in it, such only have been out of
the reach of a violent death as have fled and are
in exile.

CHAP.

CHAP. XII.

Negociations with Holland and England.

FRANCE, at that period, had no other declared enemies than Auſtria, Pruſſia, and Sardinia. She had diſplayed a ſuperiority over thoſe
powers during the preceding campaign, which
would have been entirely deciſive, if, according
to the plan of General Dumourier, Cuſtine, inſtead of paſſing the Rhine to levy an inconſider-
able contribution on Frankfort, and for which
France paid ſo dearly, had made himſelf maſter
of Coblentz, where there was no garriſon; and if
the wants of the army had been ſupplied, ſo that
the army of Belgium might have taken up its
winter quarters along the banks of the Rhine,
from Cleves to Cologne; that of the Ardennes,
from Cologne to Andernach; that of the Mozelle, from Andernach to Mayence, including
Coblentz; and that of Alſace, from Mayence to
Landau, including Spires. This poſition would
have compelled the county of Luxembourg to
have ſurrendered, by cutting off its ſupplies of
proviſions. The armies would have had behind
them a country on which, whether it were neuter
or an enemy, they might long have ſubſiſted; and,
by opening the campaign early in the ſpring,
might have paſſed the Rhine without difficulty,
and have penetrated into the center of Germany,
where the French would have been received with
open arms, if they had poſſeſſed the prudence to
have forborne from exciting terror in the inhabi-

Q 3

tants by unjuft decrees and by the fending of rapacious commiffioners to commit violence, infults
and robberies.

This great plan was neglected; yet France
might have fuftained herfelf with reputation and
effect againft her enemies who were in truth already overcome, if her conduct had not drawn
new enemies upon her.

Means exifted, at this period, for preferving
Spain in her neutrality; and by employing them
the nation would have fpared herfelf the guilt of a
great crime. The king of Spain engaged with
the Convention to remain neuter, on condition
that the life of the unfortunate Louis XVI. fhould
be fpared. This ftep does honour to the Spanifh
monarch; and it is difficult to imagine why the
French princes did not follow fo bright an example. The implacable, ignorant Convention rejected the terms of the Spanifh monarch with difdain, and thereby committed a new crime againft
the nation, by creating her a new enemy, without
confulting her on the neceffity or prudence of
their conduct.

The courts of London and the Hague, had for
fome time betrayed a hatred to the French revolution; and the death of Louis XVI. could not
but increafe that hatred. But, in England, no
part of the nation was willing to enter into a war
againft France, excepting the king, who confidered his differences with the French as a perfonal
quarrel. And in Holland, every party dreaded
to be drawn into a war. It was therefore poffible
for France to preferve peace with thofe two countries; and, till that period, fhe had wifely cultivated the good will of Holland, from whence
fhe drew fpecie and provifions; and it was eafy to
have continued that fyftem.

In the latter end of the month of November,
General Dumourier propofed to the executive
council,

council, the taking of Maeftricht, without which he could neither defend the Meufe nor the country of Leige. He thought it reafonable, after many examples in former wars, to take and hold this place, engaging by a duly authorifed manifefto, to reftore it at the end of the war. At that period his army was victorious and full of ardour. He had, after the taking of the citadel of Antwerp, affembled the whole of his heavy artillery at Tongres and Leige, in order not to expofe the horfes belonging to the artillery to die for want of forage, (as the Jacobins have ftupidly afferted) but to make himfelf mafter of Maeftricht. That place was not as yet palifadoed, nor provided with a garrifon, nor with any thing neceffary to fuftain a fiege. Venloo was in the fame condition. Caufes of complaint were not wanting to give a colour to the enterprize ; and to throw the impu-tation of being the aggreffors upon the Dutch, if they fhould refent his conduct, for they had al-ready frequently violated the neutrality, and had recently prohibited on pain of death, all exporta-tions of provifions to France, while provifions in immenfe quantities were drawn from Holland, to eftablifh magazines, on the Lower Rhine, for the Imperialifts and Pruffians, The executive coun-cil rejected the general's propofitions, and ex-prefsly commanded him to preferve the ftricteft neutrality toward Holland, which injunction the general was punctual in obferving. They then fent him an order to undertake the fiege of Lux-embourg during the winter; but, the general fhewing the abfurdity of the plan, it was not put in execution.

As the executive council had thus neglected the opportunity of feizing upon Maeftricht, which may be regarded as the key of the Netherlands on the fide of the Meufe, the general was of opinion that it would no longer be prudent to commit any

hoftility

hostility on the part of France against Holland, being convinced that a war with England must be the consequence of such hostility; and his advice was thenceforward to preserve a neutrality with both England and Holland, with the utmost solicitude.

The friendship of Holland was indispensibly necessary to enable France to hold Belgium, for if the Dutch delivered the passages of Maestritcht and Venloo to the Austrians, the Meuse would be no longer tenable, and the French would be compelled to abandon the countries of Leige, Gueldre, Limbourg, Brabant, and Namur, and retreat behind the Scheld; contracting their lines within the country lying between the citadel of Antwerp and Valenciennes. And in the case of the English and Dutch assembling an army in Dutch Flanders, the French would be further forced to abandon the Scheld, and retire behind the river Lys, and under the fortified places of French Flanders and Artois.

At this time there were at Paris many Dutch refugees victims of the Dutch revolution, and of the faithless and feeble conduct of the minister Brienne. Many among them were respectable and opulent men, who assured the French ministry that their party in Holland was much more considerable than that of the Stadtholder, which indeed was true. These representations were disregarded till the month of January, when Le Brun after giving them an hearing, referred them to General Dumourier for his opinion respecting their resources, and especially respecting a plan of invading Zealand which the Dutch patriots represented as easy to be undertaken, and certain of success. After a deliberate examination the general judged the plan to be impracticable, but wrote to the minister that he should postpone giving a definite answer till he should be at Antwerp, and be able

more

more particularly to examine the several parts of
the project; and it was resolved that the Dutch
refugees should proceed to Antwerp with their
revolutionary committee; and orders were given
to the Dutch legion, consisting nearly of 10,000
men, to garrison Antwerp, and to be ready to
form the advanced guard of the French army, in
case of a war with Holland.

An agent of Le Brun was appointed to attend
the Dutch revolutionary committee; but no positive engagement with them was entered into, and
all that related to them was rendered dependent
on the issue of a negociation which was then on the
point of commencing.

At the time that Dumourier had been minister
for foreign affairs he had sent to the Hague, as
minister plenipotentiary, Emanuel de Maulde, a
colonel in the French army, who had conducted
himself with great prudence and ability, had procured arms and horses for France, and had so well
reconciled his attention to the interests of the refugees with the respect due to the government of
the country, as to acquire the confidence and
esteem of the two factions that divided Holland.
This conduct, which was conformable to his instructions, was too moderate to be agreeable to the
temper of the present times; and de Maulde had
moreover the misfortune to be noble. Le Brun
in particular conceived an aversion to him. The
military committee disapproved of his sending
fusees to Dunkirk. His measures were opposed
on every side, and his intentions calumniated. He
was recalled; and in his room was appointed
Noel, whom the general had made principal clerk
in the office for foreign affairs. Noel, although
an extremely honest man, arriving with prejudices
against de Maulde and plans much less moderate
than those on which Maulde had acted, was very ill
received

received; and, attributing his reception to de Maulde, became his enemy and accuser.

De Maulde, on his arrival at Paris, called upon the general; and told him that, if France desired to preserve a neutrality with Holland and England, nothing was more easy; that, although the ministers of the two courts would neither acknowledge the National Convention, nor treat with Le Brun, yet the grand pensioner of Holland, Van Spiegel, and the English Ambassador, Lord Auckland, had charged him to declare that they would willingly treat with General Dumourier.

At the same time, Benoit, who had been agent of the French ministry at London, and had just arrived from that place, informed Le Brun on the part of Talleyrand, late Bishop of Autun, De Talon, and other French emigrants, who had political connections with the British ministry, that Pitt and the council of St. James's had nothing more at heart than to treat for the preservation of the neutrality, provided that General Dumourier should be charged with the negociation, and should proceed to England for the purpose of settling its terms, which he might easily accomplish before the opening of the campaign.

This overture of the English ministry was, at first, communicated to no other person of the executive council than Garat and Le Brun. Garat, who was possessed of a sound judgment, zealously embraced the offer, and proposed to send the general as ambassador extraordinary to England, without, however superseding Chauvelin, with instructions to demand a decisive answer respecting war or peace. The king's trial was not yet concluded, but the cruel catastrophe was sufficiently foreseen; this circumstance suggested new considerations to Garat, who feared that the English court might be treacherous enough to detain Dumourier in England, and thereby deprive France of
her

her beft general. Dumourier was compelled to
diffemble that he alfo faw the probability of that
event, and that it was the only thing he defired.
In order that he might efcape from the hands of
the mifcreants who governed his country, he
appeared to fubfcribe to the prudence of Garat's
precaution. It was however, determined that the
affair fhould be laid before the council, and a propofition be made by Garat to fend General Dumourier as Ambaffador extraordinary to London, in
confequence of the overtures made by the minifters of England and Holland; to give the General inftructions to conduct the negociation with
fuitable dignity and promptitude, and whatever
might be the iffue, to return inftantly to put himfelf at the head of the armies. It was refolved to
demand from the Englifh miniftry every poffible fecurity for the perfon of General Dumourier,
and for the full liberty of returning at his pleafure.

When the propofition was laid before the council, Claviere, Pache and Monge oppofed it in the
moft decided manner, undoubtedly incited by jea-
loufy and love of oppofition, for they well knew the
diftrefs of their refpective departments and their
incapability of fupporting a war that would become fo general.

Dumourier was extremely afflicted with the fate
of a meafure which feemed to have promifed his
deliverance, as well as an important occafion of
ferving his country ; but he was not difcouraged.
He was of the opinion of Garat and Le Brun that
the defign fhould not be difcuffed any more in the
council, but profecuted fecretly till it fhould be
in a ftate to infure fuccefs. It was agreed that
de Maulde fhould depart inftantly for the Hague,
under the pretence of his private concerns ; that
Noel fhould be recalled and placed elfewhere ; that
the General fhould charge de Maulde with a letter
for Lord Auckland, informing him that the Gene-

R   ral

ral would be at Antwerp on the 1ſt of February to
viſit his troops in their winter quarters, and that
having learnt from de Maulde, his friend, that
Lord Auckland had ſpoken of him with eſteem and
confidence, it would be a circumſtance of great
pleaſure to him if an opportunity ſhould offer of
meeting that nobleman on the frontiers, and that
perhaps this interview might be beneficial to the
intereſts of the two nations, and the cauſe of humanity. It was alſo determined that, ſhould Lord
Auckland receive this invitation with the good
will that was to be expected, the General ſhould
give him a meeting, and might even if it was
found neceſſary paſs into England.

It was further decided, that Maret, who had
already been ſeveral times in England, ſhould be
ſent to London, to learn from Mr. Pitt if he really
deſired to treat perſonally with General Dumourier. Chauvelin, miniſter plenipotentiary of
France to the court of London, did not at all accord with Talleyrand, who had been ſent with him
as an advertiſer in his negociation, and had not
at all ſucceeded in the object of his embaſſy, which
he was ambitious of conducting without the parti-
cipation of his colleague. Many indeed were the
ebſtacles Chauvelin had to encounter; he had
againſt him the prejudices of the Engliſh nation;
the king of England, the moſt——* in Europe,
and the moſt enraged againſt the French Revolution; the French emigrants; the perſons who had
been given him as advertiſers and aſſiſtants; the
National Convention of France; and his own inexperience. It was thought neceſſary if Dumourier's journey ſhould take place to ſacrifice Chauvelin, or rather to give him ſome other embaſſy;
for Dumourier, who had been the intimate friend
of his father, and had given him the appoint-

* Deſpotique.

ment

ment to England, infifted that he fhould be fent to
Venice or Florence, that he might continue his
diplomatic career with fuccefs.

It appears to be but juft to fay a word here of
the difpofition that Dumourier has always difplayed
in his public character.

Whether it were the effect of good nature, or of
a fenfe of juftice, he has been anxious not to prejudice the interefts of any other perfon in the public employment, and has obliged and ferved great
numbers ; and of courfe it is not greatly furpri-
fing, that he has met with much ingratitude.

Chauvelin, as it has been faid, was to be recalled,
and Maret was to be appointed to his fituation,
on the general's departure from London ; fo that
Maret was extremely interefted in the fuccefs of
the negociation, and had ftrong motives for
fmoothing the difficulties that might be in the general's way, and thereby to render his ftay at the
court of London as fhort as poffible.

C H A P. XIII.

*Departure of de Maulde, of Maret, and of General
Dumourier from Paris.*

IN purfuance of thefe plans, Emanuel de Maulde,
proceeded to the Hague, although the death of the
king, which happened while they were in agitation, feemed to be an event entirely deftructive of
them ; for the certainty that Holland was eager to
preferve peace induced Garat and Le Brun to believe that all refentment excited by that horrible
                                        cataftrophe

catastrophe would yield to the great object of preserving peace, and they were not deceived.

Maret's departure was unwisely postponed, (taking place only on the same day that General Dumourier left Paris) under pretence of first sound-
ing Mr. Pitt respecting the General's journey to
England, by the means of one of his friends, who
had already been employed in the same capacity on
a former occasion by Maret. But the General had
reason to believe that Le Brun, offended that the
Court of St. James's would neither treat with him
as minister of foreign affairs, nor with the Convention, was not sorry to undermine this negociation
by giving scope to the rash ignorance of Briffot,
and the folly of the diplomatic committee, who
seeming to think that France had not enemies
enough to contend with, studied to increase the
number, by insulting every nation.

Maret's mission was altogether unsuccessful.
Chauvelin had never been acknowledged in England as minister of the Republic, the Court of St.
James having considered his mission at an end on
the abolition of Royalty in France, and having
permitted his stay in London merely as an indulgence granted to an individual. And when the
news of the cruel death of Louis XVI. arrived in
England, Chauvelin was ordered to quit London
in four and twenty hours, and the kingdom in
eight days. It was under these circumstances that
Maret arrived in England, and received an order
from the council instantly to quit the kingdom.

But this reception of Maret by the Court of
St. James's, did not put a stop to the negociation
in Holland. General Dumourier departed from
Paris, on the 26th of January, with a mind filled
with apprehensions; he had not been able to prevent the commission of an unprovoked, fruitless,
disgraceful, and fatal crime; he had not succeeded in procuring a revocation of the decree of the
15th

15th December, nor in obtaining an exception in
behalf of Belgium, and thereby to preserve the
French army in case of retreat; nor in establishing an effective administration for the supply of
arms, subsistence, &c. for the army; nor in his
attempts to procure the necessary repairs of the
fortified places, reinforcements of the armies,
horses for the cavalry, or any of that multitude
of objects, the supply of which was necessary to
the opening of the campaign; nor (which in every
case was the greatest of his afflictions) to save an
innocent king, whose goodness was personally
known to him. He was about to resume the command of a disorganised army, abandoning itself
to robberies, and every species of excess, ill armed, in want of cloathing, and dispersed in the
impoverished villages along the Meuse, and the
Roer. New troops were daily arriving from
Germany to augment the army of General Clairfait, who with great capacity had made a stand,
and maintained himself between the Herffle and
the Roer with a comparatively small number of
troops, in want of every thing, and terrified at
the rapacity with which the conquest of Belgium
had been accomplished: That general having
counteracted all the ill effects of their long retreat.

The Prince of Cobourg, celebrated for his glo-
rious campaign against the Turks, was about to
take the command of this army. In the case of
Dumourier waiting till the Prince of Cobourg
should attack him, he was well assured that he
could not resist that General in front, and, at the
same time, the Prince of Hohenloe, who would attack him on his right flank by Namur, the citadel
of which was then repairing very slowly by the
French; and if the English and Dutch should have
time to assemble an army on his left flank, on the
side of Antwerp and Dutch Flanders, even the re-

treat

treat of Dumourier would no longer be secure, having to march through fifty leagues of flat country, with a disorderly army, pursued and almost surrounded by three armies more considerable than his own, and continually assailed by the Peasants and the inhabitants of the cities, whom, the excesses committed by order of the Convention, had driven to desperation. Deneral Dumourier, therefore had no other hope of diminishing his perplexities, but the negociation committed to the care of de Maulde. In truth, his confidence in that was considerable, since Holland had the utmost dread of a rupture with France, being quite unprepared for it, and having the greatest interest in the preservation of the neutrality.

We are about to give an account of the further circumstances of this negociation, which was broken off in the beginning of February, by the unwise and haughty impetuosity of the National Convention. The abrupt declaration of war, made by that Assembly against England and Holland, gave France an air of perfidy, respecting that negociation with which the English have reproached them with some appearance of reason ; but the same charge may be retorted on the English, and it is probable that Pitt had no other design than to amuse General Dumourier, to gain time to make the necessary preparatives for war ; and the treaty entered into by the Court of St. James's with the court of Turin, at that very period, confirms the opinion. So much truth is there in the observation, that history is but a picture of the errors and crimes of government.

IMMEDIATELY on the arrival of de Maulde at
the Hague, which was in the latter end of January,
he presented General Dumourier's letter to Lord
Auckland, who testified the greatest pleasure to de
Maulde on reading it, and told him that the interests of England and Holland being inseparable
in this affair, he should communicate the proposal
to Van Spiegle; which was no sooner done, than
the latter embraced the project of a conference on
the frontiers between the Ambassador of England,
the Grand Pensioner, and General Dumourier.

Lord Auckland dispatched three packet boats,
immediately succeeding each other, to his court,
and de Maulde sent his secretary to Antwerp,
where the General had arrived on the 2d of February, after having visited the posts from Dunkirk to Antwerp.

Throughout Picardy, Artois, and maritime
Flanders, Dumourier found the people overwhelmed with terror and grief, at the tragical death of
Louis XVI. The very name of Jacobin, he perceived, excited equal fear and horror. In all the
cities, however, there were numerous emissaries
of the Jacobins, who stirred up the populace
against the moderate and wise part of the citizens,
and collected accusations, little regarding whether
true or false, against the different administrators of
the departments.

At St. Omers and Dunkirk, there was not the
least appearance of preparations being made for the
war,

war, and there were scarcely any troops to be seen, for the minister of war had weakened maritime Flanders to furnish the augmentation of 10,000 foot and 1500 cavalry, for the army in Austrian Flanders, in consequence of the General's having demanded that reinforcement. The minister of war even drew new battalions afterwards from this country, which was part of the actual seat of the war, to form a body of 12,000 men near Cherbourg, from whence the General had observed a diversion might be made into England, in case war with that power could not be avoided.

Nieuport and Ostend, were in the same condition as St. Omers and Dunkirk, not having a single battery mounted, to prevent any vessels of war entering those ports. There were not even cannon for the purpose; nor could any be obtained, without taking them from Dunkirk, which had not sufficient for its own fortifications.

Dumourier struck with the disorder that pervaded the whole country, and seeing that his embarrassments every moment increased, was greatly satisfied with the first success of de Maulde's negociation. He instantly dispatched a courier to Le Brun, with the original answer of Lord Auckland, which stated that the British minister and the grand Pensionary of Holland, had agreed to proceed together to the frontiers to confer with the General; that Lord Auckland had sent several dispatches to his court, to obtain its sanction, and instructions relative to the conference; that he should soon receive an answer, and that his intentions were not to gain time, nor to retard the General's preparations for the campaign.

The dispatches of de Maulde, which accompanied those of Lord Auckland, gave an account of the circumstances of his interview with the British minister, and the grand Pensionary of Holland. Those ministers, as de Maulde was prepared to find

find, expressed the utter abhorrence of the atrocious barbarity recently committed at Paris; but as de Maulde gave them positive assurances that the General partook of their sentiments on that subject, and was filled with the profoundest indignation against the authors of the crime, that horrible affair did not retard the negociation; and it was settled without any difficulty, that as soon as Lord Auckland should have received the instructions of his court, the conference should take place at the Moor Dyke, on board a yatch belonging to the Prince of Orange, which would be prepared to receive the General. De Maulde concluded by declaring his persuasion, that the conference would be attended with the greatest success.

The General entertained the same hopes, and had prescribed to himself the plan he thought it his duty to follow. He resolved not to betray the interests of his unhappy country; on the contrary, it was his intention to diminish the number of her enemies, in settling the neutrality of England and Holland on a sure basis; but, after he should have rendered this last of his services to France, he resolved to free himself from the imputation of partaking in the crime of his countrymen, and no longer to fight for absurd tyrants whom he was anxious to punish, instead of aiding in the support of their hideous tyranny. He did not design therefore to return to Antwerp but to retire to the Hague, and from thence to publish a memorial in justification of his conduct.

He unfolded a part of these designs in a letter to de Maulde, which was communicated to the two ministers. They requested leave to take a copy of it, but de Maulde declined granting that permission, being unauthorised by his friend; but at the same time he delivered Lord Auckland a letter from the General, informing that minister that he should
receive

receive with great pleasure news of the sanction of the British court to these measures.

At the moment when the negociation was in this promising state, while the General consoled himself with the hope of being freed from the insupportable yoke of combating for tyrants, under the certainty of becoming one day the victim of their ingratitude and cruelty, whatever might be his success; while he thus flattered himself, on the 7th of February he learnt by the public papers that the National Convention had declared war against Holland and England, on a report made by Brissot in the name of the diplomatic committee. This news reduced him to despair, for it was altogether unexpected. He had quitted Paris on the 26th of January; had arrived at Antwerp, only on the 2d of February; Le Brun, then, had not waited to receive his first dispatches, nor intelligence respecting de Maulde's negociation. It seems that Le Brun had precipitated the report of the affront offered to the Republic in the person of Chauvelin, by order of the king of England, to excite the anger of the thoughtless Convention, and thereby raise an insurmountable obstacle to the measures he had concerted with the General.

As to Brissot, he had, as was usual with him, availed himself of this opportunity of insulting both kings and people, in which he was zealously seconded by Barrere and the Jacobins. Thus the two factions united in taking a most disastrous step without discussion and without consideration.

The war was declared, but Le Brun sent no intelligence to General Dumourier, on whom the burthen fell with the greatest weight, and little enquiry was made in the council, whether he was at all in a condition to support himself against these new enemies.

On

On the day that General Dumourier, heard of
the declaration of war againſt England and Holland, de Maulde arrived at Antwerp from the
Hague, with a ſecond letter from Lord Auckland,
congratulating him on having received an authority from his court to enter on the conference,
which was fixed to commence on the 10th, at the
Moor Dyke. The General inſtantly diſpatched a
courier, informing Lord Auckland of the declaration of war ; and obſerving, that although he muſt
admit the declaration of war to have been a little
abrupt, he muſt obſerve it had been occaſioned by
the conduct of the Engliſh Miniſtry ; firſt, in detaining two French veſſels laden with corn, not-
withſtanding the remonſtrances of the French miniſtry to the contrary ; ſecondly, in contemptu-
ouſly ordering the French Ambaſſador to quit the
kingdom, while a negociation was pending between the two nations ; and thirdly, in cauſing
Lord Auckland to publiſh, on the 2d of February,
an addreſs to the States General, which was an in-
ſult to the French nation, and equivalent to a declaration of war.

The General had alſo cauſes of complaint againſt
the Grand Penſionary Van Spiegle. He had in
vain demanded of him the liberation of Colonel
Micoud, a French officer, who, after gaining a
conſiderable law-ſuit againſt a merchant in Holland, had been thrown into priſon, through the
credit of the merchant, on a vague accuſation of
having ſpoken too freely of the government. He
had driven a troop of French comedians from
Amſterdam without even granting them time to
collect the ſums due to them ; he had permitted
Noel the French miniſter at the Hague, and
Thainville, his ſecretary, to be inſulted by the
emigrants, and had afterwards abruptly ordered
them to quit the country ; he had allowed the
emigrants to appear in military uniforms at the

Hague

Hague; and finally had suffered the greatest enmity to be expressed against France with impunity.

It is certain that the conduct of the courts of St. James's and the Hague was inexcusable, since in the midst of a negociation entered into (in consequence of overtures from themselves) with General Dumourier, whom they had demanded to conduct the negociation, they had provoked the anger of the National Convention, whom they knew to be haughty and impatient, and incapable of a temperate conduct. It is but just therefore to reproach them as well as the French with the evils resulting from this war, which is to be considered as only in its beginning, and which will be the source of other equally destructive wars.

It may be said, that providence has united all the people of Europe to inflict a punishment on the enormous crimes committed by the French nation; and perhaps to punish their own errors by the calamities they will have to endure in this long, afflicting and bloody contest. The Atheists of the National Convention, and these are the most ignorant and wicked of the members, because it is not through the influence of philosophy that they have become Atheists, but through the influence of their crimes, have considered what the General has said to them respecting Providence in his letter of the 12th of March, as an unmeaning rhapsody; to such men he has to answer, that Providence leaves us free to make a virtuous or vicious choice, but that from the first choice necessarily results the character of our actions, good or bad; that which is just is alone true; that which is unjust is the effect of error in the mind; that this is above all true with respect to governments; and that justice conducts nations to happiness, and injustice to misery; that when a nation is universally infected with a licentious spirit, as is the case with France, all her motives and actions tend to her ruin;

ruin; hence the fame phrenzy which induced France to commit the fruitlefs crime of murdering Louis XVI. and of treating his family as a herd of flaves, dictated the decree of the 15th of December, which is equally devoid of juftice and policy, which has loft the nation the good-will of every people who were attached to her, has infufed divifions into her councils, familiarifed her with accufations, robberies, and maffacres, has begotten her filthinefs and groffnefs of manners; her wantonnefs in creating of enemies, and indifference to the means of refifling them; and in fine her anarchy and total want of order, which has already inflicted upon her the firft punifhments of that long feries that awaits her. For from the moment that France became a Republic, fhe degenerated into the moft unfortunate country that the annals of the world have produced.

We will conclude this book with a melancholy reflection on the condition to which France has reduced herfelf by her errors; fhe had been prefented with a conftitution formed in a fhort and difficult period by her firft legiflature, which was not indeed perfect but highly valuable, and which every people of Europe admired and envied. The two factions that exifted in France, in combating each other, neverthelefs were of one mind to deftroy this conftitution. The court hoped to recover its former power and numerous means of gratifications; and the Jacobins entirely to beat down royalty, which they hated, but which was fo neceffary to the happinefs of Frenchmen; and while the conftitution was a theme of praife with all reafonable men in other parts of Europe, the French blamed, fpurned and rejected it. But the merits of the conftitution were unknown to the people of France, for they never permitted themfelves to judge of it but through the medium of their furious paffions.

END OF THE FIRST PART.

MEMOIRS

of

GENERAL DUMOURIER,

WRITTEN BY HIMSELF.

.... VITAM QUI IMPENDERE VERO.

TRANSLATED BY JOHN FENWICK.

PART II.

PHILADELPHIA:

PRINTED BY SAMUEL HARRISON SMITH,

CHERRY-STREET, ABOVE FOURTH-STREET.

1794.

CONTENTS

OF THE

SECOND PART.

CHAP. I.

CHAP. II.

CHAP. III.

CHAP. IV.

CHAP. V.

CONTENTS.

MEMOIRS

OF

GENERAL DUMOURIER.

FOR THE YEAR 1793.

BOOK II.

CHAP. I.

Plan of the Campaign.

WE are now entering upon the history of a campaign more rapid, more varied, and perhaps more important, in its events, than any of former or later times. The nature of the campaign was not foreseen till the first week of February; the plan was conceived and arranged between the 7th and the 22d of that month; and the campaign finished on the 5th of the following April.

The history of this short period, offers to the contemplation of the military man, Cities taken in defiance of of immense innundations, a great battle, a variety of engagements, and a retreat which excited the astonishment of the generals of the enemy, aad from which they could not withhold their praise: It exhibits an example of the two species of war, the offensive, and defensive: And it may be said to have involved consequences that will decide the fate of France, and perhaps that of Europe.

Nor is this history less interesting to the philosopher, whom it will confirm in the opinion, that the destiny of empires is often dependent on circumstances that are apparently inconsiderable; and that the character and fortune of one man may decide the fate of a nation. In the preceding year, General Dumourier had preserved

U the

the independence of France, by his success in the plains of Champagne, and rendered her name illustrious in those of Belgium : for, at that period, the greatness of the danger which threatened France united all minds under his standard, and compelled the nation to display her energy under the direction of his counsels. In the period we are now considering, the situation and character of the French people were changed. The nation or rather those who governed and misled the nation, intoxicated with success, and blinded by their crimes, no longer listened to the general, who would now have saved his countrymen, both from a foreign yoke, and from the tyranny of their own mistaken passions.

He was not seconded in his efforts. He was not obeyed. He was opposed, and betrayed ; and his campaign was unfortunate, notwithstanding his exertions to turn the fortune of war in his favour. On the point of conquering Holland, the conquest was snatched from his hands. He formed a second plan, and victory was torn from him by his own troops. In the midst of a retreat, that was as successfully conducted as it was bloody and destructive, he projected another design, which preserved his army, and arrested the ruin of Belgium, which, otherwise, would have been complete. But this design fell short of its greatest object, the deliverance of France : and, in that, it was defeated by the fierce pride of the convention, and by the fickleness of his troops ; and General Dumourier was compelled to quit his army, and to seek a retreat among strangers, who could not forbear to esteem him.

Thenceforth, the French were no longer the same people. In the soldiery, savage rage succeeded valour ; there was neither talent in the plan of the war, nor conduct in its execution ; the French slew and were slain, without remorse, or consideration. It was not war that they carried on ; and the carnage would already have been terminated, if the force that opposed them were that of a single people, or were not rendered ineffectual by the clashing of various interests and counsels.

The situation of General Dumourier was embarrassing, when he knew that England and Holland were on the point of adding their forces to those of the other enemies of France. If the persons who were at the head of affairs, had been well informed and prudent men, he directly would have advised them to evacuate the Netherlands which,

which could no longer be preserved ; and to post the troops
behind the fortified places of the north, holding for a while
the banks of the Scheld, and the citadel of Namur.
But this reasonable proposition would have been regarded
as proceeding from cowardice or treachery ; and would
have brought the general to the scaffold. Or, if it had
been accepted, it would have delivered the General
into the hands of tyrants whom it was his object to crush
for the safety and happiness of his country. Entering
France with an enemy in pursuit of him, and with the
appearance of a flight, he would have instantly lost his
military reputation, which was only to be preserved by
single successes ; and his fate would have been at the
disposal of the Jacobins of Paris, whom this retreat
would have reinforced with the whole amount of his
army. He could not therefore extricate himself from
this desperate situation, but by the hardiest and most decisive means. His military fame and the celerity of his
movements, could alone open him the way to the supply
of all that was wanting to his army. Clothing, accoutrements, horses, arms, provisions, money, all were to
be found in Holland ; and there, he was compelled to
seek them. He conceived the design of conquering
Holland by a daring blow ; and we will now rapidly review his plan, and his resources.

The Dutch refugees had formed a small revolutionary
committee at Antwerp, where was also the Dutch legion.
The committee possessed more zeal than ability ; and,
although they expended considerable sums of money in
maintaining a secret correspondence with the different
Provinces of the Dutch Republic, the information which
the general received through their means was extremely
deficient, especially respecting the military state of that
country. All that could be relied on with certainty was,
that the party of the patriots was very considerable :
particularly at Amsterdam, Haerlem, Dort, and throughout Zealand. The general pretended to reassume the
consideration of the plan, which the committee had laid
before him at Paris, of making an irruption into Zealand.
He affected to examine it minutely in presence of the
committee, and feigned to give it his approbation ; in
order to cover a plan more bold in appearance, but in
truth more certain of success, because it appeared to be
more impracticable. He did not disclose that design to
any other persons than to Mr. Koch and Mr. De Nils,

whom

whom he thought deserving of his entire confidence ; and whose zeal, probity, strength of mind, and love of their country, entitled them to be the deliverers of their fellow citizens.

The plan for the invasion of Zealand, was as follows : The refugees had learnt that the Stadtholder had formed the design of fortifying the Island of Walcheren, as a place of retreat for the States General and the members of the government, in case the French should enter the country, and should be joined by the people, whom the government mistrusted. The Dutch Committee proposed that a considerable body of men should depart from Antwerp, and proceed, with as great secrecy and dispatch as possible, by Sandvliet to the island of South Beveland, and from thence to the island of Walcheren, and, seizing upon Middleburg and Flushing, should make themselves masters of that latter island. The garrisons of those two towns, it is true, did not amount to more than twelve or fifteen hundred men, and were raw and undisciplined troops. But if the inhabitants had not joined their deliverers, the French soldiers would infallibly have been cut off. There was nothing to prevent the island receiving succours to double the amount of the French detachment ; there were already several English frigates at Flushing ; and the Dutch had a squadron of armed vessels in the Scheld, lying under the fortress of Batz, a league below Lillo, which would entirely have cut off the retreat of the detachment to the main land.

No success could be expected in this expedition, without such promptitude and exactness in the execution, as the general could not expect either from his own troops, or those of the Dutch patriots. He had not a single general officer under his command to whom he could confide so dangerous an enterprize. He could not abandon the command of the main army, to undertake the expedition himself. Had he yielded to the opinion of the Dutch patriots, he would certainly have been led into an unsuccessful enterprize ; and this unfortunate check in the beginning of the campaign would have completed the ruin of his small army, consisting of new troops, that had already suffered much by his absence, and were shortly after beaten, discouraged, and almost dispersed on the Roer and the Meuse.

But if, by the chance that belongs to military movements, this expedition had been successful, however brilliant

liant it might have been, it would have produced no real
benefit to the general. On the contrary, it would have
deprived him of five or six thoufand of his troops, who,
would have been feparated from him by an arm of the fea,
and all the places of Dutch Flanders: leaving him without a force fufficient to undertake any thing further.

The better to conceal his real defigns, however, he
profeffed to adopt that plan of attacking Holland, and he
made fome difpofitions as if he was about to undertake it
ferioufly. He had, at Antwerp, fome fmall veffels
under the command of Captain Moultfon, an American
officer in the French fervice, who had affifted in the taking of the citadel of Antwerp. This fmall fquadron confifted
of the Ariel of 24 guns, a brig of 14 guns, and three gun-
boats. He ordered thefe veffels to be fitted out, to proceed to fort Lillo, and there to caft anchor. He directed
a furnace to be conftructed on each of the gun-boats, for
the purpofe of heating balls. He commanded the fort of
Lillo, and that of Liefkenfhoeck, and the citadel of Antwerp, to be furnifhed with provifions, and put in a ftate to
fuftain a fiege. He affembled, at Antwerp, all the Dutch
veffels that on the declaration of war had been detained
in the canals of the Scheldt, and ordered them to be
prepared to ferve as fire-fhips.

He wifhed it to be believed that his object was to burn
the Dutch veffels lying at anchor under the fort of Batz;
and to feize upon that fort, which mounted forty guns.
The Dutch veffels retired to Ramekens. In fhort, every
thing feemed to indicate, during feveral days, that the
general's movements were directed againft Zealand; and
he gave the enemy reafon to imagine that the campaign
would open by the invafion of that country. Meanwhile, the general's thoughts were wholly occupied with
his own plan; which was extremely fimple, although,
had it never been attempted it muft have appeared wholly
impracticable. This plan was, to make his way with a
body of troops to the Moordyke, deceiving and evading
the garrifons of Breda, and Gertruydenburg, on his
right; Bergen-up-Zoom, Steenburg, Klundert, and
Williamftadt, on his left: and, paffing the arm of the
fea which runs between the Moor-dyke and Dort, and
which is about two leagues in breadth, to land at Dort;
where being arrived he fhould be in the heart of Holland,
and would have no obftacles to encounter in marching by
Rotterdam,

Rotterdam, Delft, the Hague, Leyden and Haerlem, to
Amsterdam. By this plan, he would take all the strong
places of Holland in the rear. Meanwhile, General
Miranda, with a detachment of the grand army, was to
bombard Maestricht, and Venloo; and, as soon as he
should know that General Dumourier had reached Dort,
he was to leave General Valence to continue the siege of
Maestricht, and to march with 25,000 men against
Nimeguen, where General Dumourier was to join him
by the route of Utrecht.

This plan, executed with rapidity, would have had
little serious difficulty to encounter, since the Stadtholder
neither had an army assembled, nor had adopted any settled plan of defence; and since, of all the enterprizes that
might be undertaken by Dumourier, this was the least to
be expected: for it seemed to be no better than an attempt
to march an army *through the eye of a needle*[*].

Dumourier's next design was, as soon as he should be
master of Holland, to send the battalions of national guards
back into Belgium; to assemble an army entirely composed of troops of the line, and commanded by generals
of whose fidelity he was assured, and to compel the
States General of the United Provinces, to order a surrender of all their towns; to make no changes in the government, but such as should be indispensibly necessary; to
dissolve the Dutch Revolutionary Committee, to the
members of which he had already signified that in case of
success, they might be severally appointed to the public
situations of their respective Provinces, supposing them
to possess the confidence of their fellow citizens; to preserve the Dutch Republic from the tyranny of the commissioners of the national convention, and from the influence of Jacobinism; to fit out a fleet with all possible
expedition at Rotterdam, in Zealand, and in the Texel,
in order to seize upon the Dutch settlements in India,
and to secure the possession of them by strong garrisons;
to offer a perfect neutrality to the English; to station, in
the country of Zutphen and Dutch Guelders, an army
of observation consisting of 30,000 men; to furnish money
and arms for the raising a body of 30,000 men, in the
countries of Antwerp, the two Flanders, and Campine,
on whose attachment he could rely; to permit the French

[*] These are the words of Dumourier.

to occupy no other part of the Netherlands, than the
country of Liege; to annul, throughout Belgium the decree
of the 15 of December; to invite the people of that country to assemble at Aloft, Antwerp, or Ghent, for the purpose of forming on a solid basis such a government as
should be agreeable to them; and after that to assemble an
army of Belgians of 40, 000 men, composed of battalions of
800 men each, together with a body of cavalry. Dumourier further designed to offer a suspension of arms to the Imperialists; and in case of its being rejected, to raise an
army of 150,000 men in order to drive them beyond the
Rhine; but if it were accepted he hoped to gain time
and means to execute the rest of his plan, which was,
either to form a Republic of the eighteen Provinces of the
Netherlands, if that should be agreeable to the people, or
to make an offensive and defensive alliance between the
Republic of the Seven United Provinces and that of
Belgium, and to raise an army of 80,000 men in the two
countries for their joint defence, till the conclusion of the
war; to invite France to enter into an alliance with the two
Republics, and to put an end to her anarchy by re-adopt-
ing the constitution of 1789; and in case of France refusing to accede to this proposal, to march to Paris with an
army composed of the French troops of the line, and a
body of 40,000 Dutch and Belgians, in order to dissolve
the National Convention, and annihilate the power of the
Jacobins.

Such were the outlines of General Dumourier's plan,
which was communicated only to four persons. It will
appear visionary to the reader; but being founded on the
circumstances of the times, and on well combined calculations, it could not have failed of success, if the most
disastrous events, entirely unconnected with the conduct
and arrangements of General Dumourier, had not broken
all his measures, and forced him to sacrifice all his hopes
to the immediate safety of the grand army, on the point
of being entirely destroyed, by the mismanagement of the
officers who commanded under him.

CHAP.

GENERAL DUMOURIER, having taken his resolution, may be still said to have had all his means to create. At Antwerp, there were two battalions of national gendarmerie, consisting of 350 men each, who were dangerous only to their officers and the peaceable inhabitants of the city, being the most detestable and undisciplined soldiers that ever entered the field of battle. These ferocious Janissaries received each 40 sols per day in specie without deduction; appointed their own officers; and comitted every kind of crime. The general, after passing them in review, declared in the strongest terms, that, should they continue to commit the excesses of which they were accused, or to be guilty of any disobedience of orders, he would instantly send them back to France. This body of gendarmerie was composed of the ancient French guards. There were also, at Antwerp, one hundred and fifty dragoons of the 20th regiment; three battalions of national guards; and about two thousand of the Dutch legion, two hundred of which were horse. Twelve battalions of national guards, newly raised, and having neither fusees, accoutrements, nor shoes, were quartered in the cities and villages of West Flanders; and had no idea that they should be obliged to take the field till the month of May.

Cannon, mortars, magazines, money, commissaries, together with their assistants, were altogether wanting. But there was not a moment to be lost. The rashness of the national convention, in declaring war against Holland, had warned the Dutch to prepare for their defence; and, unless the general had attacked them with the utmost celerity, the enterprize would have become uterly chimerical. And, indeed, had the Dutch prepared for their defence with as great activity as the general used for attacking them, the project must have been unsuccessful.　　　　　　　　　General

General Miranda had remained at the head of the army of the North during the whole winter. This general was a Peruvian by birth; and was a man of capacity, and extensive information. He was better versed in the theory of war than any other of the French generals, but he was not equally well versed in the practice. His intimacy with Pethion had been the cause of his entering the service the preceding year, as major general. He joined Dumourier at the camp of Grand-pre; and had been of great service to him, in the different attacks of the Prussians, particularly in the retreat of the 15th of September. But he had a haughtiness of disposition, and a bluntness of manner, which begat him many enemies; and he was unfit to command the French, whose confidence it is impossible to gain but by good humour and a conduct expressive of respect for them.

Dumourier had procured him the appointment of lieutenant-general, in the month of November 1792; had conferred upon him the command of the army of the North, and had promised to obtain him the rank of general, on the first opportunity. Miranda was afterward offended that Valence, an older lieutenant-general than himself, (having commanded with great reputation general Kellermann's advanced guard, and several detached corps, during the campaign of 1792) should have been raised to the rank of general on the recommendation of Dumourier. He never forgave this preference; but his resentment, unfortunately for France, did not display itself till the day of the battle of Nerwinde. At the time we now speak of, he still appeared full of attachment to Dumourier. And that general had written to him from Paris to make preparations for the opening of the campaign, very early in the spring, by the siege of Maestricht, in case a rupture should prove to be unavoidable with England and Holland.

Dumourier's own army was then under the command of general Lanouc, who was a very brave and honest man. Fifty years past in the service had rendered him respectable; but had also diminished his vigour. He was assisted by general Thouvenot, an officer of very uncommon merit.

The army of general Valence was commanded, in his absence by lieutenant-general Le Veneur, a man of great courage but of a limited capacity.

X   Dumourier

Dumourier ordered General Miranda to present himself before Maestricht with a part of his army, without too much weakening the posts on the Meuse; to reinforce himself to the number of 25 or 30,000 men drawn from the other two armies; and to communicate these orders to the respective generals, that they might contract their lines, and hold their troops in readiness to take the field, if the Imperialists, whose num'ers were daily increasing in their quarters on the Herfsle, and the Prussians who were also daily receiving reinforcements at Wessel, should betray any designs of forming a junction to relieve Maestricht, which was expected. General Dumourier thought it prudent not to point out the position that might he proper for this army of observation; and he acknowledges that, in this, he committed a great error.

In the remaining part of General Dumourier's instructions to Miranda, he confidentially unfolded his plan for attacking Holland. He desired him not to open the siege regularly before Maestricht, being too early in the season for such an undertaking, but to endeavour to carry the place by a vigorous assault with bombs and red hot balls, in the same manner as the Duke of Saxe-Teschen had attempted to carry Lisle; and, when General Dumourier should have informed him that he had reached Dort by the Moor Dyke, to leave General Valence before Maestricht, and to proceed by forced marches to Nimeguen, passing by the frontier of the Dutchy of Cleves, in order to intercept the Prussians, if they should attempt to reach Holland before him; and, to this latter purpose, Dumourier desired him to send General Champmorin (a most able engineer) against Venloo, while Miranda should besiege Maestricht, and by that means to make himself master of the lower part of the Meuse as far as Genep.

General Dumourier confined the number of men that Miranda should employ in this expedition to 25,000 or 30,000, at the utmost, that he might not too much weaken the posts on the Meuse. He recommended the greatest dispatch in the preparations, so that Maestricht might be invested by the 12th or 15th of that month; and he appointed lieutenant-general Bouchet, an experienced engineer, to assist Miranda in the siege.

Dumourier wrote nearly in the same terms to Lanoue and Thouvenot; enjoining them to inform the troops, that he should review them, after having visited the

quarters

quarters on the lower Meuse. He wrote to lieutenant-general Moreton, who commanded in Bruffels, that he was setting off immediately for that city. And to General d'Harville, ordering him to assemble his troops at Namur on the 20th of February, as he designed to review his division on the 22d of that month. Thus, in misleading such of his generals as were not to be employed in the expedition he effectually deceived the enemy, who were utterly at a loss to conjecture in what point he would begin the campaign.

Some days after General Dumourier quitted Paris, Pache resigned the war department in order to be chosen Mayor of Paris, and was succeeded by General Bournonville, for whom Dumourier had procured the rank of lieutenant-general and afterward of general in a very short space of time. Dumourier had been used to call him his Ajax and his son. In truth he had commenced his career with great spirit, and had evinced a sincere attachment to the general. Dumourier now informed him merely, that it was his design to attack Holland, without entering into any detail of his plan, lest he should be betrayed by the indiscretion or the dishonesty of the clerks of the war office.

Pache, a little while before his quitting the ministry, had ordered the demolition of the small part of the fortifications of Mons and Tournay which then remained. These imprudent orders had disgusted the inhabitants of those two cities. General Dumourier suspended the execution of the order; and, he not only desired the new minister of war to revoke it, but strongly recommended to him to repair the fortifications of those two places, with the utmost dispatch. He also counselled him to fortify with equal speed the strong place of the castle of Huy; to make ditches round Malines, which might easily be put in a state of defence by inundations; to erect strong batteries at Ostend, Nieuport, and Dunkirk, in order to strengthen our frontiers on that side, in the probable case of our being obliged to evacuate Belgium. General Dumourier further advised Burnonville to complete the lines from Dunkirk to Bergues; to form an intrenched camp at Mount Caffell; and to fortify Orchies between Lisle, Douay, and Conde; Bavay, as an out-post to Quesnoy, between Conde and Maubege; and Beaumont, between Maubege and Philippeville.

Such

Such were the counsels respecting fortifying that frontier which were given by General Dumourier, although he is accused of having betrayed his country. General Dumourier faithfully served his country till the moment that he quitted her; and he will again serve her; with the same zeal and fidelity, if he should ever see her governed by a king, under the sanction of a constitution. Had his counsels been followed, the combined armies would have been detained longer on the exterior frontier, by that line of posts and would not, have penetrated so easily into France.

General Dumourier also requested Bournonville to send him reinforcements of men, and to order General D'Arcon to join him, with some able engineers, having to make a campaign that would abound in sieges. Bournonville acceded to all Dumourier's requests, as far as was in his power, with promptitude; and General D'Arcon arrived at the army immediately afterward.

This general, although one of the best engineers and one of the worthiest men in France, had been accused of aristocracy by the well known Prince of Hesse, a contemptible Jacobin; and had been deprived of his command; but General Dumourier, who had been long acquainted with his merit, restored him to the service of his country, and found him worthy of the trust reposed in him.

General de Flers commanded at Bruges. He was a brave man; but was opinionated, and did not possess much capacity. Having received a wound with a musket ball in the camp of Maulde, Dumourier made him major-general; and afterwards sent him to Bruges, to take upon him the command in West Flanders, and had given him orders to receive the reinforcement of 10,000 men, which Pache had marched into that country on the General's request.

When Dumourier arrived at Bruges, de Flers laid before him a plan which he had formed for surprising the city of Sluys. The general pretended to adopt the plan; and sent de Flers to Bournonville, with a request to give de Flers a body of 5 or 6000 men and a small train of artillery, to enable him to menace Dutch Flanders. The request was complied with, speedily and compleatly.

The general had no design that de Flers should attack the Dutch towns in Flanders, which it was not possible for him to take; but he placed this small body of men under

his

his orders, to be ready to replace, on the fide of Antwerp
and Breda, the forces that the general fhould march into
Holland. And he knew that the affembling this fmall
army in the neighbourhood of Bruges would ftill aid in
deceiving the Dutch refpecting the general's defigns, efpecially as de Flers was himfelf deceived, and made ferious preparations for his expedition.

General Dumourier had left all the officers of his ftaff
at Liege, together with his aids de camp, and was accompanied by his faithful Baptifte. He had alfo left his
equipage with the grand army, to favour the opinion that
he defigned to return ; and had only ordered a few horfes
to attend him at Antwerp, under pretence of vifiting the
cantonments on the Meufe. To form his ftaff therefore,
he fent for four of his officers, at the head of whom he
placed Colonel Thouvenot, brother to the general of the
fame name. This officer, who, under every circumftance,
has been the zealous friend of General Dumourier,
abounded in courage, information, and refources of mind.
He was in an an eminent degree important to the general during the campaign in Holland ; and when they
quitted the army together rendered the general every fervice in his power.

The prefence of General Thouvenot was neceffary to
the grand army. He was the only officer that perfectly
underftood the details of duty in winter quarters ; and was
the only one that had influence enough to heal the fre-
quent quarrels that happened among the generals. It was
known that he poffeffed the entire confidence of Dumourier, and alfo that his merit entitled him to that confidence ; and although he was not the better beloved on
that account, it obtained him a greater degree of refpect ;
and, it being known that he was perfectly acquainted with
the general's intentions, his opinion was received with
the fame deference that was paid to the general's orders.

There was no other commiffary with the army, than
Petit-Jean, to provide magazines and every thing neceffary for the fiege of Maeftricht, and for the cantonments
between the Meufe and the Roer, and the different quarters in Belgium. It feemed imprudent to take him a moment from thefe multiplied concerns, before the arrival
of Malus, who was ftill detained at Paris, although a promife had been made to the general that he fhould be fent
to the army.

Not-

Notwithstanding these reasons, Dumourier ordered General Thouvenot and Petit-Jean to attend him at Antwerp; and, in two days, he settled with them all the necessary engagements to enable his troops to take the field for the expedition.

Dumourier at the same time sent to Liege for General La Fayette, and Lieutenant-Colonel La Martiniere, to form his train of artillery, which indeed was very inconsiderable. These two officers served him with a zeal and knowledge deserving of the highest eulogiums.

On the departure of Thouvenot and Petit Jean, General Dumourier gave them instructions for a new levy of twenty-five battalions of Belgians, consisting of 800 men each, and he charged the generals and other officers commanding in the different provinces with the execution of these orders, and appointed Thouvenot inspector general and Petit Jean commissary general; in pursuance of a decree of the National Convention, which placed those troops on the footing of French soldiers. Till that period, the Belgic Provinces had made levies of legions, regiments, and corps at their pleasure. These troops were filled with a disproportionate number of officers, and were paid on the credit of the Belgic military committee, the members of which were very ignorant and dishonest, and were governed by General Roziere, who had formerly been an officer in the service of France, and was neither a man of honour nor talents.

General Valence, on his route from Paris, passed thro' Antwerp to take Dumourier's orders. Dumourier communicated his entire plan to Valence; and informed him that he was to cover the siege of Maestricht, with the army under his command, till Miranda should depart for Nimeguen, afterward to continue the siege, if the town should not be then taken. He recommended to the general to visit all the winter quarters of the army, to choose a proper position for the covering army, to watch the motions of the enemy, and to hold himself ready to engage them if they should endeavour to relieve Maestricht, which was reasonably to be expected. Above all things, he recommended to him to act with promptness and vigour; to concert measures sincerely and cordially with General Miranda; and to consult General Thouvenot, whose knowledge could not fail to be of infinite service to him. At the same time he sent orders to Lanoue to obey General Valence.

The

The Committee of Finance of the Convention, mistrusting the general, or being desirous of counteracting and insulting them, had ordered the treasury to furnish no more money to the troops than their pay, and not to appropriate sums for the other expences, although the troops were in want of shoes, cloaths and arms. The paymaster of the army supplied no more for the troops destined against Holland, than the pay of fifteen days, which amounted to only 240,000 livres ; and the troops did not even cost the nation that sum, since they lived at the expence of the country. The expedition however was attended with prodigious incidental expences.

Notwithstanding the rapacity and unjust conduct of the French in Belgium, the whole of that nation rendered justice to the conduct of General Dumourier. In no city of Europe are there a greater number of wealthy inhabitants than at Antwerp. After the commerce of that city had fallen into decay, the inhabitants had substituted the most rigid œconomy in the place of that resource. Their expences were usually confined within the bounds of a part of their revenues, so that their fortunes could not but accumulate greatly. General Dumourier assembled the magistrates and principal citizens, and opened a loan of 1,200,000 florins. A merchant named Verbrouck was charged with the receipt of the money, and the commissary Petit-Jean with the superintendance of its expenditure. The loan produced 200,000 florins, which in the end was an inestimable resource. It served to cloath and arm the legion of the North, the hussars of the Republic, and several other French and Belgic corps. General Dumourier, who never had leisure even to examine the accounts of the expenditure, and who was in Holland while it was received and expended, has been calumniated on this ground also. He was charged in the Jacobin Society, and afterward in the Convention, with having appropriated this sum to his own use. But he whose mind is occupied with great and interesting concerns, is not liable to be greatly tempted by the love of wealth.

General Dumourier, before he entered Holland, published a manifesto, with which the House of Orange has been justly offended. That declaration, it is true, in a war of ordinary circumstances had been very unjust and unwise, although we have been accustomed to see hostilities between the most civilized nations preceded by mutual abuse and accusations. But it would be a wrong

done

done to General Dumourier, to impute to his moral character, actions that were imposed upon him by his public situation.———He was called upon to give encouragement to a very considerable party in the Dutch nation, who were dispirited by former misfortunes; and to terrify the partizans of the Stadtholder.———It became him, in the station he filled, to separate the people of Holland from the cause of the Stadtholder, since the Dutch nation, had it been left to her to determine, would have avoided the war, dreading it as altogether contrary to her interests. Dumourier's declaration resulted from these circumstances; and beside, it was necessary to screen the general from the censure and resentment of the National Convention, till he should be able to penetrate with success into Holland.

The preparations of which we have spoken were made, and the army assembled with every necessary, in ten days; and the advanced guard entered Holland, on the 17th of February. The most important difficulty was, to conceal the inconsiderable amount of this small army. And, in that, the general succeeded so perfectly, that the troops themselves were persuaded that they were not less than 30,000 strong; while the Dutch imagined they had to contend with an immense army; in which opinion, they were confirmed by the inhabitants of Antwerp, who extremely exaggerated the number of troops, which passed through that city.

CHAP.

The rear-guard of the army was composed of a battalion of National guards; a Dutch battalion; two hundred Belgians; a hundred troopers of the 20th regiment; and a hundred of the Belgic huſſars; and was commanded by Colonel Tilly, an aid-du-camp of the general. A part of the artillery was attached to each of theſe diviſions.

With this ſmall army the general undertook the conqueſt of Holland. But he had a powerful party in the country, who expected him with impatience, and were ready to declare themſelves on his penetrating into the country. He had neither time, on account of the neceſſary rapidity of his movements, nor means, for want of good officers in the different corps, to form and diſcipline theſe troops. But they were ardent, courageous, and impatient for action; and the enterprize they were undertaking had a boldneſs in it, that extremely well ſuited the genius of the nation. The general informed this little army of the rigour of the climate into which they were going; the number of ſtrong places, ſurrounded by inundations, to be taken; and the canals and arms of the ſea to be croſſed. But while he told them of theſe obſtacles, he declared to them that, being once arrived in Holland, they would be joined by numerous friends, and would find proviſions, money and every thing they wanted, in abundance.

The French ſoldier poſſeſſes great ſenſibility and underſtanding; and is not to be conducted with ſucceſs by the ordinary means of military men. If his general have the good ſenſe to unfold to him the obſtacles of an enterprize, he thinks no longer of any thing but conquering them, and actually makes the enterprize an affair of pleaſure. But if the danger be concealed from him, he is confounded in diſcovering it; and if he be once diſpirited, or rather diſguſted with being led blindly to a deſperate taſk, he gives way to miſtruſt, and it becomes impoſſible to rally him; or afterwards to controul him*.

Dumourier had cauſed General Berneron to march forward, on the 16th, with the advanced guard; promiſing that he ſhould be ſupported ſhortly by the reſt of the army. In written inſtructions which he delivered to General Berneron, he ordered him inſtantly to ſend a detachment conſiſting of 800 infantry and 100 cavalry, commanded by lieutenant-colonel Daendels, a Dutch refugee, to the

---

* This is a divine picture of a ſoldier.

Moor Dyke, in order to feize upon all the veſſels he ſhould find there, or at Swaluve, or Roowaert : to poſt the remainder of his diviſion along the little river of Merck, from Oudenboſch and Sevenbergen to Breda : and to throw a bridge over the river Merck, in order to ſecure a communication with lieutenant-colonel Daendels, and to be able to ſupport him againſt any ſorties that might be made by the neighbouring garriſons.

In Bergen-up-Zoom, Gertruydenberg, and Breda, there were three regiments of dragoons, amounting to more than all the cavalry of General Dumourier, and a ſufficient number of infantry to act with them. It is certain that if theſe had been aſſembled together, and had been joined by the cavalry of Bois-le-Duc, and Heuſden, they would have been ſufficiently ſtrong to have compelled the advanced guard to retire, and thereby to have ruined the expedition. But Dumourier knew that there was not any one of the Dutch generals charged with the defence of the country, or who had authority to draw all the cavalry together ; and he was certain that the officers who commanded in the different towns, having no plan of general defence, would attend only to the danger which threatened them reſpectively, and would not hazard any part of their garriſons, againſt an army, which each of them believed to be very ſtrong, and which appeared by the extent of its cantonments to menace ſeveral cities at once. Beſide, that the commanding officers of the garriſons were ſufficiently embarraſſed in preparing means for their defence ; not having expected ſo ſudden an attack, and in this early part of the ſeaſon.

On the 22d, the general arrived at his firſt poſt ; and was aſtoniſhed and afflicted to find that his orders had not been executed. No part of the advanced guard had yet paſſed the Merck ; by which neglect, time was given to the Dutch to withdraw all their veſſels from the Moor Dyke to the ſide of Dort, and place them under the protection of three guardſhips,. which were on that ſtation. This firſt error rendered the general's paſſage to Dort extremely difficult, and almoſt impracticable, unleſs he could obtain other boats in the place of theſe he had expected to ſeize.

He inſtantly commanded Berneron and Daendels to puſh forward ; and General d'Arcon to inveſt Breda with the right diviſion ; and Colonel le Clerc cloſely to blockade Bergen-op-Zoom, and Steenberg, with the left. The
officers

officers who commanded in those two last places abandoned all their out-posts. Colonel le Clerk made himself master of the small fort of Blaw-sluys, at a little distance from Steenberg, which place he summoned to surrender. The garrison of Bergen-op-Zoom, made two or three inconsiderable sallies ; which produced no other effect than the desertion of some of their men, who entered into the Dutch legion.

General Dumourier proceeded, with his rear guard, between the two divisions of his army, to Sevenbergen ; sending his advanced guard forward to Klundert and Williamstadt, with orders to besiege those two places. And he commanded Lieutenant-Colonel Daendels to post himself at Nordschantz, in order to cut off the communication between Williamstadt and Klundert. This officer seized three vessels at Nordschantz.

The general appointed Messrs. Koch and De Nifs to be colonels. The former of them, who was an eloquent speaker, and a man of enterprising character, was ordered to assist Daendels ; and the latter, a man of information and temperate courage, accompanied the general.

Dumourier did not conceal from himself the difficulty of passing to Dort, by the Moor Dyke. The following was the plan first projected for that purpose. Koch and Daendels, according to the instructions given to Berneron, were to proceed by the 17th to the Moor Dyke with 900 men, supported by the whole of the advanced guard, posted on the Merck. They were to collect all the vessels they could find on that side ; and, on the 21st or 22d at furthest, embarking all the men they could croud into these vessels, were to pass to Dort, which they had reason to hope would join them ; and, aided by the inhabitants, were to disarm the garrison, consisting of 250 men, unless they should be willing to incorporate themselves with the army. There were more than a hundred vessels lying at Dort. These they were to conduct to the Moor Dyke ; and, arming three or four with the largest cannon, were to send them forward to drive off the three small guard ships. Indeed it was proposed to make themselves masters of these vessels by boarding them, they being both ill-armed and ill manned.

The plan thus far accomplished, the main body of the army was to proceed to Sevenbergen, Oudenbosch, Moor Dyke and Swaluve ; and, from thence, to pass to Dort, in one or two divisions ; their embarkation being protected

by

by the rear guard, who were to deftroy the bridge that
fhould be thrown over the Merck, and to prevent the
garrifons, that might attempt to harrafs the army, from
paffing the river. The army being once arrived at Dort
there was no longer any obftacle to be feared.

On the evening in which General Dumourier quitted
Antwerp, he met, at a little village on his route, the Baron de Stael, who formerly had been Ambaffador from
Sweden to France, and was now going to Paris. The
Baron fupped with Dumourier, and informed him
that every part of Germany and Holland through which
he had paffed was friendly to the General's enterprife ;
and that at Utrecht he was impatiently expected. He
alfo confirmed the intelligence, which the General had
already received, that the party of the Stadtholder were
in the greateft confternation. Without endeavouring to
difcover the object of the Baron's journey, the General
counfelled him to wait the iffue of the prefent expedition
before he fhould explain himfelf confidentially to the
French Miniftry, that he might not too haftily pledge his
court to any certain line of conduct, or expofe his meafures to be afterwards difowned ; and he advifed him by
all means to be filent, at Paris, on any fubject but fuch
as he was willing fhould be known to the whole world.
This Minifter affured the General that he was going to
Paris on his private concerns. Dumourier before his departure from Antwerp, had given the fame counfel to a
perfonage from Poland, of very high rank and confequence ; who, being on his route, had paid a vifit to the
General at his quarters. Indeed, the General's maxim
uniformly was to take every opportunity of preventing
foreign courts from pledging themfelves to a miniftry, the
flave of an affembly of 700 men, without prudence, experience or honor.

Dumourier's original plan was totally deranged by the
negligence of the officers, to whom he had entrufted the
advanced guard, and the execution of his firft operations.
But he did not abandon his hopes of fuccefs. He concerted new means. In the canals between Oudenbofch
and Sevenbergen, he found 22 veffels from 20 to 70 tons.
He ordered one of his Commiffaries, named Bourfier, an
indefatigable and intelligent man, to make them fit to
carry 1200 men ; and to mount four of them with cannon,
for the advanced guard of this little fquadron. He im-
preffed all the carpenters and failors of the fmall ports
that

that are to be found in that part, and affigned them very confiderable pay, on the funds already raifed by the Dutch Committee, on the credit of the property of the Prince of Orange and his known partizans.

From the moment that Dumourier entered Holland, the army no longer coft the French treafury any thing more than the daily pay. The inhabitants of their own accord, furnifhed provifions and forage, as well as money to forward the expedition. Never was an army received with fuch cordiality ; nor ever did foldiers lefs merit fuch reception ; the Gendarmerie and light troops indulging themfelves in rapine and every fpecies of oppreffion. But from the difgrace of this conduct, the troops of the line, and national guards, are to be wholly exempted ; fince, on all occafions, thefe conducted themfelves with urbanity and juftice.

As it demanded time to prepare the veffels, the general made another important change in his firft plan. According to that, he meant to deceive and evade the ftrong places ; and, ftealing as it were, between them, to embark directly at the Moor Dyke. After that he would have had time to harrafs thofe places ; and relying on the weaknefs of the garrifons, and inexperience of the commanding officers, he calculated on making himfelf mafter of at leaft one of them, which event would give great relief to his army, and furnifh him with artillery and ammunition, in both of which he was extremely ill provided.

He refolved to undertake no one fiege in form.—To prefs a regular fiege forward with vigour, he muft have affembled his little army in one point, and thereby have given the enemy an opportunity of knowing its weaknefs ; and, being no longer mafter of the country, it would have been eafy for the garrifons that were not attacked to recover from their furprife, affemble troops to cut off his communication with Antwerp, drive away his workmen, and deftroy his little fleet, without which he had nothing to hope. Wherefore, while Colonel Le Clerc continued to blockade Bergen-op-Zoom and Steenberg, he ordered General d'Arcon to attack Breda, and his advanced guard at the fame time to fall upon Klundert.

Breda is a town celebrated for its ftrength. It was furnifhed with two hundred pieces of cannon, was well palifadoed, and protected by an inundation. Twelve hundred infantry, and a regiment of dragoons, garrifoned the place ; but the Governor, the Count de Byland, was a

courtier,

courtier, and had seen no service. The troops bought their bread at the bakers, their meat at the butchers, without having any magazines. The Dutch towns are most of them well protected by inundations, and abound with strong exterior works; but are greatly deficient in casemates, and the inhabitants are greatly disaffected to the government.

General d'Arcon, without opening any trenches, erected two batteries of four mortars and four howitzers, extremely near the town, on the side of the village of Hage. The enemy answered by a very brisk fire, during three days; on the fourth, General d'Arcon had no more than sixty bombs left, and must have been under the necessity of raising the siege after throwing them into the place. At this moment, Colonel Philip de Vaux, an Aid-de-Camp of General Dumourier, entered the place to summon it for the second time, and represented to the Count de Byland, that General Dumourier was on the point of arriving with his whole army, and that then no quarters would be given to the garrison, which so alarmed the Governor that he capitulated with the consent of his officers. The honors of war and all the Governor's demands were granted him. The French entered the place; which, excepting some few houses, was not at all damaged. They found two hundred and fifty *bouches a feu**, near three hundred thousand weight of powder, and five thousand fusees, of which they were in great want. This siege did not cost more than twenty men on each side. The French carried their temerity so far as to dance the *Carmagnole* on the glacis, on the side which was not inundated. Thirty dragoons of the regiment of Byland sallied out upon these men, killed some and returned with six prisoners, having lost two or three men and some of their horses.

The besieging army amounted to no more than five thousand men; and, of these, twelve hundred were detached to seize upon forts on the sluices, on the side of Huesden.

Klundert was taken in two days after the surrender of Breda. The works of this small fort were extremely regular, and the place was protected by inundations that entirely surrounded it. It was defended with great vigour, but with little judgment, by a lieutenant colonel in the

* The translator does not know what those are.

Dutch

Dutch service, who was a Westphalian. He had no more than a hundred and fifty men in the place. General Berneron had erected a battery of four cannon and a number of small mortars close behind the dyke, at a hundred and fifty toises from the place ; so that the houses of that small city were almost entirely destroyed. The commanding officer, after keeping up an almost incessant fire during several days with little effect, and having no longer any shelter for his troops, resolved to spike his cannon, and to endeavour to retreat with the remainder of his garrison to Williamstadt. He was intercepted by a detachment of the Dutch refugees, commanded by Lieutenant Colonel Hartmann, whom he shot dead, receiving at the same time a ball which killed him on the spot, and his men were made prisoners. The French carried the body of this officer to Klundert, after having taken the keys of the town which were found in his pocket.

In this place were found fifty-three pieces of cannon, some mortars, a great quantity of bombs and shot, and about eighty thousand weight of powder.

General Dumourier lost no time in sending Berneron to besiege Williamstadt. And it was with the ammunition and artillery of Klundert that the new siege was undertaken.

Dumourier also ordered General d'Arcon to commence the siege of Gertruydenberg. This small town was ill defended on the side of Ramsdoneck, having in that quarter only a slight pallisadoe along the river, and being commanded by neighbouring heights. But on the left side of the Donge, it was protected by an extensive inundation, and by two lines of extremely strong outworks, which could not have been carried in three weeks, had they been ably and vigorously defended. The garrison was composed of the regiment of Hertzel, amounting to between eight or nine hundred men, and of a fine regiment of dragoons belonging to the Stadtholder's guard. The governor, named Bedault, a major general in the service, was an old man of eighty. General d'Arcon began the attack with cannon, and mortars that he brought from Breda. All the outworks were carried, or abandoned by the enemy on the second day. D'Arcon erected batteries on some of them ; and after a few shot were exchanged, Colonel de Vaux entered the place, the capitulation was settled, the honours of war were granted, and General Dumourier,

mourier, who had arrived meanwhile, dined with the old General Bedault, who acknowledged to him that he had furrendered becaufe he had been difappointed in his expectations of receiving veffels from Dort to Gorcum, to enable him to evacuate the place. A few bombs had fallen on the city and one on the general's houfe.

During dinner, a meffenger came to inform the governor that the terms of capitulation had been violated by a lieutenant-colonel of the National guards, who, being drunk, infolently infifted on entering the city in fpite of the centinels; and had attempted to difcharge a piftol at the lieutenant-colonel of the regiment of Hirtzel. General Dumourier ordered the drunkard to be brought into the room, tore the epaulet from his fhoulder, and reduced him to the ranks, to the great aftonifhment of the officers of the garrifon, who interceded for his pardon.

General Dumourier converfed much with this garrifon, which confifted of exceeding fine troops. He has frequently fince thought of an expreffion of the lieutenant colonel of the regiment of Hirtzel, who walking with him on the ramparts, faid *Hodie mihi, cras tibi*. The honeft Swifs fpoke prophetically.

This new conqueft gave us a hundred and fifty *bonches a feu*, two hundred thoufand weight of powder, a quantity of bombs and ball, twenty-five hundred new fufees, and what was moft effential an excellent port, and more than thirty veffels of various fizes. We had alfo taken five veffels at Breda.

This was in the beginning of March. While thefe fieges were carrying forward, the general paffed the greater part of the time at the Moor Dyke, whence, it being in the centre of his operations, he directed the fieges on his right and left, and fuperintended the fitting out of his fquadron. His commiffary Bourfier having, with incredible exertions, fonnd means to arm twenty-three veffels, and to victual them for twelve hundred men, the general fent them down the canal of Sevenbergen to Roowaert, which is a fmall creek, lying a quarter of a league weft of the Moor Dyke.

On the day the general eftablifhed his quarters in this village with an hundred Dutch chaffeurs and fifty dragoons, he was cannonaded the whole day, by three guard fhips. Having pofted his chaffeurs along the Dyke, by which two men were killed on board the veffels, he compelled them to abandon their fituation. A few hours after,

ter, he ordered twelve twenty-four pounders from Breda, together with ammunition, and conſtructed ſeveral batteries, one of which was at Roowaert, to protect the ſailing of his ſquadron, and the reſt at the Moor Dyke to cover his-embarkment. He was there perſuaded that his cannon would carry more than half way over the canal; and indeed the enemy's armed ſhips did not again approach the ſide occupied by the French.

He cauſed huts covered with ſtraw to be raiſed along the ſands from Roowaert to Swaluve. There the ſoldiers amuſed themſelves and were extremely happy, but impatient to croſs to Dort. Dumourier jeſtingly told them that they reſembled beavers; and he named this aquatic cantonment, the camp of Beavers. Proviſions were in plenty; the water was not bad; and brandy was diſtributed to the troops every morning. The general gave his troops an example of firmneſs; and was lodged and lived like the reſt.

In this expedition, the general chalked himſelf out a ſyſtem for carrying on war in countries overflowed by water. It would not be impoſſible, by means of dykes, to march over any part of Holland, to conduct artillery, and eſtabliſh batteries at pleaſure: excepting in the caſe of being oppoſed by gun-boats, when it would be neceſſary to have an adequate force of the ſame nature.

General Dumourier had, among his battalions of volunteers, ſeveral men from Gaſcony, Brittany, Normandy, and Dunkirk. Of theſe men he formed a body of from four to five hundred ſailors, giving them twenty ſols per day in addition to their pay. The general's ſquadron at Roowaert was deſigned to carry his advanced guard, and he appointed an Engliſh naval officer, and a lieutenant of the Dutch navy to command it; with the aſſiſtance of ſome pilots belonging to the country. But the neceſſary delays had given time to the Dutch to augment conſiderably their ſquadron in the *Biſbos*, which is the ſmall ſea of the Moor Dyke. That ſquadron conſiſted already of twelve armed ſhips, one of which carried twenty guns; and theſe veſſels were diſpoſed of with great judgment for oppoſing the general's paſſage, and acting in concert. But Dumourier calculated, in caſe the wind ſhould be ſettled, that not more than half the ſquadron could engage him, as thoſe which ſhould be to leeward of him would not, in that caſe, be able to reach him.

The

The Dutch had also erected batteries at Stry, and all along the coast of the island of Dort; which it was said was reinforced by 1200 of the English guards, who had landed since the declaration of war at Helvoet Sluys. The general however was convinced that the enemy had no certain intelligence of his plan, because the Prince of Orange was making his greatest preparations for defence at Gorcum, and had assembled an army there to oppose his march: this army was yet inconsiderable; the reinforcements of the English and emigrants augmenting it to no more than 4000 men.

Dumourier, still to deceive the enemy respecting his real design, continued the blockade of Bergen-op-Zoom and Steenberg. General de Flers was returned from Paris, and had obtained the reinforcement that he demanded, which arrived with great dispatch. Dumourier ordered him to occupy the cantonments of Colonel Le Clerc at Rosendael, and round Bergen-op-Zoom with 6000 men, which orders were rapidly executed. He ordered the left division to approach Oudenbosch, and Severnbergen. He sent the national gendarmerie, with some cavalry, from his right, to shew themselves on the side of Heusden. A lieutenant-colonel of the gendarmerie summoned that place; and, ridiculously enough, addressed the governor by the phrase of citizen governor, instead of the usual appellation.

General Berneron continued the siege of Williamstadt; but with very ill success. He had commenced his attack at too great a distance; and consumed a great quantity of ammunition, without making any progress. There was but one front of this town which was open to attack, and that was extremely narrow: and the Dutch had thrown re-inforcements into the town by sea. Dumourier sent to the assistance of General Berneron, Dubois de Crance, (an engineer of great merit, and very different in character from his unworthy brother, the member of the national convention) and another engineer named Marescot. These two valuable officers resolved to draw nearer the town; and while they were erecting a battery at the distance of 200 toises from the place, they were abandoned by their soldiers, and were slain in a sortie, that the enemy made on the workmen. General Berneron, notwithstanding, continued the siege obstinately, which was not raised till after the departure of General Dumourier for the grand army.

The

The general having found a confiderable quantity of
shipping at Gertruydenberg, he resolved to use them in
facilitating his passage to Dort. He had a sufficient number of vessels at Roowaert for his advanced guard. Master of Breda, Klundert, and Gertruydenberg, and leaving
the corps under General de Flers to continue the blockade of Steenberg and Bergen-op-Zoom, he had secured
his rear guard from being harrassed. He therefore caused
his rear guard to advance to Swaluve, at which place there
were vessels for its embarkation; and he resolved to embark his right division in the vessels of Gertruydenberg.

The passage from Gertruydenberg to the island of Dort
is somewhat longer than that from the Moor Dyke. To
the right, and even in front of this port, the *Bisbos* is filled
with sand banks, and numerous small islands detached
from the main land of Gorcum; most of which are covered with trees and underwood. The armed ships of the
enemy drew too much water to approach these islands.
There were however, three barks each carrying four
cannon, and thirty men, stationed at different points to
guard the passage. Beyond these small islands many of
which are covered by the tide at high water, was situated
an island much more elevated above the water than the
rest, on which was a small farm belonging to an inhabi-
tant of Gertruydenberg. This island, which the enemy's
largest vessels could not approach within seven or eight
hundred toises, was separated from the island of Dort only
by a space of six hundred toises, which was guarded by a
battery mounting six cannon, standing on a low and mud-
dy soil on the island of Dort, and by a frigate of fourteen
guns, stationed under the battery.

The general resolved to land two battalions, with six
four and twenty pounders in this island; and to erect a
battery to drive off the frigate, whose guns appeared to be
small. Having done this, he designed to embark with
his right division in the smaller vessels belonging to Gertruydenberg and to pass over in the same route.

As he might be compelled to engage one of the vessels
of four guns, in his passage to the island, he designed to
fill several large shallops with chosen men on board that
vessel, and ordered two vessels each carrying two cannon
to be ready to precede him, giving the command of one to
an English naval officer named White, and of the other to
Lieutenant Colonel La Rue, an aid-de-camp of the general, who had been in the sea-service. Every preparation

was

was made with such celerity that it was the general's design to have attempted the passage on the night of the 8th or 10th. But events of a very different nature were arriving, and the rapidity of his first success was followed by a still more rapid succession of evils which decided the fate of the war.

Dumourier in the midst of his plans, and notwithstanding his successes, had for some days been a prey to the greatest uneasiness. The siege of Maestricht had been commenced on the 20th of February ; but although General Miranda had set fire to several quarters of the city, it was defended it with extreme obstinacy, by reinforcements of the emigrants, who assembled there in great numbers, headed by M. d'Autichamp, a lieutenant-general in the army of the Prince of Conde, and an excellent officer ; to whom it is said the Dutch owe the safety of the city of Maestricht.

General Champmorin had, without any opposition made himself master of the fort of Stevenswaert, on the Meuse ; and also of fort St. Michael, which commands the entrance, the left side of that river, of the bridge of Venloo. But he had not been able to take possession of Venloo, the Prussians having already entered it.

General Valence, although he possessed military talents, had not acquired sufficient authority over the troops effectually to compensate for the absence of Dumourier. He remained at Leige ; and had neither raised the winter quarters of the troops, nor drawn them closer together. And great misunderstandings existed among the generals.

General Stengel occupied the quarters round Aix-la-Chapelle. He was an officer well versed in the discipline and duties of light troops, and was excellently calculated to command an advanced guard.

General Dampierre commanded in Aix-la-Chapelle, where he was entirely taken up with his pleasures, and the means of gratifying his rapacity. He was a man of a fierce, and ambitious spirit, rash in the extreme, but was without talent, and was even timid at times through his excessive ignorance. He hated his superiors ; and machinated with the Jacobins of Paris, for the fabrication of calumnies, by which he aimed at the command of the armies.

The Prince of Coburg, who had arrived at Cologne, was acquainted with the misunderstandings of the generals, and the injudicious, and feeble disposition of the troops.

Assembling

Assembling his army he marched to Aldenhoven, where he penetrated into the French quarters without obstacle. The French instantly abandoned all their posts, without making the least stand against the enemy; and fell back upon Liege in the greatest confusion. General le Veneur, who commanded the attack of Maestricht on the side of Wyck, had the good fortune to have sufficient time to pass the Meuse with his cannon. The Imperialists entered Mastricht. Miranda, notwithstanding ought to have continued the bombardment from the left side of the river; and, collecting his army between Tongres and Maestricht, which was a tolerable position, he might then have prevented the further progress of the Prince of Coburg.

These were the orders given to Miranda by General Dumourier, on his receiving news of the disaster. This was also the advice of General Valence. That General a few days after saved a column consisting of twenty-seven battalions on their retreat from Liege, by making a vigorous charge on the enemy, at the head of his cavalry on the plains of Tongres: and Lieutenant-General Lanoüe displayed the greatest bravery, in his retreat from Aix-la-Chapelle.

But Miranda was disconcerted, and lost all presence of mind. On his own authority, he ordered the troops to abandon the Meuse. The Imperialists followed up their victory, passed the Meuse, entered Liege, and took possession of the French magazines, which were considerable, especially in the article of cloathing. So great was the consternation in the French army, that, excepting the heavy artillery which was carried off to Louvain, and from thence to Tournay, every thing was abandoned, including even the baggage of the troops.

The two generals, Miranda and Valence, assembled their forces in the camp of Louvain. Champorin, who could no longer maintain his position on the left side of the Meuse, evacuated Stevenswaert, and Fort St. M'chael, (in which places he ought to have left garrisons) and retreated to Dieft. General la Marliere, who was at Ruremonde, fell back to the same place. This retreat left the Prussians masters of the Lower Meuse. They had it in their power instantly to have crossed the country of Campine; and, by the route of Antwerp or Bois-le-Duc, might have fallen on the rear of the French army in Holland.

land. Prince Frederick of Brunswick lost this important opportunity; and General Dumourier, availing himself of the neglect, afterward placed his army in security.

The troops under Miranda and Valence, were utterly discouraged. They openly blamed and menaced their general officers, more especially Miranda, who was in considerable danger of his life. At length however General Valence, aided by the prudence of General Thouvenot, restored some degree of order in the army. But the desertion of the army was enormous. More than 10,000 men absolutely returned to France. The army loudly demanded the presence of General Dumourier. The commissioners of the Convention dispatched courier after courier, urging his departure for Louvain. The general constantly answered them, that they might maintain the army in its present position; and that still there was nothing to be feared if they gave him time to accomplish his present object. This was true. General Valence, and General Thouvenot were of the same opinion. But Miranda now betrayed a terror altogether proportionate to the rashness which had hitherto governed him, which justified the dispatches of General Valence, who from the first predicted this check, while Miranda's letters uniformly asserted, that the army of the Imperialists was not to be feared. And certainly his opinions would have been just, if the French had taken a judicious position, with an equal force, which they might and ought to have done. It was to be presumed that the Prince of Cobourg would not have chosen to hazard a battle; or, if he had, the French had no reason to fear the issue.

The commissioners of the Convention hurried precipitately to Paris. They made a report so alarming, and painted the consternation of the soldiers in such strong colours, that it was universally acknowledged that General Dumourier could alone stop the progress of the disaster, and save the army. He was commanded in the most absolute terms, to abandon the expedition of Holland, and instantly to put himself at the head of the grand army. He received the orders on the evening of the 8th of March, and departed on the 9th, in a state bordering no despair.

Dumourier gave the command of his army to General de Flers. He knew the capacity of this general to be inadequate to the task; but he had not another general officer he could put in his place. General d'Arcon was extremely afflicted with the gout, and could not keep the field,

field, and had even refused the rank of lieutenant-general, which Dumourier would have obtained for him, sa a reward for the taking of Breda. He retired to Antwerp. Lieutenant General Maraffe, an old foldier, who commanded at Antwerp, could not on account of his great age, be entrufted in an active fituation, although he was a man of courage and experience. And it was Dumourier's defign to fend General Miranda into Holland, on his arrival at the grand army.

Dumourier left Colonel Thouvenot, who was the foul of his little army, with General de Flers. He gave the colonel a copy of the inftructions he had delivered to General de Flers, whom he recommended to undertake no enterprize without the concurrence of Colonel Thouvenot. He ordered him inftantly to attempt the paffage of Gertruydenberg; and, in cafe of fuccefs, to forward difpatches to Dumourier, and to remain at Dort till he fhould receive his further inftructions.

But the departure of General Dumourier, utterly difpirited this army. Thofe who had been moft forward, impatient, and daring, on every occafion, now cofidered the undertaking to be impracticable. In truth, it became fuch fhortly afterward. The Dutch fquadron being reinforced, and the Pruffians being on their march by Bois-le-duc, de Flers, in purfuance of his inftructions in the cafe of the paffage to Dort not taking place, threw himfelf into Breda, with fix battalions and two hundred horfe, Colonel Tilly into Gertruydenberg, with three battalions, and fifty horfe, The remainder of the army returned fafely to Antwerp, owing to the good conduct of Colonel de Vaux, and Colonel Thouvenot. Thofe officers withdrew from the batteries of the Moor Dyke, with the greateft prudence, and conftancy; and although the army was thrown into diforder, they effected the retreat without lofs. The fortifications of Klundert were blown up by Thouvenot, who had not time to put that fmall fort in a ftate of defence.

And thus terminated Dumourier's enterprize againft Holland. An enterprize, projected and begun in ten days, which did not burthen France with the additional charge of one fol, and which probably had fucceeded but for the unfortunate retreat of Aix-la-Chapelle.

Two ftrong places were acquired in this expedition, by which the progrefs of the enemy might have been arrefted; and which might ferve as magazines, and a place of arms,

if

if the design of entering Holland had been resumed. In a word, France reaped no disgrace in this quarter. But, now Dumourier's projects were once more changed; and he was again compelled to form new plans, as well respecting the interior situation of France, as with respect to her enemies.

C H A P. IV.

The General arrives at Antwerp. Sends the Agents of the Executive Power from that Town. Arrives at Brussels. Addresses the Representatives of the People. Writes to the Convention. Arrests Chepy, and Estienne. Several Proclamations. Arrives on the 13th of March at Louvain. The Commissioners of the Convention come to that City to meet the General.

NOTWITHSTANDING the importance of the concerns which had occupied General Dumourier's mind, since his departure from Paris, he had not overlooked, nor failed to lament as much as the Belgians themselves, the detestable tyranny exercised over them by the National Convention, and by the agents of the Executive Power. The insolence of these latter, the Satellites of avarice and oppression, was not exceeded even by their atrocious villainies.—Their conduct was a tissue of ridiculous circumstances. Most of them assumed the military honors, and never walked the streets without a guard. They set all rules at defiance; and, finding that they were not sufficiently numerous to spread their extortions through the whole extent of those rich provinces, they augmented their means by issuing commissions to other persons like themselves.

In passing through Bruges the General was invited to a ball. One of these gentlemen, who was dancing, accosted the General on his entering the room; and announcing himself as a Commissioner of the Executive Power, he acquainted the General that he was on his road to Ostend and Nieuport, to put those places in a proper state of defence. The General sternly commanded him to confine himself to the functions of his office; to execute those with modesty; and thenceforward, to forbear intruding

himself

himself into military concerns.

Another of these personages, named, as I think, Lieu-taud, who was stationed at Ruremonde, as a task-master to General la Marliere, wrote a long letter to Dumourier, *Thouing* and *Theeing* him throughout, and commanding him to abandon every other enterprize, in order to march to the assistance of Ruremonde. The General sent this letter to Le Brun, contenting himself with adding by way of postscript, *This letter ought to be dated*, CHAREN-TON.

A third, named Cochelet, who resided at Liege, having received notice of the declaration of war decreed on the first of February, ordered a detachment of troops to attend him, and, marching on the Dutch territory before Maestricht, proclaimed the war, tore up the posts on which were the arms of the States General, and took possession of the Seven United Provinces, in the name of the French Republic.

This impertinent parade served as a warning to the Governor of Maestricht to withdraw his cavalry cantoned round the city, (together with a considerable quantity of forage) which General Miaczynsky was on the point of surprising. General Miranda naturally condemned this conduct, because he was not yet prepared to act against Maestricht. Cochelet sent the General a written order to take Maestricht before the 20th of February, on pain of being denounced as a traitor ; and he sent a copy of the letter to the National Convention, who applauded his Roman firmness. Cochelet, however, was recalled ; because, intoxicated with the honors of his proconsulship, he had treated contemptuously the authority of the deputies of the Convention.

When General Dumourier arrived at Antwerp on the second of February, he found that city humiliated and terrified by the presence of one of these subaltern tyrants, whose name he has forgotten, and whom he caused to be recalled. Every city in Belgium was governed by one or more of these execrable Proconsuls. They entered on their office by sequestering the silver of the churches, the revenues of the clergy, and the estates of the nobility. They then pillaged, or sold to their accomplices at an excessively inferior price, the furniture of the nobles and clergy. They suppressed the national imposts to flatter the people, degraded the magistrates from their seats, erect-

ed

ed clubs, and exercised an arbitrary authority, by the aid of the military, who blindly obeyed them.

Throughout the provinces of Belgium this wild tyranny was become insupportable. Dumourier had made reiterated complaints of this tyranny to the Convention, as well as to the Commissioners of the Convention, Camus, Treilhard, Merlin and Gossuin, whom he met at Ghent; but these latter either were not willing, or had not authority to redress the evil. He represented to them, that on the Prince of Coburg's appearing in force on the frontier, a general insurrection of the Belgians was to be expected, that our weakened garrisons would be massacred, and our crimes punished by the hands of those we had oppressed; and that this war was, in a manifold degree, more dangerous than the war with the Imperialists.

The route of the troops at Aix-la Chapelle, their precipitate flight to Louvain, their confusion, terror, and desertion, greatly increased the danger, which Dumourier had foreseen, of a general insurrection in Belgium.

The danger was aggravated by the conduct of the Commissioners of the Convention. They called on the provinces to express their resolution of being united to France. The people were assembled in the churches without any order or decency. A French Commissioner, supported by the commanding officer of the place, by soldiers, and by French and Belgic Clubists, read the act of union, which seldom was understood by any person present, any more than the harangue made on the occasion; the act was notwithstanding signed by the audience, generally with trembling hands; reports of the proceedings were printed, and sent to the Convention, who forthwith created another department.

These fraternal proceedings were often effected by violence. At Brussels and at Mons, muskets and sabres were employed in the assembly, and several persons were wounded. Protests were formally made against the union. Partial insurrections took place at Wawres, Hall, Braine, and Soignies. The most dangerous was at Grammont. Ten thousand peasants assembled in arms, and had possessed themselves of several cannon. They imprisoned the Commissioners, and drove back detachments of the garrison of Ghent. These tumults increased hourly. The French army, scarcely in force to resist the Imperialists, could not

spare

spare troops to put an end to these cruel contests, which were spreading over the whole of Belgium; and it had been easy for a few Flemish officers belonging to the Imperial army, with some chosen soldiers, to have insinuated themselves into the French quarters, by means of their knowledge of the language, and to have given a regular form to this intestine war.

Dumourier hated the injustice of the National Convention, and resisted every attempt to make him the instrument of its tyranny and the scourge of Belgium. A two-fold interest therefore directed his conduct at present. His objects were to deliver this unhapy country, and to save his army. As to his success in the former, he invokes the testimony of the Belgians, from whom he received the most honourable marks of esteem and gratitude, in travelling through that country, when he no longer possessed the influence of station.

Arriving at Antwerp on the 11th, he found that city in the greatest confusion and alarm. A Commissioner of the Executive Power, named Chaussart, who modestly surnamed himself Publicola, had recently removed the magistrates, and had issued orders to arrest them and the other principal citizens, to the number of sixty-seven. General Marasse eluded the execution of this order, with which he was charged by *Publicola*; but the bishop of Antwerp and the other proscribed persons were either fled or had concealed themselves. Dumourier sent a written order to Chaussart and his colleagues, to quit Antwerp, and to go to Brussels instantly, declaring, in case of disobedience, that he would give orders to General Marasse to take them there by force. Chaussart came to the General with much dignity, or insolence, and complained of this order, saying, that it seemed to be dictated by a Vizir. The General answered with good humour, *I am certainly as much of a Vizir, as you are of Publicola.*

General Dumourier compelled Chaussart to quit the town immediately. He reinstated the magistrates, and restored the peace of that important city. He issued an ordinance, prohibiting the Jacobin club in any degree to interfere in public affairs. He commanded General Marasse to wall up the door of the hall where the club assembled, to imprison every member that disobeyed this ordinance, to print the order in both languages, and to post it up and publish it throughout the city.

Dumourier

Dumourier afterwards departed for Bruffels. Having received complaints from that city of the attrocious conduct of General Moreton, he had a few days previous to his departure removed him from the command ; which he had conferred on Lieutenant-General Duval. Moreton at firft refufed to obey the General ; but in confequence of an order from the minifter at war, he took upon him the command at Douay, where he had an opportunity of purfuing his former fyftem of conduct till his death.

General Duval was an extremely good officer, and it was the ill ftate of his health alone which prevented his being with the army. He had ferved the preceding year with great reputation and fuccefs. His judgment was clear, he abounded in the qualities that beget efteem, and was perfectly calcutated to heal the wounds inflicted by Moreton's tyranny.

Duval gave the general a more particular account, than he had hitherto received, of the diforder and confternation that reigned among the troops affembled at Louvain, from which place Duval had recently arrived. Almoft all the tents had been loft in the retreat. There was not left a fufficient number to encamp half the army ; yet it was impoffible to reftore any degree of courage to the troops, or to make any movement with fafety, without encamping them for a while. A great part of the field pieces had been alfo loft.

The general officers commanding the artillery, receiving no orders during the confufion of the retreat, nor indeed demanding any, held a council of war among themfelves, in which it was refolved to carry off the whole park of artillery and conduct it into France. All the twenty-four pounders, the fixteen pounders, the mortars, and pontoons, were already at Tournay, on their route to France ; fortunately, however, the heavy artillery, and the howitzers, were ftill at Anderletcht. Thefe latter the general ordered to join the army at Louvain ; and thofe at Tournay not to proceed on their route to France.

Bruffels was filled with officers and foldiers of the army, who were on their return to France. The general fent them back to the camp at Louvain ; and difpatched orders to Tournay and Mons, and the cities in the department of the north, to arreft and fend back to the army all the fugitives returning into France.

Dumourier ordered General Stengel, who had retired to Namur, and two fquadrons of huffars, to join the army.

General

General Neuilly, who was in his winter quarters in the country of Stavelo, with the half of the advanced guard of the army of the Ardennes, at the time of the flight from Aix-la-Chapelle, had also retired to Namur, and the general ordered him to post his troops at Judoigne, to secure the communication between the grand army, and the corps commanded by Lieutenant-general d'Harville. To General d'Harville, he sent repeated orders to encamp his troops, or, if he had not a sufficient number of tents for the purpose, to make his cantonments as connected and compact as possible, in order to prevent the Prince of Hohenloe and General Beaulieu, from forcing the passage of the Meuse, or turning the right of the army, and so falling upon Brussels and Mons. The garrison of Brussels was by no means strong, yet the general was obliged to select some of its best battalions to reinforce the army.

Ten thousand men hastily raised in the department of the north were sent to the army. This reinforcement was greatly boasted of. The name of centurions had been given to these troops. They consisted of companies which were nominally a hundred men each, but were, in fact, much below that number, composed of old men and children, armed with pikes, culasses, fowling pieces, and pistols. They had been promised twenty sols per day, and were designed to garrison the towns of Belgium, but not, as they themselves said, to defend them, or to fight*. This militia, the offspring of a plan of Gossuin and Merlin, served only to heighten the embarrassment, confusion, and want of discipline, which already prevailed, and the general was impatient till he had sent them back to France.

But an object even more important to General Dumourier, than these concerns, was to calm the minds of the Belgians, and to restore public confidence throughout the country, by putting a final period to the system under which they had suffered. He was not ignorant that in this attempt he should excite the Jacobins, and the convention, to proceed to extremity with him. The time, however, for conciliatory measures, as well as for deliberation, was entirely passed : so great were the evils to be reme-

---

* ——de garder les places de la Belgique, mais non pas, disaient ils de les defendre, ni de faire la guerre.

died,

died, so enormous the wrongs that had been done to the Belgians, and so immediately was the danger of vengeance being taken by that people.

A few days before Dumourier arrived at Brussels, Chepy had urged General Duval to order several executions. He threatened to fire Brussels, or to put it to the sword. He had arrested several of the wealthiest citizens, and sent them to be confined in the fortresses of the department of the north. General Dumourier now arrested him, and sent him, under a guard, to Paris.

The legion of *Sans-Culottes*, raised by General Moreton, and composed of the lowest of the populace, held the city in awe, and daily committed unheard of cruelties and extortions. A Frenchman, a man of abandoned character, named Estienne, commanded it, with the title of General. Dumourier threw him into prison, and published an ordinance, breaking this corps, and forbidding all persons to distinguish themselves by the name of *Sans-culottes*.

He assembled the magistrates of the city. He besought them before all the people, not to attribute to the French nation, crimes committed only by individuals. He solemnly promised to punish the guilty, and to restore to their families, peaceable citizens, who had been torn from them, under the pretence of serving as hostages to France. The representatives of the people shed tears of gratitude, and caused accounts of these interesting proceedings to be published.

General Dumourier issued a proclamation to authorise the citizens to deliver complaints to the magistrates, respecting vexations committed by the French, and empowering the magistrates to verify and give a legal form to these complaints. By another proclamation, he prohibited the clubs from interfering in public affairs, and by another, he commanded all the sacred vases, to be restored to the churches, enjoining the magistrates and military officers to aid in restoring them.

These proclamations were printed in both languages, and sent into every part of Belgium. Their effect was immediate. The inhabitants of Grammont wrote to the general, that they laid down their arms. Peace was restored between the French and the Belgians. These worthy people forgot the evils they had suffered, and again embraced the French as their brethren and defenders. Indeed it is but just to say, the garrisons had always conducted themselves in a manner no ways discreditable, especially

cially

cially in the great cities ; and, had it not been for the decree of the 15th of December, and the conduct of the a-
gents of the executive power, the French character would
have been esteemed and beloved in that country.

On the 12th of March, Dumourier wrote a letter to the
National Convention, which appeared so deplorably true
in its contents, that the President and committee to which
it was referred, did not dare to read it in the Tribune.
A copy of the letter stole abroad, and was printed at Antwerp. In it the general frankly stated to the convention,
the measures he had been compelled to pursue in order to
save Belgium and the French army. He referred the
Convention, for minute information on each point, to the
minister, to whom he sent copies of the proclamations,
and an account of his proceedings, demanding of him, that
he should produce the whole to the convention, without
reserve or disguise.

He sent for the commissary Petit-Jean, and, assembling
all the administrators of provisions, &c. he informed them,
that he was on the eve of making a great movement,
with the army, and in a few days would engage the enemy ; and he made such arrangements with them as were
necessary to his purpose. He almost immediately procured provisions for fifteen days, and prepared his travelling
hospital to attend the army.

The pay-master of the army had retired to Lisle, with
two millions of Livres in specie, and the general wrote
to the commandant of Lisle, to send him back to the army
with a strong escort.

General Dumourier harranged the garrison at Brussels,
with such effect, that the different corps demanded leave
to follow him against the enemy. He departed on the evening of the 12th of March, for Louvain.

Before we enter on the history of the military operations that follow, and that we may not be obliged to in-
terrupt them, it will be necessary to speak here of the visit
which the general received at Louvain from the commissioners of the National Convention. When the dis-
after befel the army, Camus, Treilhard, Merlin, and Gossuin, retired to the frontiers of France, while La Croix
and Danton, went to Paris. When the former knew of
the general's arrival from Holland, they proceeded to Louvain to meet him, having missed him at Brussels.

Camus, and Treilhard complained of the general's proclamations, especially that which ordered the silver to be

restored

restored to the churches. They told the general that he ought not to have acted with such precipitation, but have waited their arrival, and that it was beyond the bounds of his authority to interfere with the administration of the civil government. The general answered that the first of all duties was that of attending to the public safety ; that the convention might be deceived, as indeed they had been, by their emissaries ; that the whole weight of the war, the honour of the nation, and the preservation of the army, rested upon him ; that for these he was responsible, not only to his superiors, but to posterity ; that he had undertaken no measure inconsiderately, but after the maturest deliberation ; that, had they been present, he should not have consulted them, although he should have endeavoured to have won them to act with him, in putting an end to the crimes, which had long oppressed the Belgians and dishonoured France ; and, had they opposed his intentions, he would notwithstanding have issued the proclamations.

He appealed particularly to Camus, who was religious and superstitious, on the proclamation that respected the churches. He expressed his surprise, that a man, who professed a zeal for religion, should be the advocate of a sacrilege committed on a people, whom the French considered as allies and friends. *Go to the church of St. Gudule,* Dumourier said to him, *see the host trodden under foot, and wasted on the pavement ; the altars broken : and paintings, the master pieces of art, torn into shreds ; and justify these profanations, or rather own the necessity of punishing the agents of your criminal orders. If the Convention applaud these crimes, if she have no feeling of their enormity, she is to be pitied ; and, still more, my unhappy country. Know, that if my country cannot be saved without the commission of crimes, I will not commit them. But here the crimes of France are ready to turn upon herself ; and I serve her in endeavouring to destroy them.*

Camus observed the great difficulty there would be in restoring the vessels to the churches, since they had been broken, to be heaped in coffers. *No matter,* the general said ; *since the metal remains, it will not cost us much to have them remade.*

Camus and Treilhard persisted in saying that the general had failed in respect and obedience due to the Convention. Merlin and Gossuin, more reasonable, acknowleged that the general's conduct had been just,

and

and a violent altercation arose between the two parties. Camus said, that it was a duty he muſt not decline, to report the general's conduct, to the convention.
The general exhorted him to do ſo, and ſaid that he had
already, himſelf rendered an account of his conduct.
The general produced his letter of the 12th, which became a new ſubject of contention.

It was during this interview that Camus, the moſt iraſ-
cible of men, ſaid with an air, partly ſmiling, and partly
ſerious, *General you are accuſed of deſigning to become* Cæſar:
and I deſign to become Brutus. The general anſwered, *Dear
Camus, neither am I* Cæſar, *or you* Brutus, *and your
threat is the beſt aſſurance I have of immortality.*

Theſe commiſſioners, after three or four hours converſation with the general, departed the ſame night for Bruſſels. Camus was faithful to his promiſe. He drew up
his report to the Convention, with all the bitterneſs of a
perfidious and malignant mind ; and, thenceforth, he became the decided enemy of Dumourier.

The general, on his part, returned to the conſideration
of the means left him to repair the faults of his officers,
and to reſtore vigour to an army that no longer poſſeſſed
the ſpirit which conducted them in the former campaign.

CHAP. V.

*State of the army. Its poſition. The General's or-
ders to the different diviſions. He reſolves to give
battle to the enemy.*

THE troops appeared to reſume all their courage at
the ſight of their general. Joy and confidence ſhone in
the eyes of the ſoldiers. They embraced the general.
They called him their father. They diſcovered ſhame
and ſorrow for their diſgrace, and loudly demanded to be
led againſt the enemy.

Dumourier reproached them with their want of diſcipline, but above all with their miſtruſt of generals, who,
till this fatal diſaſter, had conducted them to victory, and
who were his ſcholars and companions. He repreſented
to them, that their impatience, their want of ſubordination,
and

and the fatal consequences of these in their retreat, had
wrested the conquest of Holland from his hands, and perhaps had determined the fate of the campaign. They
appeared extremely affected by their disgrace, and difposed to repair their faults, on condition that he would
not abandon them, but would instantly lead them to recover their honour.

This disposition greatly aided the general in restoring
order to the army. But he was greatly assisted by General Thouvenot, who, with every other military talent, had
that also of conciliating the minds of the soldiery, and in-
fusing order into all the parts of a great army. With
great pleasure, Dumourier renders this testimony of the
merit of his friend, who may one day become one of the
best generals in France, if he should return to the service of his country, and prejudice do not prevent his ri-
sing to the command.

The army amounted to near forty thousand infantry,
and near five thousand horse; and this was exclusive of
the garrisons of Belgium; of a division of 5000 men (800
of whom were horse) under the orders of General la Marliere; the division of Namur, under General d'Harville,
consisting of 12,000 infantry, and 1500 cavalry; and of
the corps of the army employed in the expedition against
Holland, which amounted to 18,000 foot, and 2,000 horse,
after the junction of General de Flers.

The infantry, consisting of sixty-two battalions, were
formed into four divisions. The right was formed by
General Valence; the centre by the Duke de Chartres,
who at that period, was named Egalité; and the left by
General Miranda. Each of these divisions consisted of
eighteen battalions, and amounted to seven thousand men.
The reserve consisting of eight battalions of grenadiers,
commanded by General Chancel, was placed under the
orders of the Duke de Chartres.

Miranda had under his orders General Miaczinsky,
who commanded the left flank of the army, consisting of
two thousand infantry, and one thousand horse; and General Champmorin, who commanded a body of four thousand foot and one thousand horse. General Valence had
under his orders General Dampierre, who commanded
the right flank, consisting of an equal force with that of
General Miaczinsky; and General Neuilly, who commanded a body of three thousand foot and one thousand
horse.

The

The advanced guard was composed of six thousand men, fifteen hundred of which were horse, commanded by General la Marche. He was an old officer, who had seen a great deal of service, and had been an excellent colonel of Hussars. He was forward to undertake an enterprise, but easily discouraged. He was assisted by two excellent officers, although they were very young, who counselled him with great success, when he would suffer himself to be counselled. These were Colonel Montjoye, who was adjutant-general, and Lieutenant-Colonel Barois, who commanded the horse artillery. But the ill-health of this old general, and still more his want of capacity, rendered him very dangerous.

The rapidity with which in this war, officers rose to the highest rank in the army, inverted the order of every thing. The corps and regiments lost officers that commanded them with effect, and the army acquired inexperienced generals. Yet the army was really in want of generals. At this period it had no more than five lieutenant-generals, and twelve major-generals, six of which commanded detached corps: so that there were but six remaining to command in the line.

When general Dumourier arrived at Louvain, on the morning of the 13th, he found that the three divisions of his infantry were encamped on the heights behind Louvain, having the canal of Malines in front. The reserve, with a small body of horse, was at the distance of two leagues, beyond Bautersem; and the advanced guard at more than two leagues beyond the reserve, at Cumptich, having a small force of four hundred men in Tirlemont.

The enemy advanced and occupied all the villages between Tirlemont and Tongres. The design of the enemy was to turn our right on the 16th; and if that had been executed on the 13th or 14th, the advanced guard would have fallen back on the reserve, and the reserve on the main body, and the whole army would have been defeated and dispersed, having no known point at which to rally.

On the 14th Dumourier visited his advanced guard; and he instantly ordered several movements, by which the position of his army was much more firm and secure. He placed General Dampierre, with the troops under his command, at Hougaerde to the right of Cumptich, and ordered General Neuilly to advance from Judoigne to

Lummen,

Lummen, in order to strengthen this right wing of the army, and to extend the line beyond that of the enemy.

He commanded General Miaczinfky to take a position to the left, between Dieft and Tirlemont, on the fide of Halen, and having the river Gette in front of him. He ordered General Champmorin to occupy Dieft, with his division. This general, having informed him that Dieft was a fmall city with walls, which might be made a ftrong poft, Dumourier ordered him to add as much as poffible to its ftrength, and to leave in it two battalions and fifty horfe, when he fhould receive orders to march forward with his troops.

He commanded General la Marliere to leave a fmall body of troops at Aerfchette, in order to keep open the communication with Dieft ; and to proceed with the reft of his troops to Liers to overawe the country of Campine, to check the Pruffian column who might advance in that quarter, and to cover the retreat of the army of Holland, whom Dumourier concluded had abandoned the project of paffing to Dort, and which indeed was the cafe.

He fent orders to General de Flers to throw himfelf with all poffible difpatch into Breda ; to fend Colonel Tilly to Gertruydenberg, with the garrifons named in the orders, and to fend back the remainder of that army to the lines of Antwerp, to be placed under the orders of General Maraffe. Dumourier ordered Colonel Weftermann to take poft at Turnhout, with the gendarmerie and the legion of the north, in order to protect this retreat, to check the enemy in that quarter, and to keep open the communication with General la Marliere, and by his divifion, with the grand army.

On the morning of the 15th of March, the advanced guard of the enemy attacked Tirlemont, and the 400 men who were pofted there fell back, without engaging but with a lofs, having fuffered themfelves to be furprifed. General Dampierre, accuftomed to retreats, took upon him, on hearing the firing at a diftance, to abandon his poft of Hougaerde, where he guarded one of the paffages of the Gette, and fell back upon Louvain, at the fame time ordering General Neuilly to retire on his fide to Judoigne. Dumourier had not time to examine whether it were fear or treachery which caufed this dangerous movement on his right. Had it been known to the enemy, the French army might have been

overthrown

overthrown. Dumourier contented himself with repairing this fault, which was so much the more weighty, as it accustomed the troops to give way on the first appearance of danger; and on the same night he caused these two divisions to return to their former posts.

It was very singular, that on the left General Miaczinsky committed the same fault, and withdrew into the wood near Louvain, and was not to be found for two days. But the position he had quitted was occupied by the body of troops under General Champmorin, whom the General ordered on the 15th to proceed with the greatest dispatch to occupy the heights of Oplinter, on the left of Tirlemont. Champmorin took that position on the evening of the 16th.

Fortunately the enemy, who had fixed the 16th for their march, discovered nothing of the retrograde movements of the 15th, and were not prepared to profit by them. On the same day, the General advanced with the whole of his army beyond Bauterfem and near to Cumprich, to prepare for his revenge on the following day, and not to leave the enemy the advantage they had gained. It was absolutely necessary for him to take Tirlemont; since, otherwise, he must have fallen back, and again have subjected his troops to be discouraged and terrified.

The Imperialists, with a considerable advanced guard, occupied Tirlemont, and the space lying between the two Gettes, from the causeway of St. Tron, to the ground opposite the post of Hougaerde.

On the morning of the 16th, the General made a vigorous attack upon the Imperialists. As the heights of Oplinter commanded the high road of St. Tron, when the General had made himself master of Tirlemont, (which he gained after some resistance) the Imperialists finding their right flanked by the troops under Miranda on the heights of Oplinter, made a precipitate march, to pass a small arm of the Gette, to retire to the heights of Neerlanden, Nerwinde, Middlewinde and Oberwinde.

Between the two Gettes, at a league and a half on the right beyond Tirlemont, was a village named Gotzenhoven, which commanded the whole plain. It stood on a small hill; having hedges along the front, and ditches filled with water on the right and in the rear.

The Imperialists did not appear to perceive the importance of this post, till Dumourier had sent General la

Marche,

Marche, with his advanced guard, supported with cannon, to take possession of it. At that time the Imperialists were still in possession of the two villages of Meer and Hatten-dover, and Dumourier caused these to be attacked by his columns as quickly as they could form after filing thro' Tirlemont. The Imperialists committed a great error in not occupying Gotzenhoven in sufficient force, as that post might have defended, or might have laid in ashes, the two villages of Meer and Hattendover. The Impe-rialists collected a strong body of infantry and horse, to endeavour to dislodge the French from Gotzenhoven.— They performed prodigies of valour in this attack, al-though without success. The cuirassiers charged the French infantry with the greatest intrepidity, even a-mong the very hedges of the village, and their loss was very great. The attack was recommenced several times, The enemy attempted in vain to turn Gotzenhoven on the right, for General Neuilly, having passed the greater Gette at Dummen, had opportunely arrived in this quar-ter, with his division to take the position of Neerhelyf-fen. The engagement did not finish till four o'clock in the afternoon, when the Imperialists were in full retreat. It lasted at least eight hours between the advanced guards of the Imperialists and the French, which were nearly of equal force, and were both of them supported by the main bodies of their respective armies. The loss of the Imperialists was much greater than that of the French. The advantage remained with the latter, but they were on the point of losing their general at the attack of Gotz-enhoven.

This engagement, which cost the Imperialists more than 1200 men, entirely restored the courage of the French troops. Dumourier formed his army into two divisions, extending from Gotzenhoven to the high road, among the villages, which had been the field of battle.— General Neuilly, stationed near Neerhelyffen supported the right. General Dampierre, having arrived on the evening of the engagement, was posted at Esemael, in front of the centre. General Miaczinfky arriving with his cavalry (his infantry consisting of eight battalions being left near Louvain, was posted at the bridge of the lesser Gette, opposite to Orsmael. A part of the divi-sion of General Miranda remained behind the great Gette, to the left of Tirlemont, extending to Oplinter : at which last place General Champmorin arrived with his troops during the night.   After

After this first success, Dumourier saw that it was necessary to take a decisive step. Troops were continually on their march to reinforce the Imperialists, and the French army had very inconsiderable or no reinforcements to expect. The Imperial cavalry was double the number of that of the French, and in every respect greatly superior. It was impossible for the French to contend with a disciplined army, for the possession of the Netherlands, foot by foot; being in want of generals, incapable of executing prompt marches of bold important manœuvres, in face of a numerous and experienced cavalry, and having behind them no strong and fortified places.

There was, however, a necessity for stopping the progress of the enemy, which could not be done without hazarding a battle. Under these circumstances sound and true prudence called on Dumourier to risk every thing, before the Prince of Cobourg should have received the remainder of the reinforcements for which he waited to begin the campaign. The two armies were of equal force. That which should attack would have the advantage in spirit and confidence, which always belong to the party beginning the attack. This advantage had, during fifteen days, been in the hands of the Prince of Cobourg; but General Dumourier had regained it by the issue of the engagement of Tirlemont.

If General Dumourier should have the good fortune to gain a decisive battle and such he resolved this to be, his situation would be entirely changed: for first, it would restore him in the opinion of his army to his former superiority, and would intimidate the enemy; secondly, it would have secured the Belgians in his interest, and would have greatly forwarded the levies of twenty-five battalions which the nation had undertaken, and so would have strengthened his army by the acquisition of twenty thousand infantry, at the least; thirdly, he would have regained the ground lost on the side of Liege, for the Austrians would not have been able to have held that city, nor even Aix-la-chapelle, and would have been compelled to have intrenched themselves under the protection of Maestricht; and lastly, it would have compelled the Prince of Cobourg to have repassed the Meuse, and would have so greatly weakened his army, as to prevent his retaking the field before the month of May.

General

General Dumourier's design was, in case of success, to have formed an entrenched camp, in a strong position, between the two Gettes, under the command of General Valence, who in that situation might have watched the enemy and might have received the different reinforcements arriving from France and Belgium; while General d'Harville might have been equally reinforced on the side of Namur. General Valence would have been master of the country, and would have held the Prince of Cobourg in check, Miranda would have been posted with an army at Antwerp, and General Dumourier advancing with 30,000 men, against Bois-le-duc, would have resumed his project against Holland, and would at once have forced the passages of the Moor Dyke, and Gorcum. But if he could not have penetrated into Holland, he might at least have made himself master of Dutch Flanders, by which means he would have covered his left, and would have procured arms, clothing, money, and provisions.

In that case, he would have been independent of the National Convention, and probably might have been able to give it law, for the repose of his unhappy country, for the avenging of Lewis XVI. and for the re-establishing of the Constitutional Monarchy.

On the contrary, should the general be defeated, he designed, in the first place, to take a position behind the canal of Louvain, in order for a while to cover Brussels, and to reinforce his army; secondly, to maintain the position of Namur, raising the corps of General d'Harville to the amount of 25,000 men, and to place the division of General Neuilly at Judoigne, to cover Dumourier's retreat by the forest of Soignies, for the purpose of supporting Brussels; thirdly, to assemble a body of 25,000 men near Antwerp, and, still holding Breda and Gertruydenberg, to keep the communication open to these places by means of the posts of Liers and Diest; fourthly, to assemble a body of 14 or 15,000 men on the side of Bruges, to cover Maritime Flanders; fifthly, to negotiate with the Imperialists for a suspension of arms, and mean while to endeavour to convince the troops in the different camps, that their want of subordination, together with the disasters resulting from it, was one effect of the absurd government of the convention, that it was high time to put an end to the anarchy which

would

would otherwife caufe the entire ruin of France, and that on the army alone refted the hopes and fate of the Country. When the minds of the troops fhould have been fufficiently prepared, his next defign was to reinforce the army with battalions of Belgians, who held the Convention and Jacobins in abhorrence, to declare openly in favour of a limited Monarchy, to lay hold of hoftages for the fecurity of the prifoners in the Temple, and to march to Paris.

These were General Dumourier's objects previous to the battle of Nerwinde, and it will be feen how urgent his motives were for rifking a decifive battle, and for ufing every effort to gain the victory. He never had the bafenefs to wifh to be beaten. He earneftly ftrove to mafter events. Although he held the Tyrants of France in detestation, although he viewed with horror the cruelties that difhonored France, he was not the lefs folicitous to maintain the honor of his country, and to prove himfelf worthy of her confidence. In every cafe, and in every moment till the laft, the end of his meafures was to prevent a foe from giving law to France, and to fave his country from infult or injury, and it is this which has drawn upon him the ill founded reproach, from misinformed perfons, and in particular from the Elector of Cologne, of having changed his party only when he was vanquifhed.

Had he not previous to the lofs of the battle of Nerwinde openly declared his hoftility to the Jacobins by his proclamations at Antwerp and Bruffels? Had he not imprifoned or driven out of the country the rapacious agents of the Convention? Had he not written his letter of the 12th of March? Had he not compelled the filver of the churches to be reftored? Had not his correfpondence with Pache, Bournonville and Le Brun, (which was printed and which appeared alfo in the Monitors of March and April) declared the firmeft truths and the freeft opinions, refpecting the authors of the miferies of France. If in thofe he did not fpeak of the royal family, it was that he feared his mention of them would become a fignal for their death.

He who reads thefe Memoirs, and calls to remembrance the circumftances and the public documents of thofe times, will fee that the opinions of General Dumourier have been confiftent. He has been the zealous defender of his country. Her enemies have been his

enemies,

enemies, but the war he has made upon them has been open and generous; for his love of his country was neither fanatical, unjust, nor savage. The Emigrants, by whom he is detefted as greatly as by the Jacobins, have, on all occafions, found him humane and liberal. In a war, differing from all others in character, a war of opinion, in which inftability of principles and conduct might find excufe, he has no fhifting of opinion wherewith to reproach himfelf, no perfidy, no cruelty, no infolence in fuccefs, nor weaknefs in misfortune and difgrace. In a word, moved only by humanity, he reftored the Netherlands to the Emperor, as was acknowledged by the Archduke Charles, by the Emperor's Minifters and Generals, by his army, and by the people of the country. Nor did he make conditions or referves for himfelf. He did not demand an afylum in the Emperor's dominions. He demanded nothing of the Prince of Cobourg but his marching to Paris, with the object, and in the hope, of delivering his country.

Bafely mifreprefented to the emperor, denied a place of fafety in the Emperor's dominions, which ought to have been free to him, though all others had been fhut againft him, he expects juftice from time, which unveils the truth; and confoles himfelf in faying with Valerius Maximus,——*Perfecta ars, fortunae lenocinio defecta, fiducia jufta non exuiter, quamque fcit fe laudem mereri, eam etfi ab aliis non impetrat, domeftico tamen acceptam judicio refert.*

CHAP. VI.

Battle of Nerwinde.

THE Prince of Cobourg advanced between Tongres, St. Tron, and Landen; and the two armies were in fight of each other. General Dumourier paffed the day of the 17th in reconnoitring the pofition of the enemy, in forming his troops in order of battle, and in preparing his plan of attack. He had, in his front, the Leffer Gette, which rifes in the townfhip of Jaudrain, and runs almoft parallel with the greater Gette, into

which

which it falls below Leaw. This river ran between the two armies. Both fides of the river were extremely hilly; and the ground, on the fide occupied by the Imperialifts, formed an amphitheatre rifing from the river to the more elevated fituations of Landen and St. Tron.

Dumourier judged that the pofition of the Prince of Cobourg was by much the ftrongeft on the fide of Tongres and St. Tron; becaufe of the neceffity of his drawing his provifions from Maeftricht and Liege; and that confequently his left, which was confiderably extended on the fide of Landen, muft be more weak, and more liable to be turned, or broken.

Dumourier knew alfo, that the Prince of Cobourg had neglected to occupy the little city of Leaw, which was a very important poft, and which might either ferve as a centre to the motions of the army making the attack, or a point of refiftance for the army that fhould be attacked.

In the front of that part of the enemy's line, which extended from Landen towards Leaw, were the three villages of Oberwinde, Middlewinde, and Nerwinde.— Near Middlewinde was an eminence, called the Tomb of Middlewinde, which commanded the three villages, and a valley which feparates them from the city of Landen. He, therefore, who fhould occupy this place, muft be mafter of all the plain, and muft neceffarily, in cafe of an attack, repulfe his enemy.

On thefe facts, Dumourier laid down his plan for the battle, which was as follows: The firft column, forming the right flank of the army, compofed of the advanced guard, under General la Marche, proceeding by the bridge of Neerhellyflen, was to enter the plain between Landen and Oberwinde; and to extend itfelf beyond the left of the enemy, in order to harrafs that flank. The fecond column, compofed of the infantry of the army of the Ardennes, commanded by Lieutenant-general le Veneur, and fupported by a ftrong body of cavalry, entering the plain by the fame bridge, was to gain the Tomb of Middlewinde by a rapid movement, and to attack the village of Oberwinde, which could not withftand a difcharge of 12 pounders that were to be planted on the Tomb. And while this attack fhould take place, the third column under the command of General Neuilly, entering the plain alfo by the fame bridg, waes to fall on the right of the village of Nerwinde.

These

These three columns formed the right wing of the army, commanded by General Valence, who, in case of success, wheeling to the left, and driving the left wing of the enemy before him, was to continue his march in order of battle, leaving Landen behind him, and having his front facing St. Tron.

The centre, commanded by the Duke de Chartres, was composed of two columns. The first, (which was the fourth column in the order of attack) commanded by lieutenant-general Dietman, passing the river by the bridge of Laer, and rapidly crossing the village of the same name, which was only occupied by a few indifferent troops belonging to the Imperialists, was to press forward, and fall directly upon the front of the village of Nerwinde. The fifth column, commanded by Gen. Dampierre, was to pass by the bridge of Esemael, and to attack the left of Nerwinde. These two columns were afterward to follow the right wing, forming a diagonal line with the point of their departure.

The left wing, under the command of General Miranda, was composed of three columns. The first (being the sixth in the order of attack) under General Miaczinsky, passing the river at Over-helpen, was to charge straight forward proceeding toward Neerlanden, but being careful never to press beyond the head of the fifth column. The seventh column, under General Rualt, was to pass the river at the bridge of Orsmael, and engage the enemy by the high road of St. Tron. The eighth column, under Gen. Champmorin, was to pass the river below Neerlinter, at the bridge of Bingen, and to throw itself into the Leaw, which it was to occupy till the end of the battle.

In case of complete success, the army at the end of the action would be ranged in order of battle, with the left wing at Leaw, and the right at St. Tron, and having its front toward Tongres : which was the only point by which the Imperialists could retreat. And batteries were erected on the banks of the Gette, within reach of the bridges, to protect the retreat of the columns, in case of their being repulsed.

On the morning of the 18th of March, between seven and eight o'clock, the several columns began to move in the same instant, in great order, and passed the river without obstacle. General la Marche committed the first error of that day. He entered the plain of Landen according

cording to his inftructions, but finding no enemy there, he made a movement to the left, to fall upon the village of Oberwinde, and thence was thrown into confufion by the fecond column. Although the troops of the fecond column were retarded in their march by their artillery, yet they attacked the village of Oberwinde, and the Tomb of Midldewinde, with fuch vigour, that by ten o'clock they had carried thofe pofts.————But General le Veneur did not take fufficient precautions to ftrengthen himfelf in the latter poft.————It was foon after re-taken by the Auftrians, and the poffeffion of it difputed the whole day. General Neuilly brifkly entered Nerwinde with the third column, and drove out the Imperialifts ; but, almoft immediately abandoning the village, he advanced into the plain toward the fecond column. General Neuilly afferted, that he received an order to that effect from General Valence, who on his fide declared, it was a mifunderftanding of Gen. Neuilly.

In a fhort time, the Imperialifts re-entered Nerwinde; from which they were again driven, by the fourth and fifth columns, under the command of the Duke de Chartres. In this attack General Desforets, an excellent officer, received a wound in the head with a mufquet-ball. This part of the army fell into confufion. The infantry crowded in too great numbers into the village, and were in fuch complete diforder, that on the appearance of a fecond attack from the enemy they abandoned the place.

General Dumourier arriving in this moment, caufed the village to be once more attacked. It was again carried ; but the troops prefently quitted the village again, and all the efforts of Gen. Dumourier prevailed no further than to rally them at a hundred paces from Nerwinde, which was filled with the dead and wounded of the two parties. But the Imperialifts did not re-enter the village until the evening.

It was during the diforder in this quarter, that the Imperial cavalry rufhing into the plain between Nerwinde, and Middlewinde, charged the French cavalry ; at the head of which was General Valence, who fought with great intrepidity, was wounded, and obliged to retire from the field of battle to Tirlemont. The Imperial horfe were, however, repulfed with great flaughter.

While the horfe were thus engaged, another body of cavalry entered the plain on the left of Nerwinde, and
threw

threw themselves with great fury upon the infantry of the fourth column. General Thouvenot, who was at the head of that column, opened his ranks to the Imperial horse, and immediately caused the regiment of Deux-ponts to make so timely and well-directed a discharge of grape-shot and musquetry upon that body of horse, that almost the whole of it was destroyed.

From that instant, the fate of the battle seemed determined in favour of the French, on their right and in the centre. The troops were again in perfect order, were full of confidence and courage, and passed the night on the field of battle, preparing to complete their victory the following morning. The Imperialists have acknowledged that they were on the point of retreating, and that orders had been actually given to their baggage to retire to Tongres.

But it was quite otherwise with the French troops on the left. The fixth and seventh columns had attacked the enemy with great vigour; but, when they were already masters of Orsmael, a panic seized upon the battalions of Volunteers, and they fled, leaving the troops of the line exposed. The Imperialists, seeing the disorder, charged the two columns with their horse, which put it entirely to the rout. Guiscard, Major-general of the artillery, was killed, as well as great numbers of the Aids-de-camp and officers of the staff; and General Ruault and General Ihler were wounded.

Still, however, great opportunity remained of restoring the fortune of the day in that quarter. It was not more than two o'clock in the afternoon, when the columns fled. They repassed the bridge of Orsmael, and were not pursued further by the Imperialists. At that moment, General Miranda was informed, that the eight battalions of Miaczinsky's corps were arrived at Tirlemont. These troops were quite fresh, and General Miranda might have reinforced himself, by placing them on the heights of Wommersem, on the side of the Gette next Tirlemont. But General Miranda, either being disconcerted, or, which is more probable, seeing the success of the right wing, commanded by his rival General Valence, he yielded to his resentment, and resolving to sacrifice him, ordered his troops to retreat; and retired behind Tirlemont, at more than two leagues distance from the field of battle. Whatever be the case, his conduct was perfidious in sending no advice of his retreat to General

neral Dumourier, which exposed the right and centre of
the army to the whole weight of the enemy. But the
enemy did not avail themselves of this cowardly retreat;
either to cut off the left wing, which they might have
compleatly done by continuing the pursuit to Tirlemont,
or to renew the attack upon the centre and the right,
whose flank was entirely exposed to them.

General Champmorin, who had made himself master of
Leaw, and had remained in that position, till he saw the
retreat of General Miranda, did not abandon it till late in
the day, when he repassed the river by the bridge of Bingen, which he cut down after him, and returned to his
former position of Oplinter. And, perhaps, it was owing
to the possession of this post at Leaw, that the Imperialists
did not pursue their advantage against the left wing of the
French, on the retreat of Miranda; since, in that case,
General Champmorin might have taken their right in
flank.

General Dumourier passed the whole time of action in
regarding the movements of his centre and right wing, in
re-establishing order in the different parts that gave way,
and ensuring success in that quarter, which was the more
essential, as it was charged with the whole weight of the
manœuvres. At two in the afternoon, he observed that
the firing on his left, which till then had been very brisk,
had ceased; but he attributed this silence to success.—
The nature of the ground prevented his seeing the sixth
and seventh columns; and, during the firing of these columns, he could perceive they were advancing forward.
He had, therefore, reason to suppose that, the enemy, being driven in that quarter, had halted, that they might
not over-run the head of the columns on their right. But
no circumstances could lead him to conjecture the incredible retreat of General Miranda: and he was, perhaps,
happy in being ignorant of it, while he was repairing the
disorders of his right and centre.

Towards the close of the day, he observed, that several
columns of the Imperialists moved from their right to reinforce their left, which led him to suspect the truth; but,
it was as yet only suspicion, having received no message
from General Miranda. In this situation, he passed the
greater part of the evening before the village of Nerwinde.
At length, his suspicions, which he had communicated to
no other person than General Thouvenot, were succeeded
by

D d

by the liveliest inquietude. He departed for his left, accompanied by General Thouvenot, two aids-de-camp, and two domestics. Arriving at the village of Laer, at ten at night, he was utterly astonished to find that it had been abanded by order of General Dampierre, who after conducting himself with great valour during the engagement, had in the close of the evening without orders repassed the Gette with his division, and retired to his former position at the village of Esemael.

General Dumourier, continuing his route, arrived near the bridge of Orsmael, which he supposed to be occupied by Miranda's troops, but found it was in the possession of the Austrian Hulans, by whom he was on the point of being taken. He turned back; and proceeded, by the high road of Tongres, and Tirlemont: astonished with the silence and solitude that reigned around him, till he arrived within half a league of that city. He then learnt from three or four battalions, that were scattered in disorder, without cavalry, along the side of the high road, the disaster and disgrace of his left wing.

In Tirlemont, he found General Miranda writing to his friends with great composure. General Valence had already used every effort to induce Miranda to return to the attack, assuring him that the French were victorious on their right, and in the centre; and that, by his return, success would be altogether insured. General Dumourier commanded him, in very severe terms, to assemble his troops immediately, even during the night, and to post them on the heights of Wommersem, on the high road, and on the bridge of Orsmael, as well as that of Neerhelpen, for the purpose of, at least, securing the passage of the Gette, and the retreat of the right and centre, now in the midst of the enemy's army, with a river behind them.

Such was the fate of the battle of Nerwinde; which had been entirely successful on the part of the French, if General Miranda, instead of retreating, on perceiving the first disorder in his two columns, had lined the Gette with his troops, and had maintained the two bridges of Orsmael and Neerhelpen. This retreat was the more unfortunate, as the two columns lost above two thousand men, while the rest of the army did not lose more than six hundred men. The French had about three thousand killed or taken, and more than a thousand wounded, and lost great part of their cannon.

In

In this engagement faults were committed on both fides. The French did not attack the town of Middlewinde, which was the decifive point of the action, with fufficient vigour, and afterward abandoned that poft without any vifible neceffity. General Neuilly, after the firft fuccefs, put every thing to hazard, by abandoning the village of Nerwinde, on an uncertain order. Miranda, having already made himfelf mafter of the village of Orfinael, turned the fate of the day, by yielding to the terror of his troops, and commanding a retreat that became an abfolute flight.

The Imperialifts committed feveral errors: in not difputing the paffage of the Gette ; in not falling upon the three columns of the right, both in front and in flank, while they were marching forward to the attack, and were expofed to the fire of the villages of Laer, of Nerwinde, Middlewinde, and Oberwinde ; in abandoning the elevated and advantageous poft of the tomb of Middlewinde, and in not erecting a battery on it previous to the engagement ; in neglecting to occupy Leaw, on their right ; and, finally, in not having availed themfelves of Miranda's retreat, either in falling upon his troops, or attacking the left flank of the columns belonging to the centre of the French army, that were in the heat of the action before Nerwinde, by the whole of their right wing which no longer had an enemy in front of theirs.

CHAP. VII.

Retreat of the 19th of March. Action of Gotzenhoven.

GENERAL DUMOURIER now faw the neceffity of fecuring his retreat. The poft of Leaw, on which the poffeffion of the field of battle depended, was abandoned by his troops ; and, in the difmay which had feized upon the other two columns of his left wing, the moft he could hope was to lead them back to the banks of the Leffer Gette ; to induce them to pafs the river, and to return to the field of battle, was impoffible. Thefe two columns had loft part of their cannon in the flight ; the Generals, and fuperior

perior officers of these troops, were in no condition to undergo a fresh combat; and, independent of the real loss of these columns by the sword of the enemy, more than 6000 men had deserted, and were on the road to Brussels and France.

Dumourier passed the remainder of the night in giving orders for the retreat of his centre, and right wing, which was then commanded by the Duke de Chartres, who conducted himself with coolness, courage, and judgment.

The Imperialists had in truth gained a great victory, but they were not certain of their situation. They had been so disconcerted with the important advantages gained by the right and centre of the French army, that they made no attempt to pursue their advantage over the left. They saw the French still in order of battle and ready to recommence the action, and they really imagined that the left wing of the French was about to return to its former position. Hence they threw no more obstacles on the French in their retreat, than the day before on their advancing to the attack.

This retreat was effected in open day-light, the columns repassing the river in the order in which they advanced, and altogether with the same steadiness. Dumourier sent General Thouvenot to the right, to receive the columns, and place them in the order of battle from Gotzenhoven to Hackendower, while he took upon himself to assemble the columns of the left wing, and to post them on the heights of Wommersem, and at the bridge of Orsmael. The enemy's troops were already master of this bridge; and Dumourier, to prevent their advancing further on the causeway, sent orders to General Dampierre, posted at Esemael, to make a movement to the left with half of his division, for the purpose of flanking the causeway, and to maintain that position till the centre should have repassed the river, and then to retreat slowly to the new position that the troops were taking, with their right at Gotzenhoven, their left at Hackendower, and having the Lesser Gette in their front.

This order, completely executed by General Dampierre, preserved the army from destruction; for the two columns that had fled had acquired such apathy from the shame of the preceding day, and were so scattered, that it was ten in the morning before Dumourier could form them, so as to march with good order to take post at Hackendower, on the right and left of the high road.

The

The firſt column of the Imperial army had paſſed the bridge of Orſmael, and had already formed with its artillery in the heights of Wommerſem. But Dumourier could never prevail on histroops to attack that poſt, which commanded the ground on which they had formed, altho' they were extremely harraſſed by the artillery on thoſe heights, and ſuſtained this inceſſant firing with unſhaken conſtancy.

On this occaſion Dumourier had nearly fallen. His horſe was killed under him by a cannon ball. The readineſs with which he recovered from this ſituation was the means of preventing new diſorder, and probably a ſecond flight which this circumſtance was on the point of occaſioning.

The troops, which in the action of the preceding day, had fled with ſuch precipitation, now endured the terrible diſcharge of the Imperialiſts, with great intrepidity. But in this conduct General Dumourier perceived nothing more than a blind obſtinacy, altogether deſtitute of the daring courage that he wiſhed to excite in them. He exhorted them to charge with bayonets the enemy on the heights of Wommerſem, and ſeveral times he put himſelf at their head, without being able to make them advance; too happy, indeed in ſeeing them continue firm in their poſition, which was imminently more dangerous than a vigorous attack on thoſe troops, who, being ſeparated from the reſt of the Imperial army, and having the river in their rear, might have been totally overthrown.

The left wing of the Imperialiſts betrayed the ſame diſpoſition, occaſioned by the ſame cauſe, as that of the French. Theſe troops ſuffered the right and centre of the French to repaſs the river without moleſtation, and even to range themſelves in order of battle in the poſition of Gotzenhoven, before they could reſolve to paſs the river in order to attack them. Thus, the whole day paſſed on both ſides in manœuvring, with the exception of ſome canonnading and diſcharge of muſquets. The two armies reſted on their arms, in order of battle, the whole night, very near to each other.

This cool and ſteady retreat was the more admired by the Imperialiſts, becauſe the troops did not fall back more than three quarters of a league, and ſeemed only to be returning in great order to the ground they occupied before the battle. During the evening of the 19th, however, General Dumourier perceived by the apathy which pervaded his troops, that, ſhould he make a ſtand the next morning againſt the enemy, he would be infallibly beaten.

There has been no period when the French foldiery could be conducted fuccefsfully without great regard being paid to their temper and their feelings; and the importance of this circumftance, in conducting them to battle, has been eminently heightened by the revolution, which, having entirely deftroyed military difcipline, has increafed the force of the intractable and capricious fpirit belonging to the national character. The active and impetuous difpofition of the French is calculated to carry them forward to conqueft, and not to preferve conquefts. A defenfive and methodical war does not diminifh their bravery, but it wearies and contradicts their impatient fpirit. When once wearied and difpirited, the French troops being no longer reftrained by the feverity of military laws, abandon their leaders and their colours, and defert without the leaft thought of the confequences.

The troops of the line, ftill influenced by a remnant of their former military fpirit, an attachment to their colours, and the fear of difgrace, continued firm, and were yet to be relied on by the General; but the national-guards, compofing three-fourths of the army, declaring loudly that it was fruitlefs to lavifh their lives in Belgium, and that they ought to return and defend their own frontiers, departed by whole companies and battalions. To have attempted to retain them by force would have been ineffectual, as well as dangerous.

No courfe was now left to Dumourier but to retreat with the troops, in good order, for the purpofe of concealing their defections, and to prevent their being maffacred by the Imperialifts and the peafants of the country. In this fad condition the General was conftrained to pafs the Greater Gette during the night, and to retire to the heights of Cumptich, behind Tirlemont. All his movements for this purpofe, being performed with a precifion that fcarcely could have been expected from more difciplined, and even victorious troops, were attended with the greateft fuccefs. The Imperialifts, deceived by the fires that were carefully kept up, and reftrained by the vigour of the rear guard, did not put themfelves in motion till the 20th, when they reconnoitred Tirlemont, from which the French had had time to withdraw their magazines. However, General Miaczinfky, who was charged with the evacuation of that city, loft one of his cannon by the precipitation of his retreat.

CHAP.

CHAP. VIII.

Retreat of the 20th and 21st of March.—Engagement of Neerwelpe—La Croix and Danton at Louvain.—Engagement of the 22d of March.

DUMOURIER's position at Cumptich had the advantage of being considerably elevated above the Gette. In this camp his front faced Tirlemont ; his left was secured by the river Welpe, which turning short ran upon his rear, by Bautersem and Wertryk; his right, posted behind Hougaerde, was not so well defended. The General, however, could not maintain himself long in this position, nor was it any protection to Louvain if the Imperialists should pass by Diest ; nor to Brussels if they should turn by Judoigne. He therefore availed himself of the 20th of March, while the enemy were before Tirlemont, to pass the Welpe, and encamp near Bautersem, having his right at Op and Neerwelpe, and his left on the heights and in the woods in front of Zuellenberg.

He sent General Neuilly, with his division increased to 6000 men, toward Judoigne, with orders to prevent detachments of the Imperialists from penetrating on that side, to watch their motions, and, if they should appear with a force greatly superior, to fall back to Brussels by the forest of Soignies. Dumourier gave General Neuilly instructions respecting the means of defending this forest, and wrote to General Duval, to reinforce Neuilly with as many men as he could spare from the garrison of Brussels, and the new levies which might arrive there. He also ordered General Duval to arrest the deserters and send them back to his army.

He commanded General d'Hartville to place a garrison of 2,500 men in the citadel of Namur, and to hold himself in readiness to march with the remainder of his troops, either toward Brussels, or in such other direction as should be necessary by the motions of General Beaulieu, who was advancing with 8000 or 10,000 men by the route of Huy

Dumourier threw into Dieft a garrifon, which appeared to him to be fufficient ; General Champmorin having inaccurately reported this place to be ftronger than in fact it was. He pofted General Miaczinfky at the abbey of Gemps, in communication with Dieft. He reinforced the garrifon of Malines. He fent General Ruault to Antwerp, to affift Lieutenant-General Maraffe, and to take the command of the army in that quarter, which reinforced by the divifion of General Marliere, amounted to more than 20,000 men. He recommended to General Ruault to hold the poft of Riers as long as it was poffible, and to fall back within the lines of Antwerp, if the Pruffians and Dutch fhould advance upon him in too great force.

On the fame day, on the 20th of March, a detachment of the enemy without cannon, and inferior in numbers to the garrifon of Dieft, appearing before that place, the garrifon fled in a cowardly manner as far as Malines. But the advanced guard of the Imperialifts making an attack upon the villages of Op and Neerwelpe was repulfed.

While Dumourier was engaged in repulfing this attack, the commiffioners of the Convention, La Croix and Danton, arrived in his camp, but he fent them to Louvain, where he followed them on the evening of that day. They appeared extremely affected with the recent defeat of the army, but in a ftill greater degree with the defertion of the troops ; having met at Bruffels and in various parts of their route, entire corps returning to France. But, whatever was their concern on thefe fubjects, their minds were much more engaged, as they faid, in the execution of the commiffion with which they were charged : to prevail on the general to retract his letter of the 12th of March ; which, by its too great franknefs, had ftirred up the bittereft refentment of the convention againft him.

Dumourier anfwered that he had expreffed no more in his letter than his real fentiments ; that the difafters to which they were witnefs were the neceffary confequence of the evils of which he had complained ; that he fought only to remedy thofe evils by putting an end to the tyranny and injuftice exercifed in Belgium ; that the neceffity which they muft perceive of his retiring from a country in which he had no means of defence ought to convince them of the prudent tenor of his proclamations, againft which, the convention were prejudiced, only becaufe they were mifinformed and betrayed ; that thofe proclamations

tions had induced the peasants of Belgium to lay down their arms, and had restored a degree of confidence between the French and Belgians, and were, therefore, the means of saving the troops, who disorganized, beaten, disgusted and dispirited, were altogether incapable of defending themselves against the Imperialists, more numerous than themselves and flushed with victory, and at the same time against the people of the country, should the resentment of the latter be again excited.

The commissioners were constrained to acknowledge the justice of these representations ; but still continued to insist on the general's retracting his letter. The general, after reviewing before them all the subjects of his complaints, and setting forth in the strongest manner, the misfortunes that were on the eve of resulting from the unwise and unjust conduct of the convention, made a positive declaration to the commissioners that he would in no part retract his letter, since the loss or the gain of a battle could not effect any change in his principles, opinions or character. The Commissioners conducted this conference with much address and energy, and endeavoured to win Dumourier by the most flattering considerations. At length, after a very long contest, the general consented to write a few lines to the president of the convention, in which he requested, *that the convention would postpone their judgement on his letter of the 12th of March, till he should have an opportunity of sending them an explanation of the reasons of that letter.* The two deputies departed with this unimportant declaration.

On the 21, the general being informed of the loss of Diest, resolved to take a position nearer Louvain, left the enemy, passing the canal, should cut off his communication with Malines, or fall upon Louvain itself. He posted the division of General Champmorin on the heights of Pellenberg, flanking his left by that of Miaczinsky, posted at St. Petersroede : General La Marche with the advanced guard on the heights of Corbec, skirting the high road : eighteen battalions of the army of the Ardennes, commanded by General Le Verteur, on the heights, and in the woods of Mezendael : and the division of General Dampierre at Florival, in communication with General Neuilly's division, which fell back toward Tombeck, at the entrance of the forest of Soignies.

During

During thefe movements, the troops were harraffed by the Imperialifts, who cannonaded them the whole day. On the morning of the 22d, the enemy made a general attack on the pofts of Pellenberg, Corbec and the woods of Mazendael. Blierbeck was between the enemy and General Le Veneur, and he had thought proper to occupy it. A column of Hungarian grenadiers made themfelves mafters of this village but were driven out with great flaughter, and with the lofs of two pieces of cannon, by the regiment of Auvergne, commanded by Colonel Dumas. The attack on the advanced guard was lefs vigorous, but that on the poft of Pellenberg was extremely bloody, General Champmorin defending himfelf with equal courage and ability. He received a ftrong reinforcement during the attack, and the enemy were unable to make any impreffion on his lines. This action was extremely hot, and lafted the whole day. The Auftrian columns fuffered great lofs, and were compelled to retire.

On the evening preceding this brilliant action, General Dumourier had occafion to fend Colonel Montjoye to the head-quarters of the Prince of Cobourg, to treat refpecting the wounded and the prifoners. He then faw Colonel Mack, an officer of uncommon merit, who obferved to Colonel Montjoye, that it might be equally advantageous to both pairties to agree to a fufpenfion of arms. Dumourier, who had deeply confidered the dangerous fituation of his army, fent Montjoye again to Colonel Mack on the 22d, to demand if he would come to Lovain, and make the fame propofition to Dumourier. Colonel Mack came in the evening. The following articles were verbally agreed to; Firft, that the Imperialifts fhould not again attack the French army in great force, nor General Dumourier again offer battle to the Imperialifts. Secondly, that on the faith of this tacit armiftice, the French fhould retire to Bruffels flowly and in good order, without any oppofition from the enemy. And laftly that Dumourier and Colonel Mack fhould have another interview after the evacuation of Bruffels, in order to fettle further articles that might then be mutually deemed neceffary.

This ftipulation, the firft that was entered into between the two generals, became hourly of more importance to Dumourier. His army was greatly diminifhed, efpecially in officers. He had fcarcely ammunition for a battle; and

and unfortunately, he was well perfuaded that, in cafe of a ferious attack, he fhould be abandoned by his army.

He had fufficient proof of this on the following day. The Imperialifts thought themfelves fo little bound by the articles agreed to by Colonel Mack, that General Clairfait (who was ignorant of thefe articles) fell upon the advanced guard and the troops pofted at Pellenberg. The action became general along the whole front of the army. Champmorin defended himfelf with the fame obftinacy as before ; but toward the clofe of the action, when the Imperial infantry were actually retiring, and there was no longer any enemy before the army, excepting fome light troops, old General La Marche became fuddenly terrified; and, notwithftanding the intreaties of Montjoye, De Barois, and other officers of diftinction, he retired in great confufion, firft to the abbey of Duparc, and afterwards to the other fide of the river Dyle, behind Louvain.

The Imperialifts, who acknowledged a lofs of 700 men, (that is to fay 2000 in both actions) were fo much difcouraged that they took no advantage of this cowardly retreat, which left a very dangerous interval between General Le Veneur and General Champmorin.

General Le Veneur had fought with great vigour during the whole of the action, but, feeing himfelf abandoned by La Marche, he alfo paffed the Dyle, without waiting for any orders, and pofted himfelf between Coorbeek and Heverle.

After the defection of thefe two divifions, Dumourier was compelled to order General Champmorin to abandon Pellenberg, and to retreat alfo behind Louvain, paffing through the city, and by the abbey of Vlierbecke.

General Miaczinfky retired by a bridge on the high road of Dieft, being protected by a battery of cannon placed on the heights above.

Dumourier availed himfelf of thefe two days, to remove his wounded, and the flour for his army, in boats, to Malines. Other articles belonging to the troops were thrown into the river ; but the confufion attending the evacuation of Louvain, and the avarice of individuals, caufed a great quantity of thefe articles to fall into the hands of the enemy, who entered Louvain that very evening, as the general retired with the garrifon, confifting of five battalions, which formed his rear guard.—— The Imperialifts alfo took fome boats laden with wounded, ed, which the escort abandoned on fight of a few huffars. These wounded soldiers were treated with great humanity, notwithstanding the atrocious calumnies of the Jacobins, spread with a design of irritating the French troops, and of instigating them to make war without quarter, and with greater barbarity.

The disgraceful retreat of the French from Louvain, is among the instances that prove how delicate and dangerous is the situation of the generals commanding the French armies. Having determined on their plan of attack or defence, and having given orders for its execution, they will be continually subject to defeat and ruin, if they have not other plans in reserve to stand in the place of orders ill executed or disobeyed: they can have no reliance on the generals under their command, who are frequently the first to give the example of disobedience, and sometimes of cowardice; they can never depend for a moment on the real strength or position of the corps that are not in their fight, since officers, as well as men, defert or change their position at pleasure; they have no means of remedying these ills, since they dare not punish, being certain of making most dangerous enemies of those whose faults they do but reprove: they are ever in danger of wanting even food for their troops, because the ancient system of providing necessaries for the army has been changed, to ferve the purposes of ignorant and selfish men: and, they will seldom dare to hazard the great movements that decide the fate of war, with soldiers, who, though presumptuously brave, are destitute of good officers, are ill armed, inexperienced, easily discouraged, mutinous, fond of reasoning, and altogether let loose from military law.

But, if a General be notwithstanding successful, the calumnies of the Journals and Clubs await him, and he is sure of being accused before the suspicious, blind, and imprudent Convention. If he be unfortunate, the whole weight of responsibility is thrown upon him, and he is branded with the name of coward or traitor.

Such is the situation in which the Republic of France places her generals in a war, on which depends, not only the political existence of the nation, but the individual liberty of every citizen. Dumourier has been replaced by Dampierre, who had the good fortune to be killed in battle; Dampierre by Custine, who perished on a scaffold; the latter by Houchard, who was disgraced

the

the moment that he had defeated the Duke of York, and raised the siege of Dunkirk; and it is the detestable Jourdan* who now commands the army, which alone stands between Paris and the vengeance of the powers of Europe.

In Alsace, on the southern frontier, and in the interior part of France, we have seen the same succession of generals. Every old and experienced officer has been driven from the service; and physicians, painters, and postillions command armies. It is said that Caligula made his horse consul. People of France, become as degenerate as you are cruel, you yourselves prepare the instruments of your destruction!

* We are assured by emigrants, arriving here from the army, that it is not Jourdan, of Avignon, who commands the armies.——*Note of the Editor†.*

† By the above note it appears that Dumourier had mistaken Gen. Jourdan, who defeated the barbarians of Maubenge, for Jourdan the assassin of Avignon,
                                                            T.

CHAP. IX.

Retreat to Brussels.—Evacuation of Brussels.—Camp of Enghien.—Camp of Ath.—Conference at Ath with Col. Mack.—The Arrest of Gen. Miranda.

THE disorder accompanying the retreat from Louvain utterly checked the energy the army had displayed in the two preceding combats. Happily, night concealed this universal defection of the troops from the enemy, who, notwithstanding the verbal stipulations agreed to by Col. Mack, would probably have seized upon this opportunity to destroy or entirely disperse the French army.

Dumourier with great difficulty prevailed on the troops to halt on the heights of Coztenbergue, half way on the road to Brussels. And this new calamity induced him to make an entire change in the disposition of the several corps under his command. He sent an order to General Duval to prepare for the evacuation of Brussels. He removed old General la Marche from the command of the advanced

advanced guard, which he gave to General Vouille. He formed this advanced guard, which was now become the rear-guard, of a strong body of the artillery, of all the cavalry of the army, and of twenty-five battalions, almost the whole of which were troops of the line. He himself took post in this rear guard, which amounted to near 15,000 men, and which indeed might be said to be his army. The other part of the troops marched under the protection of this chosen body, which behaved in a manner worthy the importance of its station.

Dumourier established his camp under the walls of Brussels, by the side of the little river of Woluwe, having his right at San-peters-waluwe, and his left at Vilverde.— Having taken the precaution of transporting his park of artillery to Anderlecht, he sent it off on the 23d to Tournay, by the road of Enghien and Ath, keeping only the cannon necessary for his rear guard.

The Prince of Cobourg, who was ignorant of the deplorable condition of the French troops, no doubt deemed himself happy in the suspension of arms, which procured him possession of the Netherlands, without further combat. But resistance on the part of Dumourier could only have tended to lay waste the country, without enabling him to keep his footing in it.——Since the Emperor Joseph demolished the strong places of those Provinces, they are destitute of any point that can resist an invading army; a battle gained gives the conqueror fifty leagues of country, or perhaps drives the vanquished to the extreme frontier.

The engagements entered into by Colonel Mack were faithfully observed by the Prince of Cobourg, who remained three days at Louvain, sending only small detachments to hang upon Dumourier's rear guard. The General was therefore at liberty to provide for the safety of Brussels, and of the other great cities through which the French army were compelled to pass on their retreat. Justice and humanity demanded that the Belgians should not be pillaged, and it was essential to avoid every means of irritating them. They had pardoned the excesses committed by the French, and had rendered them new services, and it was a duty to avoid opening the recent wounds of the country, since in that case despair would have again driven them to arms, and the French, surrounded by the Austrians and Belgians, had been entirely sacrificed.

On

On the 25th, the army paffed through Bruffels, obferving the greateft order and good conduct, and proceeded to Hall, from whence the General defigned they
fhould march in two columns to the frontiers of France.
No pillage was committed by the troops, nor were
any infults offered, or reproaches made on either part.
The inhabitants of Bruffels did not forget this fervice rendered them by General Dumourier. They have
expreffed their remembrance of it by marks of public
efteem[*]. Dumourier reflects on the juftice they have
done him with pleafure, and he would not have been
profcribed, and a fugitive, had he every where found
equal juftice.

The General's object now was to provide for the fafety
of the different detached forces, and to concert fuch
movements as that their retreat might keep pace with his.

While General Beaulieu was penetrating with feven
or eight thoufand men by Huy, the Prince of Hohenloe
was advancing by the province of Luxemburg againft
Namur, which was occupied by 15,000 men, under the
command of General d'Harville. But this divifion had
been formed at the expence of the garrifons of Givet and
Maubeuge; and the Prince of Hohenloe, turning by one
of thefe places, might make himfelf mafter of it, and
penetrate into France.

Dumourier commanded General d'Harville to leave
2,500 men with provifions and ammunition in the citadel
of Namur; and, dividing the remainder of his troops
in two columns, to fend one to Givet under the
command of Lieutenant-general Bouchet, and to retire with the other toward Maubeuge; halting firft at
Charleroy, and afterward pofting himfelf on the heights
of Niny above Mons. In this pofition General d'Harville would cover Maubeuge, la Quefnoy, Conde and
Valenciennes; and, as he would then be reinforced at
Mons with the divifion of General Neuilly, confifting of
6000 men, his divifion would be augmented to 12,000
men, befide the reinforcements daily arriving.

In anfwer to thefe inftructions, General d'Harville informed Dumourier, that he had neither provifions, ammu-

[*] Dumourier will ever be loved and refpected by the Belgians. It was in
the attempt to fave them from the decree of the 15th of December that he
fell. They will never forget the courage and humanity that he exerted in their
behalves. The EDITOR ventures to make this promife in the name of his country. Note by the British Editor.

nition

nition nor money sufficient to provide for the citadel of Namur scarcely for fifteen days order ; that he must either abandon the citadel or defend it with the whole of his division ; and demanded of General Dumourier determinate orders in what manner to conduct himself. With these dispatches from General d'Harville, came also letters to the same effect from General Bouchot, and documents from the Commissary Barneville that justified his statements.

Dumourier had no need to deliberate upon the orders it was necessary to give General d'Harville. To leave this division at Namur, was to risk the loss of Givet or Maubeuge, both in want of troops, and had either of them fallen into the hands of the enemy, the division of Namur would have been easily surrounded ; and to leave 2,500 men in the citadel, without money and ammunition, was in effect to deliver them to the Austrians. He therefore ordered General d'Harville entirely to evacuate Namur, and retire in good order to Givet and Maubeuge.

Dumourier considered the six battalions posted in Breda, and the three in Gertruydenberg, as lost, yet their having provisions for four or five months, and great store of ammunition, would, he knew, enable them a considerable time to stop the progress of the Prussians and Dutch. In order to keep open a communication with this division of his army, Dumourier saw it was necessary to secure the citadel of Antwerp, and commanded General Berneron to post himself in that citadel with 2000 men, and six months store of provisions.

Dumourier appointed Lieutenant-general Omoran to the command at Dunkirk, and along the sea-coast of the department of the North ; and ordered him to repair the lines and forts of the intrenched camp between Dunkirk and Bergues ; to form an intrenched camp on Mount Cassel ; to go in person to Courtray to take upon him the command of the army of Holland, and to post it in the camp of Haerlebecke, having the Scheldt in front.

He sent orders to General Marasse and General Ruault, to make their retreat, passing the Scheldt by the extremity of Flanders through Ghent, to the camp of Courtray, or Haerlebecke, while the garrison of Malines should retire to the same place by Dendermonde along the Scheldt ; being careful not to precipitate their retreat, and to cut down the bridges after them.

General Dumourier's design was, if he could have held the citadels of Namur and Antwerp, to have formed a

strong

strong line, without the territory of France, running from the right to the left by Namur, Mons, Tournay, Courtray, Antwerp, Breda, and Gertruydenberg. In this situation, if the suspension of arms should have continued, he hoped to have greater influence on the re-establishment of order in France. In the case of the suspension of arms being broken, the Imperialists finding themselves in the centre of a semicircle, would be compelled to commence their attack at the two extremities to proceed with safety, which would turn the campaign into a war of sieges on their part, carried on at the expence of their own territory. Thus Dumourier would have gained time to reorganise and reinforce his army: which, having the strong places of France behind it, might have been restored to its former confidence.

On this supposition Dumourier would have occupied the city of Tournay, and the camp of Antoing; from which place if the enemy had been greatly superior, he could have retired to a very strong position in his former camp of Maulde.

In pursuit of this plan (which had undergone no other change, than that of the evacuation of the citadel of Namur) he marched on the 26th to Enghien, and on the 27th to Ath, while the division of General Neuilly marched to Mons by Hall and Braine.

At Ath, he received orders from the Convention to arrest the colonel of the 73d regiment of infantry, (who had abandoned the army without orders, taking with him his two battalions, and returned to France;) and also General Miranda. Dumourier executed the order that respected General Miranda with regret, since he was persuaded, that this rigorous measure was less an act of justice than the effect of the hatred of the Jacobins against Pethion and the Girondists, who were the friends and protectors of Miranda. This General found means to escape the danger in accusing Dumourier, after his quitting the army; an event which was extremely favourable to Miranda.

On the same day Colonel Mack arrived at Ath; a verbal agreement was again entered into between that officer and Dumourier; but this was in much more formal terms than the former. The colonel began by expressing the acknowledgments of the Imperialists, for the peaceable manner in which the retreat of the French troops was conducted, in consequence of the prudence of General

Dumourier's

Dumourier's orders; by which means the country was spared the most frightful disasters. On the other hand, he noticed the moderation shewn by the Imperial general, who, while he forbore to harrass the French troops on their retreat, took care, nevertheless, to conceal from both armies the connivance between the two generals.

It was agreed upon by Dumourier, and Colonel Mack, that the French army should remain some time longer in the position of Mons, Tournay, and Courtray, without being harrassed by the Imperial army; that General Dumourier, who did not conceal from Colonel Mack his design of marching against Paris, should, when their designs were ripe for execution, regulate the motions of the Imperialists, who should only act as auxiliaries in the execution of their plan; that, in the case of Dumourier's having no need of assistance, which was to be greatly desired by both parties, the Imperialists should not advance farther than the frontier of France, and that the total evacuation of Belgium should be the price of this condescension; but if Dumourier could not effect the re-establishment of a limited monarchy, (not a counter-revolution,) he himself should indicate the number and the kind of troops which the Imperialists should furnish, to aid in the project, and should be entirely under Dumourier's direction.

Dumourier made Colonel Mack acquainted with his design of marching the following day to Tournay, with the march of General Neuilly to Mons, and of the army of Holland to Courtray.

It was finally decided that in order to combine the operations of the Imperial troops under the Prince of Cobourg, and those under the Prince of Hohenloe, at the time when Dumourier should march to Paris, Condé should be put into the hands of the Austrians, as a pledge; that the Austrians should garrison the town, but without any pretensions to the sovereignty, and on the condition that it should be restored to France, at the conclusion of the war, and after an indemnity should have been settled by the two parties; but that all the other towns belonging to France, should, in the case of the constitutional party needing the assistance of the Imperialists, receive garrisons, one half of which should be French troops, and the other half Imperialists, under the orders of the French. General Valence, General Thouvenot, the Duke de Chartres, and Colonel Mountjoye, assisted at this conference.

CHAP

CHAP. X.

Camp of Tournay.

ON the 28th, Dumourier marched to Tournay, and took the position of Antoing, having his advanced guard in Tournay, and the flanking corps of the left, commanded by General Miackzinsky, on Mount Trinity. He sent General le Veneur with the army of the Ardennes, to occupy the camp of Maulde.

In this was Madame de Sillery, with Mademoiselle d'Orleans, whom the general had never till then seen.—These ladies had taken up their residence at Tournay, on the advice which Dumourier had before this given to Lieutenant-General Omoran, who then commanded in the Tournaisis; because Mademoiselle d'Orleans, who was no more than fifteen years of age, was proscribed in France by the decree against the Emigrants. This young Princess (who as well as her brothers, the Duke de Chartres, and the Duke Montpensier, is perfectly well bred, and well informed) is an example of virtue, resignation and constancy.

The Duke de Chartres, who had served the preceding campaign with distinguished valour, and a pure and disinterested patriotism, and who had recently displayed a degree of courage, and civism, reflecting honour on the French name, was included in the decree of banishment, rendered against the house of Bourbon, and would have been subject to the cruelest vexations the moment that he should enter France.

Dumourier, during the two days that he passed at Tournay, testified by every circumstance in his power the lively concern that he took in the fate of this unfortunate and amiable princess. As both she and Madame de Sillery were greatly in dread of falling into the hands of the Imperialists, because of the influence which they supposed the emigrants to possess with the Emperor, Dumourier on his departure from Tournay, caused them to be conducted to St. Amand. When the general's protection, far from serving, might have been fatal to those

F f 2

ladies

ladies, they accepted of an asylum in Mons, offered them by the Imperial generals. If the virtues of Mademoiselle d'Orleans do not find their recompense, at least, may she find protection from the hands of a beneficent Providence.

While Dumourier remained in the camp of Tournay, he received intelligence, that General Neuilly's division, on ariving at Mons, instead of encamping on the heights of Nimy, had pillaged the magazines, and afterward fled in total disorder (without however, being attacked by the enemy,) to Condé and Valenciennes. The Cavalry only remained with General Neuilly, and Dumourier commanded him to retreat with those to Condé, spreading over as much ground on his march as he could, between Binche, Roeux, Soignes, and Leuse; carrying off with him the forage, horses, and carriages, and cutting down the bridges behind him.

The evacuation of Mons rendered Dumourier's situation at Tournay very dangerous, his right being altogether unprotected; but, independent of the suspension of arms, his knowledge of the country made him secure of his retreat, which he was unwilling to undertake, till he should have known what movement was made by his left. He, therefore only took the precaution of commanding General d'Harville to confine himself within the camp of Maubeuge and Givet, in order to prevent the enemy from penetrating on the French territory, on that side.

On the 29th of March, three deputies from the Jacobins arrived at Tournay. They introduced themselves to the General by saying, that they bore a commission from Le Brun; and, presenting a letter from that minister, conceived in vague and uncertain terms; they declared they had communications to make to him respecting the affairs of Belgium. These three men were Proly, a contemptible adventurer, born at Brussels; Desjardines, a writer of little note, who had formerly been driven from Brussels; and Pereira, a Portuguese Jew. The first of these we have seen was already known to the general; the second called himself a man of letters, and the third was a furious Jacobin. They were offended that the general refused to enter on the subject of their embassy, before Mademoiselle d'Orleans, to whose apartments they had expressly come to utter a Philippic against the general. He made an appointment to meet them at his own quarters.

The

The conversation that took place between Dumourier and these men, is pretty nearly such as they have reported it to be. They agreed with him in his opinion of the imbecility of the convention, and on the necessity of dispersing that assembly, and establishing some other legislature. After that, they founded the general respecting the persons who should succeed the convention in their authority; and one of them ventured to say, that the Jacobins had their president, registers, tribunes, orators, as well as the habit of discussing or determining great concerns; and that therefore, there was no need to look further. Dumourier, in his usual sincere and decisive manner, utterly rejected this idea; grounding his objection on the immorality, rashness, cruelty, and incongruous qualities of that society; to which all the misfortunes of France he declared were to be attributed.

Proly said, *how then will you be able to replace the present representatives of the people, and at the same time avoid the delays and other defects of the mode of election by primary assemblies?* The general answered, *nothing is more simple, or more easily accomplished. The patriotism of the administrators of the departments and districts is, at present, well tried and approved. For this one time, it is but to take all the procureurs-general of the departments and districts: and to complete the number by members of the departments and districts. These will form a very competent legislature: they will re-establish the constitution of 1789: all divisions will be healed in France: the Royalists will lay down their arms: foreign powers will no longer have any colour for carrying on the war, and France, having a solid government with which they can treat, will listen with readiness to terms of peace. For do not you imagine,* the general added, *the Republic can continue to exist: your crimes and your ignorance have destroyed its possibility.*

These three men made some objection to the general's propositions, but they listened very tranquilly to those *blasphemies* of the general, of which they afterward gave so dreadful an account. Desjardines, who proceeded further than the rest in his address and artifice, said that he should return to Paris to give an account of his mission; and that he hoped soon to see the general again. They took their leave of Dumourier without molestation; and certainly, he never thought of arresting emissaries of such little consequence.

General

General Dumourier has no doubt that, had he seconded their idea of replacing the National Convention by the society of Jacobins, he had entirely gained the confidence of that society; but he acknowledges that his temper, perhaps too sincere in this instance, robbed him of the possibility of seeming to yield to their measures. He instantly perceived that he could not turn this instrument to his purposes, but by plunging into a series of horrid crimes; and the events that have succeeded, have proved to him that his judgment was not erroneous.

On the same day, he received a letter from the seven commissioners of the convention, met at Lisle, who commanded him to appear in that city, to answer to the charges alledged against him. He answered, that being in sight of the enemy, employed in re-organizing his army, and in restoring its courage, (which was indeed true) he could not quit the army for an instant; but if the commissioners would come to him at Tournay, he would answer every accusation with his usual frankness; that when he should have accomplished his retreat, and the army should be safe in the French territory, he would have more leisure to take into consideration his personal affairs; in a word, that he would never enter Lisle, excepting it should be with troops to punish cowards, who had abandoned their colours and calumniated the most intrepid defenders of their country.

C H A P. XI.

Retreat to the Camp of Maulde.

GENERAL DUMOURIER was extremely uneasy respecting the fate of the troops at Antwerp; having received no intelligence from that quarter, and fearing indeed, that General Rualt who bore his orders to General Marassd, had fallen into the hands of the enemy.

The retreat from Antwerp across the Scheldt, by the extremity of Flanders, was long and difficult. But Dumourier knew that the enemy were less numerous in that quarter than the troops at Antwerp. The Prussians and Dutch were before Gertruydenberg and Breda; and Colonel

lonel Mylius, who prefented himfelf before Antwerp had not more than 2000 men, and thofe were irregular troops of the Imperial army.

But the French troops at Antwerp had fallen into ftill greater diforder than any other part of the army. They were feized with a panic, and the generals were no longer mafters of them. On the 26th Colonel Mylius had the audacity to fummon the city. Part of the French troops had already croffed the Scheldt, but, inftead of waiting for the remainder, they precipitately retired by Bruges to Dunkirk, excepting a fmall body of them, which Colonel Thouvenot prevailed upon to halt at Ghent. General Maraffe had funk the Ariel frigate according to Dumourier's inftructions, after fending away her mafts, rigging, and guns, by the canals to Dunkirk. He had alfo fent away part of the magazines of the garrifon, but a great part ftill remained, and more than 8000 men.

As the terror and confufion which before had fpread among the troops redoubled on the approach of Colonel Mylius, a council of war was held, in which it was unanimoufly decided, that it was more prudent to fave this part of the army together with the magazines and other effects belonging to the French nation, than obftinately to rifk the lofs of the whole.

It is impoffible for Dumourier to form a candid judgment of this capitulation, fince the rapid fucceffion of important events that followed, prevented him from any perfect knowledge of the circumftances of the garrifon. The Imperialifts are extremely dextrous in the difpofition and conduct of their advanced guards, multiplying them to the eyes of an enemy, and milleading the enemy refpecting their real force. It is alfo to be prefumed, that the French generals, embarraffed and difconcerted by the diforder prevailing among the troops, imagined the whole Pruffian and Dutch army to be before the place. No excufe, however, is to be made for their having furrendered the citadel, which was altogether independent of the city, and in no one cafe ought to have been included in that capitulation.

On the 27th or 28th of March, the French troops quitted Antwerp. None of them paffed by Courtray, and they were not at liberty to encamp at Haerlebeck, as had been defigned. They entered the French territory in different bodies, and at different times, and part of them

them were difposed of by General Omoran in the camp of Caffel and the lines of Dunkirk, and the remainder helped to form the camp of Madelaine, near Lifle.

It was not till the 29th that Dumourier received intelligence of this difperfion of more than 20,000 men of his army, and even then his intelligence was unaccompanied by any detail. The difperfion of the body of troops under Neuilly, and the evacuation of Mons, had expofed his right, and that of Courtray now expofed his left to ftill greater danger, which the enemy might turn, approaching by the left of the Schelt, and if he fhould be compelled to retreat before the enemy in the prefent difpofition of his troops, he had nothing to expect but to be completely routed.

For thefe reafons, he refolved to raife the camp of Tournay in the morning of the 30th. He had before this, fent General le Veneur to occupy that of Maulde. He fent the army of the North, by the bridge of Mortagne, to encamp in the ftrong pofition of Bruille, which he ordered to be joined by three bridges to the camp. He fent General Miaczinfky with 4000 men to occupy Orchies, to fecure a communication with Lifle, and he eftablifhed his head quarters with his park of artillery at St. Amand.

By the unexpected furrender of the citadel of Antwerp, the garrifons of Breda and Gertruydenberg were entirely cut off from all communication with the army. They amounted to near 6000 men, that were on the point of being facrificed without the hope of affiftance, and without any fervice to enfue to France. Dumourier, therefore, fent orders, through the medium of Colonel Mack, to General de Flers, and to Colonel Tilly, who commanded in thofe two places to capitulate, on condition of being at liberty to march to France with arms and baggage. This was accordingly done; and was an important fervice rendered France, fince one half of the army had already deferted.

At this period the fafety of the frontier towns in France was entirely owing to the fufpenfion of arms; for had the Imperialifts preffed forward, fuch was the diforder prevailing in the French army, they muft have penetrated the frontiers.

In the midft of this chaos of things, and of the difcontents and diforders that refulted in the French army, the

troops

troops never ceafed to exprefs an attachment to their general, rendering juftice to his efforts to preferve them from ruin. The rear guard, and the troops of the line especially, who had always feen him the laft in every retreat, in the day or at night, and always expofed to the greateft danger, were moved with refpect, and even compaffion for the general, and with extreme refentment againft his enemies, the Jacobins and the National Convention. A wifh for the re-eftablifhment of a limited Monarchy was almoft general in the army. A few of the battalions of volunteers only dared openly to efpoufe the Republic. The cavalry, and the troops of the line were altogether decided; and the artillery declared that in every cafe, they would defend their general. It was openly propofed to march to Paris, and to overthrow the Anarchifts, to whom the army juftly attributed the whole of their difgrace and misfortunes. It being faid that the general was to be commanded to appear at the bar of the National Convention, their conftant language was, that they themfelves would conduct the general to Paris, and would fhare his fortunes.

Dumourier attentively obferved this difpofition in the troops, which he faw was fupported by the complaints of the generals, and of the greater part of the other officers. Thefe latter, feeing the generals under whom they had been conducted to victory, outraged in the Jacobin Journals, accufed of treachery, arrefted, and treated without regard to decency or juftice, naturally concluded, that their own elevation to the fuperior ranks, would but expofe them to the fame difafters. Some of the generals, however, among whom was Dampierre, kept up a perfidious correfpondence with the leaders of the Anarchifts; and, hoping to fupplant their fuperiors, by the aid of the prefent diforders, they loudly proclaimed the fame doctrines as their colleagues of Paris, and by their falfe infinuations kept alive the Jacobin phrenzy that infected part of the army.

The two parties were now in the greateft fermentation, and the conteft tended to an iffue which could not but be prompt and violent. Three Commiffioners of the Convention, Lequinio, Cochon, and Bellegarde were in Valenciennes; thefe already treated the army and its generals as rebels, would not permit any communication between them and the garrifon, and ftopt their convoys

of

of provifion and money. They were bold enough to hazard a manifefto againft Dumourier, which they fent to the army, and the garrifon of Conde.

The garrifon of Conde, confifting of four battalions and a regiment of cavalry, under General Neuilly, were extremely divided in opinion, but they feemed to incline to fupport Dumourier, to whom General Neuilly was altogether attached.

At Lifle, the conteft was ftill more marked and more violent. The Comiffioners of the Convention, who had made this place their point of union, and the Jacobin Club inftigated an extremely numerous populace againft the higher rank of citizens. On the other hand the foldiers, efpecially the troops of the line, broke out into tumults, and fpoke loudly in behalf of their general, and againft the Anarchifts. But they were without leaders, and their meafures were void of plan and conduct. Affignats were alfo fuccefsfully diftributed among thefe troops, and the fame means were employed in the army under the general's immediate command, and even with thofe neareft to his perfon.

The Commiffioners of the Convention alfo endeavoured to accomplifh their defigns by affaffination. On the 31ft of March, fix volunteers, of the third battalion of La Marne, demanded leave to fpeak to the general, who ordered them to be introduced. They entered with their hats on, the back part being placed in the front, having the word *Republic* chalked on them. They made a long and fanatical harangue to the general, the purport of which was, that they, and many others of their comrades, had fworn to fend him to the bar of the National Convention, or, in imitation of Brutus, to ftab him. Dumourier anfwered with great compofure and gentlenefs, that they were blinded by a miftaken zeal; that they could not but perceive the unfortunate condition of France; and that the rage with which remedies were applied, ferved only to prove the impoffibility of maintaining the republic, fince an unjuft and unreftrained government could not long exift. While the general fpoke, they approached with a defign of furrounding him, which, perhaps, would have been effected, but for the intrepidity of the faithfull Baptifte, who feized upon the foremoft, and called the general's guard to his affiftance. The volunteers attempted to refift, but they were

overpowered

overpowered; and the general not only saved their lives but prevented their being ill treated. He contented himself with securing their persons in prison.

The indignation of the army was general; and on the same day the different corps presented addresses signed by individuals of every rank, professing an inviolable attachment to their general; and the greater part of them expressing their desire of marching to Paris to re-establish the constitution.

After hostilities had been thus commenced by the Commissioners of the Convention, and after the troops had thus declared their wishes, Dumourier set about the means of making himself master of Valenciennes, Condé, and Lisle; without which he could strike no blow of importance.

He now readily acknowledges that, although he did not for a moment lose sight of his object, he failed in neglecting means which, doubtless were necessary at that period; but which he was induced to reject by his aversion to perfidy and cruelty. He relied too confidently on the strength of his legitimate means, and on the good faith and conviction of his troops; and he neither counteracted his enemies by corruption, nor destroyed the more inveterate of them when it was in his power. A measure was proposed to him that was probably essential to his interest. It was to assemble the troops of the line in a camp apart from the rest, and to disarm and disband the national guard. But this could not be accomplished without a dreadful effusion of blood; for there had long existed an extreme animosity between the national guards, and the troops of the line. There were many of the battalions of national guards, who had served under his command with great valour, and had lately presented addresses to him, couched in loyal and strong terms; and he could not prevail on himself to recompence them with disgrace, or perhaps, with death. And, if he should make exceptions in the execution of the plan, those might include disguised anarchists; and he could no longer rely with safety on his troops.

History presents no example of opinion having agitated the passions of men to so excessive a degree, of having so greatly disfigured their characters, and having so completely bereaved them of all the social affections, as in the French revolution. The love of liberty was a noble
passion

paſſion in 1789. It became licentious in 1790 and 1791. By the ſucceſſes of the year 1792, the love of freedom, inſtead of being exalted into heroiſm, degenerated into a blind, inſolent, and barbarous phrenzy ; and the period that we are reviewing in theſe memoirs added to the ferocity of its ſpirit.

The ſtruggle for aſcendancy was not equal between Dumourier and the Jacobins. His means were enfeebled by his ſcruples. The crimes of the Jacobins were not to be cruſhed but by crimes more incredible than theſe ; corruption was to be oppoſed by corruption, and treachery and cruelty to the attrocities and horrors of the Jacobins. The ſect of the Jacobins was not to be annihilated but by a monſter more frightful than itſelf ; or by a foreign ſword. And hence the ſequel of this hiſtory is no more than an account of the miſtakes of Dumourier ; who embraced the incompatible deſigns of preſerving his own eſteem, and purging the nation of her crimes. In a converſation he had formerly held at Louvain with Danton and La Croix, on a propoſal made by thoſe Commiſſioners relative to a conduct they wiſhed the general to adopt in Belgium, by no means very reputable ; the general obſerved (and he has ſince repeated the obſervation to Camus) that he would never commit an action which he regarded as a crime, even for the ſalvation of his country. He has ſince been told that Danton ſaid *General Dumourier wants energy ; his mind has never riſen to the true revolutionary pitch.* The revolutionary pitch roſe, after that period ; and, Dumourier, who has not changed, could not but fail in the ſtruggle, ſince to ſucceed it was neceſſary to diſplay crimes greater than thoſe with which he had to combat.

Dumourier ſent orders to General Miaczinſky, who was at Orchies, to march with his diviſion to Liſle ; to arreſt the Commiſſioners of the Convention, and the leaders of the clubs ; to proceed from thence to Douay and remove General Moreton from the command of that town ; to proclaim there and at Liſle the unanimous reſolution of the army to reſtore the Conſtitution : and afterward to proceed by Cambray to Peronne, where he was to take poſt. This unfortunate General did not ſufficiently perceive the importance of his charge. He ſpoke of it to various perſons, and among the reſt to St. George, the celebrated Mulatto, Colonel of a regiment of Huſſars, who betrayed the general and drew him into Liſle with a very ſmall eſ

cort

cort. The moment Miaczinfky entered the town, the
gates were fhut upon him. He was arrefted, conducted
to Paris, and brought to the fcaffold. This officer was a
native of Poland, and was one of the chiefs of the confede-
ration, at the time that Dumourier was charged by the
court of France to direct its operations. Miaczinfky had
been made prifoner in an engagement with the Ruffians;
and afterward, claiming an indemnity from France, in
which the general could not find means to ferve him, he
had obtained for him the rank of major-general, and per-
miffion to raife a free corps, and had afterward employed
him with great utility in France and the army. Miaczinfky, brave in war, did not difplay the fame courage
in his perfonal defence when he was taken, nor at his
death. He accufed Dumourier of various crimes againft
the nation; and even of fome grofs frauds, that were no
doubt fuggefted to him by the enemies of Dumourier. He
alfo accufed La Croix, which was the caufe of his ruin.

Miaczinfky's troops, after they were quitted by that
officer, wandered on the Glacis of Lifle, into which
place the garrifon would not admit them. Dumourier, receiving intelligence of this, fent one of his aids-de-camp,
Colonel Philip de Vaux, to put himfelf at their head, and
to conduct them to Orchies and Douay. De Vaux was
arrefted through the treachery of a brother officer, taken
to Paris, and executed. He died with great courage and
conftancy.

Philip de Vaux was born at Bruffels, had ferved in Auftria, and had afterward taken part againft the Emperor
in the revolution of his own country. Dumourier had
known him at Paris, and appointed him his aid-de-camp.
He was a man of capacity, of great courage, and of an
exalted and feeling mind. In fine, he poffeffed the qualities neceffary to make a general officer.

The garrifon of Valenciennes was commanded by Major-General Ferrand, whom Dumourier had raifed to the
rank of Colonel, and afterward to that of major-general;
and whom he believed to be attached to his interefts. This
officer was of an age not very liable to be heated with
opinions; and, till this period, had appeared to be well
informed and moderate. But characters moulder away
before opinions, and Ferrand became one of the moft intemperate of Dumouriers accufers, and one of the firmeft
fupporters of the anarchifts.

The

The grand provost of the army, named l'Ecuyer, demanded of Dumourier as a favour, the charge of arresting the Deputies at Valenciennes. He was no sooner in that city, than he became their confident, and instrument: although by a strange accident he perished afterward on the scaffold. While he was in Valenciennes, he had written a circumstantial letter to the general, respecting the arrangements he had made for arresting the deputies, and this letter was found in the pocket of the general's great-coat on the 4th of April.

These two men, Ferrand and l'Ecuyer, undermined the general's plan for making himself master of Valenciennes; these being at first confidentially communicated to them; and they effected an entire change in the disposition of the troops which he had contrived to send there.

Dumourier's design on Lisle and Valenciennes, being thus suddenly defeated, he had no other resource than to make himself master of Condé. The situation of the army, on the extreme frontier of France, was become altogether embarrassing. The army depending upon the strong towns for subsistence, Dumourier was compelled either to disband them, or to join the Imperialists, unless he could obtain possession of one of the strong towns. The first of these measures would have deprived him of all resource, and given a decisive victory to the anarchists. The second was repugnant to the feelings of the general, and the troops, inspired by the laudable principle of national honour; and he could not have obtained the universal consent of his army to this measure, since the opinions of the troops were divided, and since the indefatigable intrigues of the Jacobins had wrought such a change in the disposition of the soldiery. And the latter was impracticable, because the General had no artillery to undertake a siege; his artillery being sent to Lisle when he retreated from Belgium. The third of these measures also, must have produced a civil war. A regular siege would have demanded great length of time, during which the soldiery would have made the same reflections that operated on the mind of Dumourier, and which continually restrained him in the plans that seemed necessary to his object: these reflections regarded the horror of seeing Frenchmen combat each other, having foreigners for spectators, to whom both parties would have become a prey, when they should be mutually incapable of further resistance.

Dumourier

Dumourier therefore thought of leading his army to Paris. But he could succeed in that, only in having a majority of opinions with him. Every other expedient was at once painful and uncertain. Every day, every hour diminished his hope. He beheld his situation, without deceiving himself, and being subdued by his difficulties. He regarded them under every aspect, and he cannot now recollect the first five days of April without horror.

CHAP. XII.

Arrest of the Commissioners of the Convention, Camus, La Marque, Bancal, and Quinette; and of Beurnonville, Minister of War.

ON the first of April, General Dumourier, in order to be nearer his army, and to favour a project of surprising Valenciennes, (which had been proposed to him, and which failed by the misconduct of the general officer who was charged with its execution,) removed his head quarters from the city of St. Amand to the suburbs; where was stationed a chosen body of cavalry, and where he was also nearer Conde. Various circumstances had prevented his proceeding in the first instance to the latter city, but in that neglect he committed a great error, and perhaps it was the cause of compleating the ruin of his affairs. Perhaps it had been better if he had at first established his head quarters at Conde; but the events that passed in that period were so sudden and unforeseen, he was so effectually shut out from intelligence, and was so compleatly ignorant of all that passed beyond Valenciennes and Lisle, and he was so entirely occupied in observing and moulding to his purpose the dispositions of his army, that to blame or justify the conduct into which he was driven by this strong chain of circumstances, it is necessary to have been in his situation.

Perhaps even it is well for him that he did not make himself master of Conde, for if the inconstancy of the French character had then caused a strong defection in his army, being in the centre of that strong city, he had been delivered up to his enemies, or massacred by his own troops.

The

The commissioners of the Convention availed themselves of Dumourier's hesitation in this respect to visit Conde, and to issue proclamations, circulate assignats, and fill the town with emissaries of the Jacobins. The sixth regiment of infantry, the only corps of troops of the line which had discovered a decided spirit of Jacobinism, and a battalion of National Guards of Versailles, struck terror into the mind of General Neuilly, who thenceforward was no longer master of the place; although he persuaded himself that he was, and continued to assert it to Dumourier, who too long relied on his ill founded confidence.

In this battalion of Versailles, was a captain of the artillery company, named Le Cointre, son of the celebrated deputy of that name of Versailles. This young man declaimed vehemently against the advocates of the constitution; and, being rudely handled on that account by some dragoon officers, he quitted the garrison to lay his complaints before Dumourier, who caused him to be arrested, that he might have an hostage for himself, in the person of the son of one of the most furious among the members of the *Mountain*. Dumourier also caused to be arrested a lieutenant-colonel, an officer belonging to the staff of the army, who declaimed openly and vehemently against him: and having no secure place in which he could keep these prisoners, he sent them together with the six volunteers, who had attempted to assassinate him, to Tournay; requesting General Clairfait to keep them as hostages in the citadel.

Lieutenant-General le Veneur, who at the time of La Fayette's desertion had followed that officer, and who was indebted to Dumourier for his pardon, and his re-establishment in his rank, now came to Dumourier to demand permission to retire from the army, on the pretence of being in an ill state of health. His object was, to obtain the command of the army of the Anarchists. Dumourier granted him permission to retire, and also to a general named Stetenhoffen, a foreigner whom Dumourier had made major-general. Dampierre was at Quesnoy with his division, and carried on a treaty with the commissioners of the Convention, as did also General Chancel, who was cantoned at Fresnes. And their example was followed by General Rosiers, and General Kermorvan, who had the command of the Belgians in the camp of Bruille.

Dumourier

Dumourier was the more affected by these inftances of treachery, becaufe all thofe officers had been indebted to him for their rank, had complained more loudly than any others againft the Anarchifts, and had preffed with more feeming impatience the execution of his defign of reftoring order. Excepting Dampierre who died in the command of the army, and Chancel who replaced Neuilly at Conde, and was obliged to furrender after a long fiege, thefe officers have been punifhed for their ingratitude, by the fufpicions and difdain of their patrons, and the lofs of their employments. This unhappy example of treachery of fuperior officers, who were in appearance moft attached to the caufe of the general, could not fail to produce a pernicious effect on the foldiery, and add ftrength to the party of the Jacobins.

Dumourier now faw that he could no longer hope to march to Paris without oppofition from his army, as the temper of his troops at firft feemed to promife. He faw that he would have to commence by a civil war, which he had always thought of with repugnance ; and to compel one part of his troops to combat the other, a dreadful extremity for a general who regarded his foldiers as his children, and who had never conducted them but by his kindnefs, and the influence of a mutual affection.

Another circumftance rendered him timid, and deprived all his meafures of energy. This was, the danger of the prifoners in the temple. It was to be feared that the Jacobins would inftantly facrifice the unfortunate victims, whom they already treated too unworthily to afford any hope that they would fpare them in the firft moments of their fear and refentment. Had thofe prifoners been facrificed in confequence of Dumourier's march to Paris, he would have incurred the reproaches of Europe, and hiftory would have configned him to infamy ; while he would have prepared for himfelf an anguifh, that would have endured through the remainder of his life.

General Dumourier from the time of his being at Tournay, inceffantly meditated on this dreadful circumftance. Befide General Valence, the Duke de Chartres, and General Thouvenot, who partook of his councils, he alfo confided his thoughts on this fubject to Colonel Montjoy, and Colonel Nordmann, colonel of the regi-

ment

ment of Berchiny. He propofed to fend thofe two officers with three hundred huffars to Paris, on the pretext of arrefting deferters, and fending them back to this army. He meant to have given them difpatches to the minifter of war, which would have juftified their going to Paris, and would have given it a natural air, in the cafe of their being interrogated. They were to proceed as covertly as poffible by the foreft of Bondy; and afterward, reaching the prifon by the Boulevard of the temple, were to force the guard, making falfe attacks in feveral different points, carry off the four illuftrious prifoners, placing each of them behind an huffar, and having a voiture ready in the foreft, to pufh forward with the utmoft fpeed to Pont St. Maxence, where another body of cavalry were to be pofted to meet them.

But to this end it was neceffary to be in poffeffion of either Valenciennes, or Lifle; and the circumftances that followed defeated the project, to which thofe two worthy officers whom we have juft named, were altogether devoted. There remained no means of faving the illuftrious prifoners from the rage of the Jacobins. To form a confpiracy in Paris demanded time, and the emigrants had fo ill fucceeded in attempts of that nature, that it had been madnefs in the general to have placed any confidence in fuch a plan. Deprived then of all hope of delivering the prifoners, the general had no other refource in their behalf, than to poffefs himfelf of hoftages for their fafety. Hence he had fo anxioufly fought to feize upon the Commiffioners of the Convention at Lifle, and Valenciennes; and he was now determined to detain fuch as might put themfelves into his power.

On the morning of the 5th of April, a captain of Chaffeurs, whom Dumourier had pofted at Pont-a-Marque, on the road between Lifle, and Douay, with fifteen trufty and refolute men under his command, with orders to arreft any couriers, but above all the Commiffioners of the Convention, if they took the road from Lifle to Paris, brought him advice that Beurnonville the minifter of war had paffed them on the road to Lifle, and had informed him (the captain of Chaffeurs) that he fhould afterward proceed to the head quarters of his friend General Dumourier. The intimacy that fubfifted between this minifter and the General was known.

Dumourier

Dumourier was aftonifhed that he had received no courier from Beurnonville, nor any manner of advice refpecting his journey, at a time when the General could no longer doubt of his being profcribed, and when the *Rubicon* was already paffed. This was the firft and the only intimation which Dumourier received to prepare him for the important fcene that followed.

About four o'clock in the evening, two courfiers came to the General to announce the arrival of the minifter of war with four commiffioners of the National Convention: Terror and defpair were painted on the countenance of thefe meffengers. Interrogated by fome of the ftaff officers refpecting the caufe, they did not hefitate to fay that General Dumourier was utterly loft, that the commiffioners came to conduct him to the bar of the Convention in virtue of a decree, but that the general would never reach Paris, fince affaffins were planted on the road by bands of twenty and thirty, at Gournay, Roye, and Senlis, in order to murder him. They even indicated who thefe affaffins were, being foldiers belonging to two new regiments, called the Huffars and dragoons of the Republic. The general had broken a fquadron of the Huffars, for having refufed to obey their colonel, and had fent them back to France on foot and without arms, which the Jacobins had reftored them in order to affaffinate their general. The regiment of dragoons confifted of men who had committed numerous crimes at Paris, from which they had been fent with great difficulty to join the army, where they attempted to repeat their crimes. Their conduct was cowardly and attrocious, and the general was compelled to act with feverity toward them on his retreat from the Netherlands. They afterward deferted and fled to Paris, when they were now difpatched to be the accomplices of the Huffars.

Immediately afterward the minifter of war appeared, followed by the four commiffioner, who were Camus, La Marque, Bancal, and Quinette. The minifter after embracing the general with expreffions natural to their mutual attachment, informed him that the commiffioners came to notify to the general a decree of the National Convention. General Valence was already with Dumourier, and the reft of the ftaff officers now crowded into the apartment. Partaking of the opinions of their general as they had partaken of his fatigues, dangers, victories and defeats, his fate was not to be feparated from theirs; and indignation rather that inquietude was expreffed in their looks. Dumourier faw that this temper of mind might break out into violent confequences, which induced him the more to preferve the compofure with which he was determined to act in this critical moment.

Dumourier would be unjuft if he did not offer the homage of his efteem and gratitude, to thofe generous men, who in the midft of his difgraces preferved the conftancy of their friendfhip to him, and their attachment to principle, by facrificing emolument and honors, to follow him in his retreat. Nor can he forbear here to record the magnanimity of General Valence, who being offered the command of the Armies on condition of arrefting Dumourier, not only fpurned at the offer without hefitation, but concealed the dangerous temptations laid before him by the commiffioners of the Convention from the knowledge of Dumourier.

Camus fpoke for the members of this deputation. In a manner that expreffed fome degree of irrefolution, he requefted the general to go into another room with the deputies, and minifter of war, in order to hear a decree of the Convention refpecting him. The general anfwered, that as all his actions had ever been public, and as the fubject of a decree paffed by feven hundred perfons could be no myftery, he faw no reafon for complying with the requeft, and that the officers who were prefent ought to be witneffes of whatever fhould pafs in this interview. Beurnonville, however, as well as the deputies, urged the requeft with fuch appearance of refpect that the General went with them into an inner room, but his ftaff officers would not permit the door to be clofed, and General Valence entered the room with him.

Camus prefented the decree to Dumourier; who, having read it with perfect compofure, returned it, and obferved, that forbearing within certain limits to condemn a decifion of the National Convention, he could not but judge this order to be untimely, fince the army was diforganized and difcontented; and fince his quitting it in that condition would be followed by its total diffolution; that it would be prudent to fufpend the execution of the decree, till he fhould have reftored the army to its proper footing, when he would be ready to render an account of his conduct; and when it might be decided whether circumftances required or permitted his appearance at Paris; that

that he read in that decree, an article empowering the
Commissioners to suspend him from his functions and appoint another General, in the case of his disobeying the
order ; that the Convention having charged them with a
commission including such severity toward the general,
and of so delicate a nature with respect to themselves, had
certainly relied no less on their prudence than on their
firmness, that therefore he would throw himself on their
discretion, and would not positively refuse obedience, but
merely demand a delay in the execution of their order :
that, in fine, being now judges of all the circumstances,
they could easily resolve on the conduct that became
them, and if they were determined upon suspending him,
he would meet them half way, by himself offering his resignation to them, which he had so often tendered during
the last three months to the Convention.

Camus replied that the deputies had no authority to receive the General's resignation ; and then said, *But if your
resignation were accepted of, what would be your conduct
afterwards ? I should act as became me*, the General answered ; *but I have no hesitation in declaring to you, I
will neither by going to Paris subject myself to be treated
unworthily by fanatics, nor to be condemned to death by a
revolutionary tribunal.—Then you do not acknowledge that
tribunal*, said Camus.—*I recognise in it*, replied the General, *a tribunal of Blood and of Crimes, to which I never
will submit while I have a sword that will not deceive me,
I moreover declare, that had I the power I would abolish it,
as being a dishonour to a free Nation*.

The other three deputies who were men of much more
temper and moderation than Camus, perceiving that the
conversation became intemperate, interposed, and endeavoured to convince the general that the Convention
had no inimical designs against him ; that he was loved and
esteemed by every one, and that his presence in Paris
would destroy the calumnies of his enemies ; that his absence from the troops would not be long, and that the deputies and minister of war would remain with the army
till his return. Quinette offered to accompany the general to Paris to be the pledge of his safety, and to return
with him, making the most fervent protestations that
he would personally expose himself to all danger in the
general's defence. After this the conversation became
more cool and temperate, Bancal, a man of reading and
talent,

talent, endeavoured to win the general by his regard for his name, and cited examples of obedience and resignation to the laws of the Greeks and Romans. *Let us have done with mistakes, Sir,* said the general; *we degrade the Roman history; and disfigure the Roman virtues, that they may serve as an excuse for our crimes. The Romans did not massacre Tarquin. The Roman republic possessed a stable government and just laws. They neither had a Jacobin club, nor a revolutionary tribunal. We are in a state of anarchy. Ferocious men thirst for my blood, and I tell you that I have often acted the part of Decius but never will that of Curtius.*

The deputies assured Dumourier that he had formed an unjust idea of the state of Paris; and that indeed he was neither called before the Jacobins, nor the revolutionary tribunal, but to the Bar of the National Convention, and that he would speedily return to his post.

I passed the month of January at Paris, said the general, *and surely that city has not become more reasonable since, especially in the moment of public danger. I know by the most authentic of your journals, that the Convention is governed by Marat, the Jacobins, and the tumultuous tribunes filled with the emissaries of the Jacobins. The Convention has not the power of saving me from the fury of these men; and, if it became the respect that I owe myself to appear before such judges, even my deportment would provoke my death.*

Camus then returned to his categorical question. *You refuse to obey the decree of the Convention?* The general answered that he had already stated to the deputies his view of the subject. He urged them to take a moderate course, and exhorted them to return to Valenciennes, and from thence to make a report to the Convention, setting forth the general's reasons, and supporting those by shewing the impossibility of taking the general from his army at this instant, without incurring the greatest risk of disbanding it.

Dumourier acknowledges that, had they yielded to these counsels, he should have been imprudent enough to have permitted their departure. The colleagues of Camus appeared by no means unwilling to listen to reason, altho' on his part he rudely repulsed every conciliatory measure. *Call to mind,* said one of them, *that your disobedience in this case will cause the ruin of the republic. Cambon said in your tribune amidst bursts of applause,* answered the general,

ral, *that the fate of the republic rests not upon any one man. I have, beside, to observe that the name of the republic does not belong to us ; our condition is absolute anarchy. I swear to you that I have no desire to elude enquiry. I promise you on my honour, a pledge that is inviolable with military men, that when the nation shall have a government, and laws, I will give a faithful account of my actions and motives. I will myself demand a trial. At present, it would be an act of insanity in me.*

The conference lasted more than two hours, but that which has been stated was the exact purport of it. The deputies retired into another chamber, to decide on the course they should pursue.

Dumourier was at this period deceived respecting the designs, and the conduct of Beurnonville ; in consequence of which he has made unjust complaints of that minister. He learned afterward from a virtuous and impartial man, that Beurnonville was constant in his friendship to Dumourier ; and the gross accusations of Marat against that minister is an additional proof of the fact : and Dumourier is eager to make this public avowal of his error.

It is certain that Beurnonville, being several times appealed to by Dumourier respecting the conduct he would observe in this case, constantly said, *I cannot advise you. You know what it becomes you to do.* As soon as the deputies were withdrawn, the general complained that Beurnonville had forborne to give him intelligence of the approach of this important event, at the same time however requesting him to join the army, and again to take upon him the command of the advanced guard. Beurnonville answered, *I know that I shall fall a sacrifice to my enemies, but I have resolved to die at my post. My situation is terrifying. I see you are decided, and that the step you will take is of the most desperate kind. I demand as a favour at your hands that you will not separate my fate from that of the deputies.*—*Be assured that I will not,* answered the General. Dumourier was at that moment unjust to the magnanimity of Beurnonville, whom he considered to be perfidious, or at the best unworthily carried away by circumstances. May he receive some consolation in this justice rendered to him by Dumourier. And may his heart, justly offended, be open to receive the attonement of his friend !

Beurnonville, Valence, and Dumourier returned to the officers, who impatiently waited the result of this long conference.

conference. But their inquietude was not entirely dissipated, for the general did not then acquaint them with the resolution he had taken. These officers have since told him that, had he consented to go to Paris, they would have prevented it by violence.

When the deputies first arrived at the general's quarters, the regiment of Berchiny was drawn up in the court yard; and the general had commanded Colonel Nordmann to select an officer on whom he could rely, together with thirty men, and to hold them in readiness to execute his orders. The passions by which the troops were agitated were forcibly expressed in their looks, and the general exerted his influence to moderate them.

In this interval while the Deputies were deliberating, Dumourier in walking met doctor Menuret, surgeon to the army, and said to him, *Well doctor, what remedy shall we apply to this wound?* Menuret answered quickly, *the same as in the preceding year at the camp of Maulde, a grain of disobedience.*

In about an hour the deputies returned to the General's room, Camus much agitated, said harshly, *Citizen General, are you ready to obey the decree of the National Convention, and go with us to Paris?* The General replied, *Not in this instant.*—Then, said Camus, *I suspend you from your functions. You no longer command the armies. I forbid all persons to obey you, and command every one to assist in arresting you. I will go myself and place the seals on your papers.*

A murmur of indignation was heard. *Give me the names of those persons,* Camus cried out rudely, pointing to the officers around him. *They will themselves give you their names.—I have now other employment,* replied Camus, who no longer knew what he said : *I demand your papers.*

Dumourier now saw that the emotion of his officers was at its height and on the point of producing some rash action. He said, in a firm tone, *This is insufferable. It is time to put an end to such insolence.* And, in the German language he commanded the Hussars to enter. He then ordered the officer of the hussars to arrest the four deputies and the minister of war, but not to do them any personal injury, and to leave Beurnonville his arms.

Camus then said, *General Dumourier, you are about to destroy the Republic.*—*Say rather it is you, old madman,* the General replied to him.

They

They were conducted into another chamber ; and after having dined, were conveyed in their own carriage to Tournay, escorted by a squadron of the hussars of Berchiny. Dumourier sent a letter to General Clairfait, saying that he sent him hostages, who would be responsible for the excesses that might be committed at Paris. He requested General Clairfait to treat the minister of war, with more distinction than the rest.

Such were the facts relative to the arrest of the Commissioners of the Convention, which was a measure forced on the General by circumstances. As to the act of delivering them into the hands of the Imperialists, it is to be remembered that Dumourier had no fortress in which he could keep them in safety, and that the Imperialists being as deeply concerned as himself in the fate of the prisoners of the Temple, they could not be placed in any hands so sure. They could be detained merely as hostages, nor was there any danger to their personal safety, their detention being simply an act of precaution on the part of Dumourier. Besides, it is to be recollected, that the Prince of Cobourg consented to act on the footing of an auxiliary to General Dumourier, in this war, for the overthrow of the Jacobins, and for the re-establishment of the Constitution. Hence these hostages were not really prisoners of the Imperialists, but those of General Dumourier, for whom they held them. The deputies and the minister of war were sent to Maestricht, where they were kept till a change of circumstances required their removal.

This event is one more instance of the blind precipitation attending upon all the measures of the National Convention. It is to be remarked also, that Camus, who went post from Liege to vote for the death of Louis XVI. had in this last instance, suddenly quitted the frontier, to procure the arrest of General Dumourier, had himself dictated the decree, and had demanded to be charged with its execution. It was therefore that he was so unrelenting during the conference, lest his colleagues should have yielded to persuasion, and should have returned to Valenciennes, as they were counselled to do by the General.

CHAP.

CHAP. XIII.

Attempt to assassinate General Dumourier on the 4th of April. Events of the 5th of April. Departure of General Dumourier.

IMMEDIATELY after this important event, Dumourier sent Colonel Montjoye to acquaint Colonel Mack with the circumstance; and to appoint a time and place, for a conference between the General and Colonel Mack, for the purpose of finally concluding upon the terms of their treaty, and for settling the measures that should be reciprocally taken, according to the conduct that should be adopted by Dumourier's army after this decisive period. Being informed that a congress of the Ministers of the Combined Powers would speedily be held at Antwerp, Dumourier sent General Valence to Brussels that he might be nearer the neighbourhood of the Congress. During the night, Dumourier composed a short manifesto, which was digested and put into form the following day. In this, he drew up a recital of the facts of that day, and exposed his motives for arresting the Commissioners of the Convention. He particularly insisted on the necessity of possessing hostages, a regard for whose safety might prevent the crimes in which the Jacobins might otherwise indulge on learning the event.

On the morning of the 3d of April, the General went to the camp, and addressed the troops on the part he had acted, who appeared to approve of it with enthusiasm. He afterward went to St. Amand, in which place were the corps of artillery, who testified the same approbation of the General's conduct, as the troops in the camp, although the most indefatigable zeal to seduce this corps was employed by the emissaries of the Jacobins of Valenciennes, and especially by two of Dumourier's superior officers, one of whom, a Lieutenant-colonel named Boubers, had received very particular obligations from the General.

Dumourier

Dumourier deemed it prudent to sleep at St. Amand, for the purpose of marking his confidence in the troops there; and at this place Colonel Montjoye brought him the answer of Colonel Mack. It was agreed that the following morning the Prince of Cobourg, the Arch-duke Charles, and the Baron de Mack should meet General Dumourier, between Bossu and Conde, for the purpose of resolving on the movements of the two armies, and respecting the direction of the succours that should be granted of Imperial troops in the case of Du-mourier having occasion to demand them.

The whole day of the 3d of April passed with as great success as the General could expect. The army appeared of one mind, with the exception of some mur-murs that were heard among some of the battalions of volunteers: and a movement which the General prepared to make on the 5th, was calculated to banish the secret means of intrigue. The General designed to take a new position with the greater part of his army near Orchies, by which means he would remove the troops from the dangerous neighbourhood of Valenciennes; would de-stroy the leisure that belongs to a permanent camp, and in which intrigues have the greatest scope for action; and would be able to menace Lisle, Douay, and Bouchain. He acknowledges that, had he adopted this plan imme-diately on his entering the territory of France, he would probably have been more successful. But, at that peri-od he relied on Valenciennes and Conde; and, perhaps, it is to this error that the sequel is to be attributed.

It is, however, difficult to determine at present what would have happened in that case. The character of the events of that period, is such as no prudence could fore-see; since they were the sudden acts of the caprice of the people, which were subject to no calculation, and that followed each other with a rapidity to which neither foresight nor talent could oppose any obstacle. And it must be acknowledged that the principle which so abruptly detached the French soldiers from a General whom they had previously adored, has an aspect that cannot be regarded without aprobation. They were in arms for the liberty of their country. They saw their General treat with the enemy. They thought themselves betrayed, and they passed from an esteem for their General to the hatred of him. They were not

informed

informed of the purport of his negotiations, nor of the care the General had taken in that treaty, of the interests, and honor of his country. He had not been able to do more, with respect to his troops, than to state to them in general terms the necessity of changing the government, and putting an end to anarchy. They applauded the design; but, as the General had not aided his plan by seductions, nor by terrors, the first impression wore easily away; and the activity of the Jacobins, more constant, more vigilant, and of a nature much more adapted to make impressions upon them, was employed with the utmost success.

The grossest calumny takes root speedily in the minds of men; but more than in any other time, in a period agitated by the dœmon of anarchy. Suspicion ripens in times of revolution, The word *Traitor* being once pronounced, the multitude endeavoured to find in the definition of this word, the exact portrait of the General, whom proclamations, but still more the baser intrigues of corruption, devoted to disgrace. His prudence was now artifice; his love of the public welfare, personal ambition; and a silence dictated by his judgment, knavery. One quarter of an hour employed in the concealed labour of falsehood, supported by the powerful engine of corruption, effaced all sober reflection in men, whose condition precludes them from much thought, and who delight in barbarous and bloody scenes.

If we cooly examine the progress of the revolution, we shall see that the activity of the *Guillotine* is the motive of the high patriotism of the French. The spectacle of severed heads, of torn limbs, carried in procession throughout Paris and other cities, has begotten a terror in some, and in the rest an audacious barbarity; and in both cases has produced a decisive effect, leading the former by fear, and the latter by the necessity of providing for their impunity, to the endless multiplication of murders. The consequence is that the blood spilt by this dreadful engine has converted the nation into a mass capable of effecting astonishing objects.

Frenchmen, do not be led to suppose that the indulgence with which Dumourier judges you, is an eulogium on your conduct! He detests your crimes. He regards the species of liberty you enjoy, as wild and incompatible with the interests of society; and he would rather perish on your unjust and permanent scaffold, than be the apologist or partaker of your phrenzy!

This

This digression faithfully paints the feelings of Dumourier's mind, at the dreadful period which perhaps decided the fate of France. Agitated by the various passions springing from his situation, but still directed by principles, he resisted the temptations of ambition. His justice would not permit him to be Cromwell, nor Monk, nor Coriolanus. His power was extreme, but his wishes moderate. And it is now a consolation to him that he is unfortunate rather than criminal.

Dumourier received various reports every instant, respecting the disposition of the garrison of Conde. Previous to his moving with his army to Orchies, he saw the necessity of assuring himself perfectly of Conde; in order to arrange the movements of the Imperialists, his treaty with whom he dared not avow, till he should have made a declaration to his troops of his ultimate views, and should have commenced his march to Paris.

On the morning of the 4th, he departed from St. Amand for Conde. He had left General Thouvenot at St. Amand, to regulate various details relative to his projected movement, and to watch the public temper. An escort of fifty hussars, which he ordered to attend him, not arriving as he expected, and the time for his conference with the Prince of Coburg approaching, he left one of his aids-de-camp to follow him with the escort, and departed with the Duke de Chartres, Colonel Thouvenot, Colonel Montjoye, some aids-de-camp, and eight hussars; forming together a company of about thirty persons.

Dumourier proceeded towards Conde without any apprehension, his thoughts being deeply engaged on subjects far different from the fatal event which was about to arrive, and of which he had not the least presentiment.

Being within half a league of Conde, between Fresnes and Doumet, he met an officer dispatched by General Neuilly, to inform him that the garrison were in the greatest fermentation, and that it would not be prudent for him to enter the place, till the commotion should have ended, whether it should be in his favour or against him. Dumourier sent back the officer with an order to General Neuilly, to send the 18th regiment of cavalry to Doumet to escort him.

He had a little before overtaken a column of three battalions of volunteers marching towards Conde, with their baggage and artillery. Surprised at this march, for which he had given no orders, he demanded of the officers where
they

they were going. They answered to Valenciennes, and he observed to them that they had turned their back on Valenciennes, and were proceeding to Conde. At this time he was in the midst of them, and had stopped by the side of a ditch to suffer them to pass. He does not conceive why they did not then arrest him.

While they were yet in fight it was that General Neuilly's messenger arrived. Then comparing in his mind the tumult of the garrison of Conde, and the unexpected march of these three battalions, he withdrew an hundred paces from the high road, with a design of entering the first house in Doumet, for the purpose of writing a formal order to these three battalions, to return to the camp of Bruille, to which they belonged.

At this instant, the head of the column suddenly quitted the high road, and ran toward him, uttering dreadful cries. He then remounted his horse, and proceeded at a moderate pace toward a broad ditch, on the other side of which was a marshy ground. Shouts, insults, reproaches, and above all the words, *stop, stop*, forced him to pass the ditch. His horse having refused to take it, he was obliged to clear it on foot. He was no sooner on the other side, than a discharge of muskets succeeded the former tumultuous cries. The whole column was instantly in motion ; the head and centre endeavouring to overtake him, and the rear quitting the high road with equal rapidity, to get between him and the camp of Bruille, which he was endeavouring to regain.

He was now in the most imminent danger. He was on foot. The Baron de Scomberg threw himself from his horse, and insisted on the general's mounting, though with the certain sacrifice of his own life. The general refused. At length he mounted a horse belonging to a domestic of the Duke de Chartres, who, being extremely active, fled on foot. Dumourier's horse was taken and led in triumph to Valenciennes. Two hussars were killed, as well as two of the general's domestics, one of whom carried his great coat. Colonel Thouvenot had two horses killed under him, and saved himself at last by mounting behind the faithful Baptiste, who also lost two horses. The unfortunate Cantin, the general's secretary, was taken and perished on a scaffold. This young man possessed great understanding, courage, fidelity, and patriotism. The three battalions fired more than ten thousand ball.

The

The general, unable to regain his camp, proceeded along the Scheldt, and arrived, still pursued, though not so closely, at a ferry, a little distance from the village of Wihers, which was situated on the Imperial territory. He passed the river, accompanied by five other persons. The remainder gained the camp of Maulde, through a discharge of musquetry. As soon as the general had passed the river he proceeded on foot through a morass, to a neighbouring house ; where, at first he was refused admittance, but on announcing his name was immediately received by the worthy owner. Thence he continued his route on foot to Bury, where was quartered a division of the Imperial regiment of dragoons of la Tour. Here he wrote to Colonel Mack, and took some refreshment, of which he stood greatly in need. He was already joined by the faithful Baptiste, who, passing through the whole of the camp, had turned by Montagne, and had every where spread an alarm.

Dumourier learnt from Baptiste, and other persons during the course of the day, that the designs of the three battalions were entirely unknown to the troops ; that, on the news of their desertion and attempt to murder the general being spread, the strongest indignation was expressed by the soldiery ; and that the escort of hussars and some other horse had pursued the three battalions, who suddenly wheeling, had fled to Valenciennes. Baptiste added, that the whole camp was in a state of the greatest inquietude, and importunately demanded the return of the general.

It was now too late to rejoin his army, and it was necessary that he should wait for Colonel Mack, to whom he owed an account of the reason of his failing in the appointment in the morning. That officer arrived in the evening ; and Dumourier having recited to him the attempt which had been made on his person, observed, that this was the crime of individuals, which far from corrupting the disposition of his troops, would necessarily strengthen their attachment to their General, and destroy all their remaining connection with the anarchists ; that consequently, far from being discouraged, his design was to return to his camp by day-break the following morning, to put himself at the head of his soldiers who loudly demanded his return, and to pursue his plan openly and with the utmost vigour.

Colonel

Colonel Mack, to whom the military virtues were familiar, has since acknowledged that this species of courage then appeared to him more astonishing than that which is displayed in the dangers of a battle. Had he then seen all the soul of Dumourier, he would have found this apparent security mingled with apprehension, excited by the example and fate of La Fayette. But the general's resolution was taken. He resolved to sacrifice himself throughout ; and would not give his army occasion to say, that the desertion was on his part, or that, being recalled by his soldiers, he had resisted their wishes.

Dumourier passed part of the night in digesting, with Colonel Mack, the proclamation of the Prince of Cobourg, which appeared on the 5th of April, with that of General Dumourier. The Imperial General in his proclamation declared, that he was now no more than an auxiliary in the war, against the anarchists of France ; that it was not the intention of his sovereign to make conquests, but to co-operate, in restoring peace and order to France, with General Dumourier, whose principles, as they were expressed in his proclamation, he adopted.

It was again agreed by Colonel Mack, and Dumourier, that, as soon as the latter should be master of Conde, he should deliver it to the Austrians, in order to serve as a magazine and place of arms for the Imperial army, in the case of aid being demanded by Dumourier ; that he should be instantly furnished with such succours as he should demand ; that he should specify the number of infantry and cavalry to be granted him, the mode in which these should serve, whether by a junction with his troops, or by making one or more separate diversions in behalf of the cause ; that, however, Dumourier should not call for succours, but in case of absolute need, it being more agreeable to the mutual object of the parties, that he should endeavour to accomplish it by his own troops only ; and that, in case of his being able to do so, the Imperialists should remain neuter, and should not pass the frontiers of France.

The proclamation of the Prince of Cobourg, made in consequence of this negociation, has been condemned but unjustly. Of what real advantage had it not been to the Imperialists, and what solid glory had they not acquired, if, by enabling Dumourier to march to Paris, they could by this noble moderation have spared the blood and treasure that will be wasted in this quarrel, for which the towns

that

that may be acquired with infinite difficulty will be no manner of compensation.

It is to be feared that an avidity for conquests among the belligerent powers is the real obstacle to the termination of this destructive war. By this passion they were prevented from seizing upon the occasion offered, by the departure of General Dumourier, and the consequent annihilation of his army, of pressing forward to Paris. The combined powers have since lost their time in making a methodical war, while the French have been able to recover themselves, and their armies have become more numerous, and better disciplined.

On the 5th of April at day-break, Dumourier proceeded with an escort of fifty Imperial dragoons to the advanced guard of his camp at Maulde, where he was received with the greatest joy. He harangued the several corps, by whom he was answered with expressions of affection. Notwithstanding, he remarked that there were some indications of a contrary spirit, and several factious groups assembled in different parts.

His next design was to go to St. Amand, to prepare for the movement of his troops to Orchies, according to his former plan. As he was entering the city, one of his aids-de-camp came toward him on the full gallop, and informed him that during the night the corps of artillery, excited by the emissaries of Valenciennes, who had spread the report that the general was drowned in the Scheldt in flying to the enemy, had sent a deputation to Valenciennes, and that on the return of their deputies they had instantly rose upon their generals, driven them from the place, and were preparing to march to Valenciennes.

Dumourier had with him, two squadrons of the regiment of Berchiny, a squadron of the hussars of Saxe, fifty curiassiers, and a squadron of the dragoons of Bourbon. Yielding to his emotions of passion, he resolved to fall upon St. Amand with this body of cavalry. His officers, however, represented the danger and inutility of this step, as he had no infantry at hand, and would subject his escort to be mown down by the artillery. He gave way to their reasoning. He learnt shortly after that the corps of artillery went to Valenciennes. The money belonging to the army and the equipages of the officers remaining in the city without guard, he commanded them to be conducted to Rumegies, at the distance of a

K k   league

league from his camp, on the road to Orchies; that village being protected by a part of his advanced guard cantoned there.

The corps of artillery was the flower and strength of the French army. Feeling its importance, it abounded more than the others in clubs and orators, and indeed, might pass for the Pretorian guard of the revolution. When its desertion was known in the two camps, part of the troops followed, and confusion and dismay were spread among the rest. Several of the general officers who waited for the opportunity were eager to lead entire divisions to Valenciennes. Those who still remained attached to the person, or principles of Dumourier, instead of shewing themselves to their troops, and setting an example of courage, were struck with terror, concealed themselves, or thought only of their own safety. General La Marlier had been among the most forward of the enemies of Anarchy, and possessed the entire confidence of General Valence; who, when he departed from Brussels, confided the whole of his baggage and effects to him, with a request that he would send them after Valence to Tournay. La Marlier appropriated the money, horses, and property of his general to his own use, and deserted to Valenciennes.

Dumourier was at Rumegies, dictating orders to be issued to the different parts of the army, when he heard of the defection of the troops in camp. Nothing was left him now but to provide for his personal safety. He mounted his horse, attended by General Thouvenot, and his brother the colonel, the Duke de Chartres, Colonel Montjoye, and Lieutenant-colonel Barrois, two or three others of his staff, and some Aids-de-camp, having no escort; and retiring to Tournay alighted at the quarters of General Clairfait. He was followed in about an hour afterward, by fifty Cuirassiers, half a squadron of the hussars of Saxe, and the whole of the regiment of Berchiny. Those brave and worthy men, brought with them the equipages belonging to the general and the staff officers, excepting the saddle horses of the general, which were stolen by one of his grooms, who joined the anarchists.

The troops of which we have just spoken and a few others that arrived shortly afterward, amounting to about seven hundred horse, and eight hundred infantry, followed the General without any solicitation on his part;

and.

and this circumstance renders him the more anxious respecting the fate of those men, the companions of his former glory, and of his last disgrace.

Dumourier in retiring from France invited no one to follow him. His plan had totally failed, and a few men more or less on either side would not influence events. The individuals attached to his cause had ties of family and of interest in France, and he resolved not to multiply misfortunes without benefit. Those who followed him, therefore, had the real merit of being guided by principle.

In the confusion that succeeded the General's departure, none of the orders that had been issued were executed. Lieutenant-general Vouille, who commanded the advanced guard, did not receive the order of withdrawing it within the camp of Maulde till the 6th, when it was no longer in his power. The General retired to Tournay, as did also Major-general Neuilly, who had abandoned Conde, Major-general de Bannes, Second, and de Dumas, and some of the principal officers of the battalions of Volunteers; where they were afterward joined by Lieutenant-general Marasse, Major Generals Rault and Berneron, and Colonel Arnaudin.

The treasury of the Army contained two millions of livres in specie. It had been carried from St. Amand to Furnes, between Conde and Valenciennes, by a battalion of Chasseurs, who at first deliberated respecting the dividing of it among themselves, but afterward being likely to quarrel, in order to avoid the bloodshed that would ensue, made a merit of their patriotism and conducted it to Valenciennes. Soliva, a commissary of the army of the Ardennes, pursued these troops with a squadron of the dragoons of Bourbon, retook the money on the Glacis of Valenciennes, and led it back to Furnes; but being pressed by new battalions was again obliged to abandon it. Soliva and the dragoons retired by Mons. They might have brought off the money had they passed by Bruille, and Mortagne, but the confusion of the moment prevented recollection and foresight. If the treasury of the army had been saved, the General's situation had been very different; and the little army that followed his fortunes, would have encreased rapidly, being in a state to pay them, instead of being as he really was, without money. This circumstance proves, that the pay of the army was not embezzled by him, nor em-

ploye

ployed as a means of corruption. Dumourier placed little confidence in means of corruption, in which as the leader of a party his conduct was greatly erroneous.

Dumourier had not the qualities that were requisite for the leader of a party. It is probable that he would have filled the station of a General or an Ambassador with success, under a stable government, whether monarchical, or republican. But the violent state of things in France, destructive of all his pre-conceived ideas of justice, and injustice, threw him entirely out of his sphere. His activity, so greatly spoken of even by his enemies, was repressed by his dread of committing crimes ; and he preferred his own esteem to success. Thus in his first reflections, after his retreat among the Imperialists, he saw the cause of his failure in himself, but he felicitated himself on the fact. To have swayed the fortune of France, had undoubtedly given him a noble place in history ; but to have been indebted for it to the flagitiousness of his conduct, was too severe a condition ; and he was happy in resigning one to escape the other.

He invites men of high stations to examine themselves with the same austerity ; and moralists, to study the influence which character has on events. Cæsar and Pompey, determined a noble quarrel by noble means, and on both sides were displayed greatness of mind, virtues, and talents. Had those men been surrounded with the lowest vices of the meanest classes in society, they would have fled, or would have fallen victims. It demands a Maaniello to conduct the populace. But when a great nation becomes an entire populace, neighbouring nations are thrown into the greatest embarrassment ; because the electric spirit spreads with more rapidity among the people, than among the higher orders of men.

C H A P. XIV.

Dumourier at Mons.—Establishment of the French at Leuze—Congress of Antwerp.—Second Proclamation of the Prince of Cobourg.—Departure of the General for Brussels.

GENERAL CLAIRFAIT gave orders for the reception of the French troops which might arrive in the villages round the town of Leuze, which was fixed upon for the residence of the French general officers ; and Dumourier departed for

Mons, accompanied by the Duke de Chartres, Colonel Thouvenot, Colonel Montjoye, and Lieutenant Colonel Barrois, passing by Bury, to concert measures with the officer commanding the Imperial advanced post, for protecting the retreat of such of the French as should join the Imperialists.

The Imperialists were faithful to their truce. It is certain that had they fallen on the French camp on the 5th of April, they might have utterly destroyed the army. Their conduct was therefore highly honourable ; yet, without incurring the blame of perfidy, perhaps on that day they ought to have made a movement with their army, taking possession of the camp of Maulde, and shewing themselves at St. Amand : they not only would have found no resistance, but probably would have been joined by several battalions of the French, which during more than four-and-twenty hours, appeared by their movements to be irresolute as to the conduct they should pursue. But however this may be, the fidelity of the Imperialists to their engagements, is to be applauded. Their motives were most worthy, as well as the generosity with which they received the French refugees, who had certainly been among the bravest of their enemies.

Dumourier found Colonel Mack at Bury, from which place they departed together for Mons, in the general's carriage. It was agreed between them, that the Imperialists should instantly besiege Conde, and that the place should be summoned in the name of General Dumourier, who accordingly wrote the summons and sent it the following day to the Imperial head quarters. It was further agreed that a return should be made of the officers and soldiers which accompanied or followed Dumourier ; that considering their having unfortunately lost their military chest, they should receive the pay of their respective ranks, at the rate that officers of the same rank in the Imperial service were paid, and should be placed on the same footing ; that a commissary of war belonging to the Imperial army should be attached to these troops, together with a French commissary, to certify the justice of the returns ; that an advance should be made from the Imperial treasury of 30,000 florins, which should be put into the hands of the French staff officers for the pay of their troops, that Dumourier should have the rank, and establishment of *Feld-zeugmeister* (general of the artillery) ; and that finally, this pay and advance should be regarded as a loan to the party of Dumourier, and that the general should engage, as soon as any progress should be made in France, to reimburse this sum to the Imperial treasury.

It is a confolation to General Dumourier, that the companions of his misfortunes continue to enjoy this eftablifhment. Indeed they have, fince that period, been fubjected to the condition of taking an oath, which was not in the firft inftance required ; but at that period they were the foldiers of a party which no longer exifts, and it has been fince deemed neceffary to demand that fecurity for their fidelity. Dumourier would himfelf become their pledge with readinefs, having throughout the war tried their fidelity, courage, and refignation. Let them accept of this teftimony of the efteem and affection of their general, and may they be recompenfed for their virtues in contributing to the fuccefs of the power whom they will faithfully ferve.

In purfuance of thefe arrangments, Dumourier caufed, by the order of the Prince of Cobourg, 10,000 florins to be advanced to the French troops at Leuze ; unwilling, through motives of delicacy, to take the whole of the money agreed to be advanced, becaufe in penetrating fpeedily into France this fum would have ferved till they could have proceeded further into the interior part of the country ; and Dumourier appeals to the Prince of Cobourg, Colonel Mack, and the other principal officers of the Imperial army, refpecting the clearnefs and difintereftednefs of his conduct. It was further decided that the general, till he fhould be employed with his troops, fhould be provided with quarters, near thofe of the Prince of Cobourg; and the Imperial head quarters being eftablifhed at Bouffu, General Dumourier's quarters were fixed at the abbey of St. Ghiflain.

Dumourier makes here an avowal of his gratitude to the general officers of the Imperial army, by whom he was treated with diftinguifhed marks of regard, and more particularly by the Archduke Charles, and the Prince of Cobourg. At this time was formed a friendfhip between Colonel Mack and Dumourier, which on the part of the latter will never be diminifhed. Colonel Mack is an officer of uncommon virtue, and military talents, and the unbounded confidence placed in him by the Imperial army is the juft recompence of his fervices. It is greatly to be hoped, for the intereft of the houfe of Auftria, that the health of this officer will be reftored.

During two days that Dumourier was at Mons, he was treated by the inabitants in a manner that is flattering to his own honour ; and his reception was the fame at Tournay, Leuze, and indeed, throughout the whole of that country ; thefe worthy people being fenfible of the fervices he had rendered them, especially on his return from Holland, and during the retreat of his army to France.

It would be injustice not to name an instance of the delicate attention of the Prince of Cobourg to Dumourier's situation. The General seeing a corps of two hundred chasseurs belonging to the emigrants, as they passed thro' Mons, on their route to join the advanced guard of the army, represented to the Prince of Cobourg, that this mingling of the emigrants with his troops could not but produce fatal effects, especially on entering France ; and the Prince of Cobourg instantly gave counter orders to the chasseurs ; sending them by Namur, to serve in the advanced guard of the Prince of Hohenloe.

The Prince of Lambesc-Lorraine testified also to the general his gratitude for the essential service rendered to his house by Dumourier when he was Minister of Foreign Affairs, in preventing an unjust confiscation of his property, and of that of the Princess of Vaudemont.

On the 7th of April, the Prince of Cobourg departed, with Colonel Mack, to attend the Congress, held at Antwerp ; from which place he returned on the evening of the 8th. Dumourier passed those two days at Leuze, in the midst of his comrades, whose uneasiness he dissipated by informing them of the establishments made for them by the Imperialists. General Vouille took the command of these troops ; and Dumourier, assisted by General Thouvenot, began to reform them, according to the regulations of the Imperial army ; which was the more necessary, as the refugees were composed only of fragments of the different corps ; with the exception of the regiment of Berchiny. Dumourier quitted the companions of his misfortunes on the evening of the 8th, and felt some presentiment that he should not return to them. On the morning of the 9th he arrived at Mons, where he found the Prince of Cobourg, setting off for his head quarters. Dumourier went there also ; and after treating further on what regarded their mutual interests, he went in the evening to the quarters which had been prepared for him at the abbey of St. Ghislain.

On the morning of the 10th of April, a proclamation of the Prince of Cobourg was brought to Dumourier, dated the 9th, which entirely annulled the former proclamation of the 5th; and expressly declared, that the Prince of Cobourg would thenceforth carry on the war against France, in behalf of his sovereign, and would hold such towns, as he might take, by the right of conquest, and on the ground of indemnity.

The emigrants have had the imprudence to rejoice at the issuing of this latter, and to condemn the former. It might be demanded if these emigrants were Frenchmen. But, setting aside the influence of passions, by which not only individuals, but also the governments interested in this war are influenced, it will appear but too true, that the second proclamation of the Prince of Cobourg, in depriving Dumourier's party of all means of acting in concert, and in setting forth the belligerent powers as rapacious conquerors, has attached the whole of the French armies to the interest of the National Convention, which the greater part of them had previously detested ; has compelled the cause of royalty to be forgotten, in the danger of the country ; has pointed out the salvation of France as resting on the existence of the Republic ; has rallied the different parties round the standard of the national honour ; and has certainly been injurious to the success of the campaign, and rendered the issue of the war extremely uncertain.

This second proclamation was issued at the conclusion of the Congress at Antwerp, in consequence of the determination of the ministers of the combined powers. Dumourier now saw that his treaty with the Imperialists was entirely destroyed ; and, without offering useless complaints of this sudden change in the councils of the Imperialists, he consulted only his character, and principles, and resolved to sacrifice all his personal interests.

He repaired instantly to the head quarters, and told the Prince of Cobourg frankly, that he came to thank him for the personal kindnesses he had rendered him, and that he hoped to continue to merit his esteem ; that when he entered into a treaty with the Prince of Cobourg, his object was the regeneration of France, and not its dismemberment ; that he would not enter into any discussion concerning the motives of the combined powers ; but that for his part, he could have no share in lessening the territory of France, or employ either his influence, or his moderate talents, in that task ; and that therefore he felt himself obliged to withdraw from the coalition, and must beseech the Prince of Cobourg to grant him a passport.

The Prince of Cobourg could not forbear to express his high esteem of his delicacy. The Arch Duke Charles, and Colonel Mack, also expressed their esteem for the general ; and he departed for Brussels. Dumourier can have no doubt that, after a direct violation of the principles of the treaty that had taken place, and after an open disavowal of the proclamation issued in consequence of that treaty, his presence must have been embarrassing to the Imperialists, and that they regarded the resolution he took with pleasure. But it was not long that he left them in any perplexity, his resolution was taken the moment he perceived ther designs.

Before Dumourier quitted the Imperial army, he had the satisfaction of knowing that his former companions would be continued in their rank and employments. They are well treated and serve in the Imperial army, where assuredly they will support their reputation.

Being arrived at Brussels, he explained the motives of his conduct to the Count de Metternich, the emperor's minister in the Netherlands, who received him with the greatest friendship, and gave him a passport for Germany.

. In this place the memoirs of the public life of General Dumourier are concluded. The remainder of his life has been filled up with difficulties, dangers, persecutions, and calumnies of every kind, of which he may one day render an account to the public. But this history can only interest those who are truly his friends, and they are not many : or, real philosophers, and such are indeed rare.

CHAP. XV.

Conclusion.

SUCH is the series of events in three of the most disastrous months of General Dumourier's life. In this short period he has experienced all the miseries, and all the dangers, that the weakness and wickedness of man can inflict upon a public character. Calumny and injustice form the outline of this dark picture, which may serve as a lesson to men of every description, and from which philosophy alone can extract those consolatory reflections which propriety of conduct and rectitude of motive supply. He hates, neither those who have defamed his character, nor those who have pursued his life, nor those who have refused him an asylum, and whose ungenerous and ill founded resentment persecutes him wherever he flies. The first, are ignorant of the true state of those facts, which, from their very singularity, are exceedingly liable to misrepresentation. The second, are actuated by that spirit of fanaticism, which is reasonable proof. The third, are prejudiced by calumny, and confider him as a dangerous character.

The Ministers of foreign courts have given it out, after the Emigrants, that he is a proper object of suspicion, and that they can never be sure he will not veer about and put himself at the head of the French. His proscription, and his three declarations, ought to be a sufficient pledge of his firmness: those three pieces have raised him many enemies by the perverse misconstruction given to his expressions.

He avows that he passionately loves his country, and that he will never hesitate a moment to sacrifice his life to its welfare; but he declares, at the same time, that whilst it is polluted with crimes, and delivered over to the horrors of anarchy, he will never enter it again: that, proscribed, as he is, and an outcast of society, he prefers all the miseries and all the dangers he may incur, to the most splendid situation in which the oppressors of his countrymen, and the inciters of their mad excesses, could place him.

He has been the open enemy of those powers who wished to interfere in the internal affairs of his country, both whilst he was a minister, and whilst he was a general; because he was most firmly persuaded, that the Revolution, which was doubtless, expedient and inevitable, would have been accomplished, not only with innocence, but glory, if foreign interference and the open incouragement given to the emigrants, had not exasperated to madness a people by nature impetuous and violent. After licentiousness and anarchy had destroyed every thing in France, he wished to avail himself of the same foreign powers to re-establish order, not merely without injury to his country, but with the most tender regard for its interest and its glory.

When he saw that this became impracticable, he formed the plan of a diversion, by which he conceived he might essentially serve the cause of his country and of Europe. Distrust, or other motives, prevented its execution. He grieves at the protraction of the sufferings of human nature: he sighs impatiently for the termination of this calamitous war, without foreseeing the means of its accomplishment, as for nothing which now takes place in Europe, with respect to France, can be reasoned upon after the common maxims of policy and prudence.

It has been said that he was bribed over by the Dutch Patriots, and afterward sold to the Prince of Orange a list of the principal conspirators. This absurd imputation appears in a German work on the French Revolution, called Minerva, much esteemed for the beauty of its style. The author has certainly been deceived in this as well as in many other circumstances, of General Dumourier's life, which the natural love of the marvellous has constantly magnified and blackened. He declares, that he never possessed a list of the Dutch Patriots, that he knew only a very small party of these refugees in France, that he knew these only because they formed a Batavian Revolutionary Committee at Antwerp; that he does not know the names of any of those who may entertain the same opinions in Holland; that he has never had any communication, either before or since, with the Stadtholder's party; that it is even impossible such a communication should have existed, as that court never forgave the manifesto which preceded his expedition into Holland; that he never received a bribe; that he is poor, and glories in being so.

He will conclude these Memoirs with some observations on the three classes of French emigrants. Foreigners are surprised, that they should not unite in their distress, because they are unacquainted with their distinguishing characters. Their divisions are a great misfortune, but they are almost without a remedy.

The first class, of which the Princes of the House of Bourbon are the leaders, consists of the old court, the higher order of ecclesiastics, the parliaments, and the principal financial department. Allured by the seductive influence of this party on the one hand, and terrified by the extravagance of the Jacobins on the other, the low noblesse have been induced to join them in military array. This class is composed of pure Royalists: they wish and demand the re-establishment of the ancient monarchy, and of course, of absolute despotism; and regret the old institutions with all their abuses, institutions which it is impossible should ever re-appear, since a new order of things has rendered France no longer the France of former days, but a new nation, requiring as a new nation, a new moral and political constitution, to re-establish on the broad basis of general utility the security of the government, and the confidence of the people.

The

The second class, of which Fayette is the apparent leader, consists of the constitutional monarchists, men who desire a great reformation, or rather a total reformation, in the principles and forms of the old government. The greater part of this class were employed in the first National Assembly in the great work of forming the New Constitution; but falling, as they soon did, a sacrifice to the cabals of the people of Paris, and above all to the frantic excesses of the Jacobins, paid dearly for the propagation of those principles of Liberty and Equality, which, having been originally laid down by themselves without any modification, and taken up by the people in too gross and literal a sense, were pushed to that extravagant extent, which has brought about the subversion of all the estates, and the general anarchy of France.

The third class, which is scarcely distinguishable from the former, but by the later date of their defection consists of the military who followed General Dumourier: and all the nobles proscribed on this occasion, who could escape from their country. This class includes all those members of the National Convention who had the courage to vote in favour of Louis XVI. and against all the abominations which resulted from his execution; and who, having attested their wishes in a protest, had the good fortune to escape.

The first class, the most numerous, the most splendid, the most diffused over Europe, and the most favoured by its attentions—by little effectual aid, but great promises, and still oftener by humiliations and caprice, possesses the most decided aversion to the two others; and confounds them in its ignorant presumption with the Jacobins themselves. The unjust imprisonment of Fayette excites in their bosoms no mercy for that unfortunate General. But against Dumourier, they level all their rage: and the zeal with which they calumniate his character, augment his distresses, and encourage his universal proscription, is truly surprising.

This class has preserved all its pride and all its pretensions. It will have every thing or nothing. The last success of the Combined Armies fills them with frantic joy; and nothing is heard but offensive schemes of revenge and personal ambition. If the operations of the same armies slacken for a season—they are betrayed—they are deserted, they are undone—and this moment the king of Prussia and his Generals, and the next the Emperor's, are assailed with their loud and unseasonable reproaches. Always extravagant and always difguftful to the people where they refide, who coolly obferve their motions, and conclude, with fome plaufibility, that felfifhnefs is their fole leading principle, they have the prefumption to think that all Europe is only armed for their fakes, and that when they re-enter their country, where they will recognife nothing—not even the veftiges of their demolifhed villas, they fhall take poffeffion of their town-manfions, their country cottages, their elegant luxuries, their domeftics, their dependents, and above all their power, and their credit.

The intolerance of this clafs of emigrants towards the two others precludes that union which is fo effentially neceffary in their prefent unfortunate fituation, were it only to excite the attention and compaffion of the feveral States where they have fled for protection, and rove without a fettlement. There are notwithftanding in this clafs, fome few individuals of fenfe borne away in the general mafs by their unlucky fituation, and the prejudices of their birth, who form an exception to the general rule, and fincerely reprobate the extravagance of the reft, but they are little attended to. This clafs is divided too, within itfelf, into factions as active, as intriguing, as full of bickerings and jealoufies, as when it glittered at Paris or Verfailles. It is a court itinerant, which has loft nothing of its occupation, though deprived of its ftability.

The other two claffes of emigrants are infinitely more moderate and reafonable, and might foon be brought to coalefce. Fayette and Dumourier, if they met in any other place than a prifon, would foon underftand each other ; and the fhades of difference, which have hitherto only feparated them, perhaps for want of a due explanation, would melt away, and vanifh before the common intereft of their country, and the common fufferings of themfelves. For thefe two chiefs, and thefe two claffes have both been ftrenuous for the eftablifhment of liberty in their country, and the reformation of abufes. They have fupported with firmnefs the great caufe of human nature, and, if they have differed in the means, they have agreed in the principle.

General Dumourier declares to the emigrants of every defcription, whom force or inclination has feparated from their country, that it is only by a well cemented union they can acquire that confideration, which alone can better their fituation at the clofe of the war, whether they fucceed in returning to their country, or whether they are doomed to relinquish it forever: that it is the advantage of misfortune to purify the mind, and to temper it for the hardier virtues: that it is time to renounce the language of prejudice, since it is no longer understood in France: that, that country is more different from the France of 1788, than from Gaul in Julius Cæsar's time; that it even changes every six months; and, that unfortunately the Jacobins have been more prudential in the gradations of their crimes, than the emigrants, who, without giving themselves the trouble to examine the progress of the national genius, build all their schemes on the state of France at the point of time that they left it.

Their unfortunate situation may continue a long time; it may become utterly without a remedy: the worst should always be supposed, that we may not be misled by fallacious expectations. If they don't persist in shaking off their arrogance, their extravagance, their imprudence, their internal discord, they will soon disgust the people who give them shelter, and whose temper will infallibly be soured on a thousand occasions by the war; their minds will not be fortified to bear the triumphs of success, or the desperation of a failure: in the first case, they will abuse their return, and be driven into a banishment more hopeless than their present one; in the second, they will become the most wretched men upon the face of the earth.

Banishment, like every other condition of human nature, has its advantages. It gives us objects of comparison, of which we would never otherwise have an idea; it gives us information; it calls forth our energies by its difficulties; it renders us indulgent and sociable; it excites between ourselves and our protectors a reciprocation of sensibility and benevolence. The upright man, the man of wisdom and reflection, brings back from this involuntary pilgrimage, a store of those hardy and of those gentle virtues, which qualify him better to benefit his country, and lead to that universal philanthropy which diminishes the dismal effects of national partialities.

General Dumourier gives them another piece of advice, which he carefully observes himself——to be indulgent to their countrymen, and not to revile a whole nation by too indiscriminate reproaches. It is *imprudent*, at least, to brand as rebels twenty millions of men who rise against a hundred thousand. These twenty millions form such an immense majority, that the hundred thousand are more deserving of the name of rebels. The emigrants of every description, who love their country, and are worthy of returning to it, may fairly—under the dismal apprehension, lest anarchy should produce the total subversion and disorganization of the empire—may fairly detest five or six hundred scoundrels who lead that amiable people astray, and hurry them beyond the reasonable bounds of true liberty, of true patriotism, of feasible equality, and of the possible means of public happiness and order; but they should surely preserve, in misfortune especially, that love for their country which maintains their title to its blessing.

They should never calumniate the nation at large: they may justly lament that the French are blindfolded, and led through crimes into every extravagance. But there is one point of view which is consolatory to every true Frenchman: he sees through all this anarchy, a most determined courage, and the greatest frankness of opinion. With these qualities the French may be brought back from their errors; but it is by reason, and not by reproaches, that this can be accomplished. Let those among the emigrants whose situation, whose influence, and whose knowledge, may one day call them to the important duty of re-establishing order in France, let these men fit themselves for reclaiming the public opinion, by instantly sacrificing their resentment, of whatever nature, or however just, and ceasing to exasperate by invectives the whole of the people of France. The character of that people may be eclipsed for a time, but will never be entirely obliterated; and what is crime in some few individuals, is energy in the nation at large.

The history of the world does not present an instance of a nation assailed by so many enemies at once, less terrified at the thunder of the charge, or keeping them at bay in every quarter with such obstinate resolution. The last campaign, which was enough to have crushed them at once, only displayed one general mass of valour; and if they yield, the next campaign, they will be subdued, but they will not be degraded. It is greatly the interest of the emigrants that the French should not be despised; for whatever their nation may suffer in the estimation of Europe, will be a loss to themselves. They have already, for the last two years, been guilty of a great mistake in representing to foreign powers that the French armies were contemptible, and utterly incapable of making any resistance. This mistake, which has proved so fatal to the Prussians, has taken away all credit from their reports. Let us never hear such misrepresentations again—They are much too serious.

The French nation, collectively taken, will always be amiable. She is labouring at this mment under a moral diftemper, whofe dreadful convulfion only render her a greater object of alarm. Foreigers may employ the fword, but her emigrant offspring fould only approach her with the foothing accents of pejuafion :—it is their intereft to do fo : their defign of fuperiducing order on that confufion which has driven them fron their country, will, otherwife, every month and every veek, become more perfectly hopelefs.

This advice is not the refult of bat compliance, or perfonal intereft, or ambition. Genera Dumourier declares, and his Memoirs will prove, that he reprobates the prefent ftate of things in France ; that he fees in them only the fubverfion of every rational priciple, and the utter impracticability of promoting puble happinefs ; he declares, that he will never warp to fuh an order of things ; and that he would chufe beggary, pofcription, wretchednefs and perpetual exile, in preferene to any re-eftablifhment in his country that muft be purhafed by the facrifice of his moral principles,——but he declares, too, that he loves his countrymen, and that were he poignarded in their delirium tomorrow, he woul breathe out his laft accents, in a lamentation of their errors, and a benediction to his country.

FINIS.